About the Author

Fiona Veitch Smith was born [in] South Africa with her family [...] in Cape Town before return[ing ...] continued her journalistic an[d ...] History, Journalism and M[...] Writing. She lectures in media and script[...] universities. She also writes books for children. She lives in Newcastle upon Tyne with her husband and young daughter. In her spare time Fiona enjoys walking with her dogs, gardening, and playing the clarinet.
http://fiona.veitchsmith.com

About The Peace Garden

"Definitely not your run-of-the-mill romantic thriller. What started off as an investigation into missing plant theft in suburban Newcastle turns into an international thriller set against the background of post-apartheid South Africa and the birth of the internet. A triumph. I couldn't put it down."

Abidemi Sanusi, Commonwealth Writers' Prize nominee for *Eyo*.

"A great story, with a compulsively page-turning conclusion, which also gives the reader an inside look at many of the conflicting issues of racial prejudice in its most notorious institutional expression - apartheid South Africa."

Dr Steve Pillinger, linguist, Wycliffe, Southern Africa.

"A cleverly-plotted novel with nice comic touches."
RS Downie, New York Times bestselling author of the *Ruso Medicus* novels.

"A tense, funny, fascinating and moving book."
Gillian D'Achada, Sanlam Award-winning author of *Sharkey's Son*.

"You won't find stereotypes or cardboard cut-outs in this story. Each character is fully-drawn and has depth and compassion. The Peace Garden is for an intelligent reader: a cross between a coming-of-age story and a crime thriller, the story is complex and will make you think."

Julie Compton, author of *Tell No Lies*.

The Peace Garden

Fiona Veitch Smith

First published 2013 by
Crafty Publishing
6 Lynton Way
Newcastle upon Tyne
NE5 3TN
United Kingdom

www.craftypublishing.com

© Fiona Veitch Smith 2013

The Peace Garden is also available as an e-book.
© Fiona Veitch Smith, 2011, published by Crafty Publishing.

The right of Fiona Veitch Smith to be identified as author of this work has been asserted by her in accordance with the Copyright, Designs and Patents Act 1999. All rights reserved.

British Library Cataloguing in Publication Data:
A catalogue record for this book is available from the British Library,

ISBN 978-0-9569141-6-3

Section heading quotes from Hugh Johnson, The Principles of Gardening, Mitchell Beazley, New Edition, 1984.

Cover image © Amy Barnes, 2011 www.amybarnes.co.uk

www.craftypublishing.com

For Rodney:
my husband, my anchor,
my best friend.

Part One:

"New Friends"

Part Two:

"Old Enemies"

Part Three:

"Lovers"

Part One:

"New Friends"

"Every natural community of plant has an inherent stability born of competition. Its inhabitants hold their ground in due relationship with each other by constant warfare. The only plants (and animals) present are those which have found an ecological niche for themselves; somewhere where their needs and characteristics dovetail with those of their neighbours."

(Hugh Johnson, The Principles of Gardening)

Chapter One

July 1990: eleven years ago

"I CANNUT BELIEVE it! Me plants have gone again!" Grandma Iris was pacing to and fro on her neat front lawn, pointing to gaping holes in the colourful flowerbeds. "Over here Natalie!" She summoned me from my sun-stained refuge on the step. "D'ya remember that hydrangea we planted a couple of years back? Well …" Her lips pulled together like a draw-stringed bag. Arms folded, nose pointed, eyes ranging across her floral kingdom. "And those gladioli were just beginning to bloom. Who could do such a thing? And just a few days before the judging as well!" Her accusing finger quivered from leathery palm to cracked nail. It certainly was a mystery, I agreed.

Grandma had told me about the missing plants as soon as I stepped out of the taxi from Newcastle Airport. I had slept in the car, so by the time I got to Jasmine Close my half-speed mind was not quite ready to absorb the finer details of the case. But after a cup of tea in Grandma's kitchen, and cold water splashed on my face, my freckles were finer and my mind sharper. I took out my Nancy Drew notebook and pieced together as much as I could.

Fact One: In two days time, on Saturday 16th July, Grandma Iris and three other gardeners in the cul-de-sac would be judged in the annual 'Most Beautiful Garden' contest run by the Evening Chronicle.

Fact Two: Grandma Iris had come in the top three of this most prestigious contest for the past five years.

Fact Three: For the past month, Grandma Iris and the other residents of Jasmine Close had woken up on certain mornings to discover that various plants had been dug up from their gardens during the night.

Fact Four: Last night was one such night.

Fact Five: Apart from the hydrangea and the gladioli, Grandma Iris' garden had been pillaged of a patch of geraniums, a selection of lilies and an indeterminate variety of seedlings from the potting shed, despite the fact that the latter was secured with two padlocks.

"Eeeee, me plants. Who would take me plants?" I closed my notebook and put it in the worn back pocket of my jeans. Mum called them my 'play jeans' as opposed to the smart Levis that I was allowed to wear to discos. I had left all my smart clothes at my latest home in Washington DC as Grandma Iris wasn't much for 'airs and graces', which was fine by me. I really looked forward to these summer holidays in the North East of England, where I could just be myself, not worrying about what the children of the diplomats would think.

There was nowhere I could get dirty in the array of apartments that had been my home for as long as I could remember. Before Washington we lived in Paris, then before Paris, Canberra. Or was it Wellington? My dad, Jimmy Porter, was an auditor with the British Foreign Service. It was his job to make sure that Her Majesty's embassies around the world were complying with budgetary constraints. My mother, Danielle Gilbert (French pronunciation, not English), was a photographer and didn't seem to mind the rapid-fire change of scenery. Grandma said she was flighty and got what she deserved when she married my dad. Perhaps he got what he deserved too: a wife who didn't hold him down and gave him as much freedom as he gave her. Sometimes I thought that I was the only thing they had in common.

I was twelve years old and still waiting for 'the effects of that kind of lifestyle' (as Grandma put it) to creep up on me. Teachers predicted it while Grandma Iris claimed to have already seen it, but as far as I could tell I was a pretty normal kid. Apart from my breasts, that is. My left one was considerably larger than my right. I was quite worried. My mum said that it was not unheard of and if it still persisted in a couple of years she would take me to see someone about it. Simon, a cousin from Mum's side of the family, thought he'd put the whole matter in perspective for me: "Who cares if a grape's bigger than a pea?" Well, I did.

"What're we going to do pet?" Grandma asked.

"Wait a few years and see if it grows," I suggested.

"Aye, that might do it. But it won't help for the contest." She knelt beside a mutilated azalea that the plant thief had damaged when digging out its neighbour. I stooped my shoulders a little more than usual, grateful for the oversized sweatshirt that I wore over my jeans.

"I see he got you too, Mrs Porter." I helped my grandma to her feet and together we walked towards the pavement where a man and boy were standing watching us.

"Aye, he did Mr Storey. And you?"

"Why aye. Didya think the blighter would leave us alone?"

"What did he take?"

"Those two new dwarf conifers that we put beside the garage door."

"Oh no, he didn't!"

"I'm afraid he did. Pots 'n all. Ya see it's not just old folks who he's preying on." Grandma and Mr Storey stood shaking their heads as I jotted down this new evidence in my notebook. Roger, a spotty thirteen-year-old with a skinhead haircut, tried to get a closer look. I closed the book and started to put it away. Roger grabbed my wrist. "Give 'ere!"

"No, it's a secret."

"I want to see."

"Well you can't."

"I will if I want to." His thick fingers tightened over my skin. I yelped.

"Roger, ya little bugger! Whadya think you're doing?" Mr Storey grabbed his offspring by the collar and pulled him backwards. "Now say sorry to the lass!"

The skinhead, looking at his feet, muttered.

"I didn't hear ya!" his dad said loudly and slowly, as if talking to a deaf person or a foreigner.

"I'm sorry."

"That's all right. Isn't it, pet?" I nodded to my grandma, taking pity on the boy.

"It's a Nancy Drew notebook," I said. "I'm investigating the case of the missing plants. Do you have any theories about who the thief could be?"

"It's that black bugger at the end of the road!"

"Watch yer language boy!"

"Sorry Dad. But you even said that it was the darkie."

"Aye, I did. He's the logical choice."

"I'm afraid you're right Mr Storey," said Grandma with a firm nod. "He's the only one in the whole street with a fence around his garden. What's he got to hide? I ask ya.

"I noticed a tall elderly lady coming out of her driveway from across the road. "What do *you* think, Auntie Rose?"

"About what, petal?" I smiled, and stood a little closer to my favourite great aunt who joined the huddle of neighbours in front of her sister's house.

"Natalie's doing a little detective work, Rose. She wants to know who's stealing all our plants." Grandma took my hand, pulling me back. I looked quickly to see if Auntie Rose had noticed, but there was no change on her delicately made-up face.

"Well whoever it is, he paid me a visit last night too."

"What did he take, Auntie Rose?"

"Two tea-roses from under my bedroom window."

"That's not too bad then, that bed could do with thinning out."

Auntie Rose didn't seem to hear her sister as she pointed to my notebook with a pretty pink nail. "That's one yellow and one white, dear." I looked up and noticed another resident of Jasmine Close coming out of the house next door. "Morning, Mr Rashid."

"Good morning Natalie! It's good to have you visit us again. Are you staying long?"

"Most of the summer; aren't you pet?" said Grandma.

"Who's this?" I asked, bending down to stroke the young golden Labrador that was walking with the Pakistani man.

"His name's Gazza. He's the latest addition to the family."

"Are you sure he's not the thief, Mr Rashid?"

"Oh, I don't think so, Mrs Porter. He'd have a hard job removing those large pots from Mr Storey's driveway!"

The Peace Garden

Mr Storey laughed. "Did you lose anything Abe?"

"He tried to get one of my pink azaleas, Bert, but he gave up after a while."

I checked my notes. "He tried to get one of Grandma's azaleas too. Didn't he Grandma?"

"Yes pet he did," said Grandma, eyeing Gazza with suspicion.

I went over my notes again before I went to bed. Well, so far, it seemed as though the man at the end of the cul-de-sac was the main suspect. I wondered who he was. He was obviously a black man, but beyond that I didn't have much to go on. I'd have to do some more investigating.

What would Nancy think? I picked up one of four books that I'd brought with me from Washington. They were all about the famous titian-haired detective, Nancy Drew. I didn't really know what titian hair looked like, but by the picture of Nancy on the cover, I presumed that it was a golden red, like mine. In fact, I looked a lot like Nancy, I thought: the same red hair; the same green eyes; the same dusting of freckles. Now all I had to do was get rid of these braces on my teeth, and pray that my right breast would grow. Every boy was in love with Nancy!

Of course, they were attracted by her razor-sharp mind and matchless detective skills too. I'd work on those while nature decided what to do with the rest of me.

Chapter Two

"IT'S BEST TO plant them as deep as they'll be high." Old, worn hands covered mine as we put the bulb in the soil. "It's a little early to be planting daffodils, we usually do it in October, but I remember how much ya liked it last time. Compost then soil then a good soaking from the can."

Rising on her knees, hands on back, the old lady stretched and grimaced. "I think ya'll have to do the rest yerself, pet, or I'll have nowt left in me." I helped her to her feet then settled her on the step. Back to work. I dug some holes, about a ruler's depth, then half the same from each other. A bit of compost, then the bulb, more compost, then soil. Grandma said we were putting them to bed for winter.

"But why do we have to plant them so far in advance, Grandma?"

"They need time to get used to things pet. When ya cover 'em they spend time getting familiar with their new home. They check out how much moisture there is, what kind of minerals are in the soil, how much sunshine gets in, and if they're happy, they'll grow. They'll spend all winter getting ready to come out in spring. Then when the time's right nothing'll keep 'em down."

"Just like people."

"What's that pet?"

"Oh nothing," I said, looking at the house at the end of the street.

"Well, I think I'll go put the kettle on then. You come in when yer ready." She shuffled down the path, her grey perm shifting in the breeze. She stopped suddenly then turned smiling: bright blue eyes poked through pale crinkles like bluebells in the snow. "I've got scones for ya," she said.

The Peace Garden

Finishing the last of the daffodils I lay back on the grass. The sun was lulling, my eyes heavy. We'd spent most of the morning trying to repair the damage left by the thief. Oh it wasn't vandalism; he'd been careful how he dug out the plants. But to get enough root support he'd taken a lot of earth with him. The gaps were few, but like a mouth with a lost tooth, you noticed the difference.

With only two days until the judging it was too late to replant properly. We had managed to get some potted marigolds and geraniums from the garden centre at Ponteland and placed them in the gaps; but it was harder to disguise the spaces in the shrubs. The missing azalea and some of the gladioli caused jarring disruptions to the carefully graded back line.

Grandma Iris's was a traditional English garden; a good, old-fashioned design that could be found anywhere in England. Plants sloped inwards from the tall shrubs (rhododendrons and potentillas) at the back, hydrangeas and lilac in the middle, and a mixture of annual and perennial flowers at the front. All this was padded with ground-covering geraniums and stonecrop. The whole thing was backed by a five-foot wall, adorned with sweet peas, honeysuckle, clematis and summer jasmine. The front garden, being open to the road, consisted of a square of lawn, surrounded by jam-packed beds of daisies, chrysanthemums, delphiniums, carnations, irises and lilies.

The entire display was carefully planned to produce colour throughout the year. When the spectacular array of spring daffodils and tulips died off, the primadonna marigolds and petunias emerged to waltz in the summer heat. Then, just in case the others refused to perform, the perennially perfect foxglove and phlox were guaranteed to turn up every year. Autumn was ablaze with spectacular foliage, winter garnished with holly and yew.

Reliably English though it was, Grandma Iris's was not a cottage garden, and she was proud of it too. Grandma had nothing but disdain for the designer-cottage gardener who, in her opinion, was far too haphazard in approach. The self-seeding, quick-spreading hodge-podge of plants that made up a cottage display lacked the discipline and structure that she demanded of the piece of earth under her dominion. "How do you know how it will all turn out, Grandma?" I once asked.

"Well, pet, ya need a bit of faith. Ya have this idea, ya see, of what it'll look like in the future. Each bulb, seed and sapling, has the potential to become something great. Some work, some don't. Ya help them the best ya can, but in the end, they've gotta decide to do the job themselves."

By the look of it, Grandma's garden was filled with high achievers, suspecting, perhaps, that any slacking off would see them cast out of Eden.

The custodian popped her head out of the kitchen door: "We're short of sugar pet. I'll just go to yer Auntie Rose's. Back in a tick!"

"Back in a tick" I knew, meant more like "back in an hour". Despite Grandma's apparent dislike for her sister, she spent an enormous amount of time visiting her. "I won't hear the last of it if I don't," she explained, not explaining a thing. In fact there was a lot about my grandma's relationship with Auntie Rose that I didn't understand.

If you didn't know they were sisters, you'd never have guessed. Grandma, at seventy-five, was three years older, four inches shorter, twenty pounds heavier, two bra sizes bigger, and, in her opinion, a great deal smarter, than her only sister. Both were widows, but their lives could not have been more different if they were characters in a novel.

Iris always had a good head for business and had inherited the family hardware shop when her father died. By the time she retired she had developed a small chain. She had married the local piano tuner, George Porter, but George was more interested in playing the piano than opening a music shop.

George, it seemed, was a great disappointment to Iris. His early death, soon after my dad Jimmy was born, seemed to be more of a blessing than a curse, as in Grandma's day, divorce was never really an option. At least that's what she said after a couple too many sherries at Christmas.

Rose, on the other hand, had had it easy (at least that's what the sherry said). She'd still been at school when their father died and did not have to work in the family business like Iris did. She even went on to university in Durham. Paid for, my grandma never ceased to remind her, by brass tacks and elbow grease: Iris' elbow grease.

She married a minor aristocrat who was later injured in the war. She nursed him but he never regained his health and they never had a child. Years later, widowed and retired, the two sisters bought houses in the same cul-de-sac but that seemed to be all they had in common.

"I'm back pet. Come and have that tea and scones then." I opened my eyes and left my pool of sunshine, joining Iris Ludlow Porter at the kitchen table.

Chapter Three

WE SPENT THE next day, the eve of the great garden competition, at the hairdresser. Grandma was intent that if her perennials didn't impress the judge, our new hairdos would have to do the trick. The 'hairdresser' was vertically opposite Grandma's at Pam Storey's house.

The Storeys were relatively new in the neighbourhood, only having lived there for two years. They had moved to Jasmine Close from a council house in Wallsend. "I won't hold it against them, mind," my grandma declared magnanimously. "They're hard workers ya know, and deserve a chance to better themselves." This was very generous coming from a woman who believed that one's evolutionary development was reflected in whether one was 'council' or 'private'.

Bert Storey had worked his way up the food chain as a plumber: from apprentice to artisan to entrepreneur. He had the opportunity to buy his current business after his former employer had the misfortune of getting a flat tyre outside St James' Park five minutes after the Magpies had been thrashed 3-0 by Sunderland. The plumber, fatefully wearing a red-and-white striped shirt, was spotted by a group of grieving black-and-white clad fans taking his tyre-iron from the boot. "We thought 'e was after a bit o' aggro, yer honour," one yob put forward. Six of the seven hooligans were confined to jail for ten years, and the unfortunate man to his wheelchair for life.

Bert took over the business at a reasonable rate and had the satisfaction of putting into practice all the dreams and innovations of fifteen years of serfdom. He consolidated the domestic plumbing and municipal drain maintenance, hired a supervisor then diversified into small to medium industrial hydraulics, which

The Peace Garden

had been his pet subject at college. With the money rolling in, Pam resigned her position at Betty's Unisex and encouraged Bert to buy a house in a better area.

She had spent the first year in Jasmine Close sorting out young Roger's adjustment problems in his new school and redecorating the three-bedroom bungalow. The former consisted of frequent visits to the headmaster's office to apologise to irate mothers of black-eyed and red-nosed youngsters, the latter of a rather fetching scheme in lemon and teal.

Grandma was having a set. Adorned with red, yellow and green curlers she looked like a geriatric Rastafarian. Going under the dryer, Grandma could be mistaken for the first Rasta in outer space. Then Pam lit up a Benson 'n Hedges Special Mild. The setting lotion and nicotine were frying my brain so I decided to take a look at the garden.

Pam's lemon and teal theme was continued in the front yard. Surrounding the perfectly manicured lawn were dozens of yellow, blue and cream containers in a myriad of shapes and sizes. Arranged in graded clusters were evergreen shrubs, dwarf fruit trees, roses, annual impatiens, geraniums and zinnias, as well as a stunning array of begonias, dahlias and lilies.

Pam stepped out of the house. Her unnaturally blonde hair was cut in a stylish bob, with no tell-tale roots showing through. She walked over to where I stood on the lawn, her Lady Di heels sinking into the grass. She smiled. "It'll be your turn soon, pet. Any ideas?"

I shook my head, tossing my thick red ponytail over my shoulder. Peering through an overlong fringe, I asked her if she had any suggestions.

"Well, yer a young lady now, so why don't we try something a little mod." She lifted my ponytail, holding it this way and that against my face. "Bobs are in now ya know. Well 'ere in the UK anyway."

"In America too," I said.

"Well, why don't we cut it to shoulder length? A little shorter at the back then sloping down to points at the front. I'll thin yer fringe a bit, then feather it on top. It'll be long enough to tie out of the way, but short enough to give ya a bit of body when ya want it."

At the mention of 'body', I slumped forward and cut off eye contact with the 38 D's that Pam wore with pride. "Sounds great," I said, deciding to change the subject. "Why don't you plant your flowers in the garden instead of these pots?"

"It's all the rage," said Pam. "'Container gardening', they call it. I brought a lot of these from me old house. Ya couldn't do that if they was planted deep."

You couldn't steal them as easily either, I thought. "Suppose not," I said instead.

Pam continued like she'd memorised a feature from *Home and Garden*: "Ya see, ya can move em around a bit. Mix-'n-match. I don't know about you, but I get bored if things is the same year after year. And that's the problem with planting 'em. This way I can change me displays to look like new. And ya can keep up to date with the latest fashion colours."

"Fashion colours? In the garden?"

"Oh aye. They change from season to season. Bright colours for roses are out right now," she said, tucking a happy yellow hybrid tea rose behind a more favoured dusk pink one. "This way I'll never be caught out. And if I ever have to move again, well …" her voice trailed off as Bert's plumbing van pulled up the driveway.

"Yer home early, pet," said Pam.

"Aye, I thought I'd give the rock garden an once-over before tomorrow." Bert came up behind us, pulling my ponytail in a way that let me know that nothing I said would be taken seriously until I was at least fifteen.

"Cut it off then Mrs Storey."

"What's that love?"

"My hair. I think you're right. A bob is just what I need."

"All right then. Give me a minute though. I'll just make some tea for Uncle Bert, then finish off yer Grandma. Why don't ya look at the back garden? I'll give ya a shout when I'm ready."

"Okay," I said, and skirted around the back.

I could hear the Storeys chatting through the open window as I strolled towards Bert's recently constructed rock garden and pond. Small, cemented cliffs sloped down towards a figure-eight pond with a hydraulic fountain bubbling happily in the far corner. Despite only being built six months ago, according to Grandma the garden looked good enough to enter this year's competition.

I climbed into a weeping willow that predated the Storeys by thirty years and heard Bert reading aloud from the Evening Chronicle.

"That Mandela fella's in the paper again. I know he had a hard time of it and all but why do they have to keep harping on about him? It's been over four months since they let him out. Oh, aye, here's something interestin'. They mention the competition: 'Amateur gardeners from all over Newcastle are putting the final touches to their annual displays in anticipation of tomorrow's contest'. Any idea when they'll get to us, Mrs Porter?"

"About noon, Mr Storey. That should give us a fair chance to show off in good light."

"That it will, Mrs Porter. See 'ere, Pam, they're planning on building on that piece of wasteland soon. A shopping centre."

"That's good news, Bert; perhaps we can look at renting a space for the salon."

"No need for that pet, I earn enough for both of us."

Pam's reply was stifled by the kettle letting off its steam. I climbed a little higher in my willow: I could now see over the six-foot wall into the neighbour's garden. Shuddering with pleasure, I realised that I was looking directly into the enemy's lair, and there, inside a greenhouse, was the man-at-the-end-of-the-street.

I didn't think he could see me behind the curtain of branches, but pulled a little further back just in case. Out came my Nancy Drew notebook. Yes, he was a black man. It was a little hard to tell through the tinted glass, but he looked about five-feet-ten, of medium build and middle-aged. He peered through thick glasses at what looked like a flowering cactus.

I checked my list of stolen plants then quickly looked around to see if they were tucked away somewhere. Like Nancy Drew, I refused to condemn anyone until I had absolute proof. However, the large greenhouse dominated most of the backyard and it wasn't giving up its secrets easily. I needed to take a closer look. But just as I began to plan how to clamber out of my tree and over the wall, I heard Pam calling me from the kitchen. I wondered if Nancy Drew ever had a bob.

Chapter Four

GRANDMA WENT STRAIGHT to bed after *Coronation Street*, saying she needed an early night to prepare herself for the competition. With deceit born of necessity, I told her that I would like to watch the latest *Ruth Rendell* mystery as I needed to do a book report on it for school. She didn't notice the holes in my story and I bought myself a two-hour alibi. Fortunately my room was just off the living room so I didn't have to alert Grandma's suspicion by walking past her door when I dressed for my fact-finding mission.

I still wore my play-jeans and pulled a black anorak on top. With my not-so-easy-to-tie-back new hairstyle tucked into the hood, I tied the laces on my trainers and filled my pockets with notebook, camera and torch. Something-is-about-to-happen music was playing on the TV as I quietly opened the front door and stepped outside.

Directly opposite, Auntie Rose's lights were blazing, but I knew it was just to ward off potential burglars. Grandma had told Pam and me earlier that afternoon that Rose was out gallivanting with some of her toffee-nosed friends again. They looked fine to me when they came to pick her up in their Audi.

I turned left out of the driveway and walked quickly past the Rashid's house. Gazza the Labrador was scratching around in a flowerbed and looked up as I approached. He wagged his tail then barked out a welcome. I ducked behind a low hedge. That was all I needed, having to explain to Grandma's neighbours why I was traipsing around in the middle of the night. Mr Rashid appeared, silhouetted against the warm glow of the hall light. "Come in, boy," he said. Fortunately, Gazza seemed more interested in joining the family gathering than pursuing strangers. The door closed behind the two friends as I scooted across the road to the

Storey house.

I slipped down the alleyway between their property and the house-at-the-end-of-the-street, ducking as I passed the living room window where the family was watching *Match of the Day*. I climbed a sturdy trellis and was soon in Bert's alpine garden. There was the willow in the corner furthest from the kitchen door, shrouded in darkness. It was perfect. I propped my torch in the crook of the tree, shining it upwards. The dim cone of light inside the willow curtain was just bright enough to allow me to find my way, but not to attract attention from inside the nearby houses.

I scaled the wall then walked along the top until I reached a crab apple tree on the other side. I tucked the torch in my belt then clambered down the conveniently placed tree into the target area. Mission accomplished: I was in enemy territory. Taking out my list of stolen plants, I shone the torch into the dark corners of the garden: nothing out of the ordinary. There were one or two shrubs that had clearly been there a long time, the crab apple tree and a small vegetable garden. Rather boring really. I turned my attention to the large greenhouse that dominated the plot. Perhaps the evidence I needed was behind locked doors.

Unfortunately the entrance to the greenhouse was only a few feet from the kitchen door. A little risky, I thought, but I'd come too far to back out now. Hugging the wall, I skirted behind the bushes until I was level with the house. There was no light on in the kitchen, but I wasn't taking any chances. I got down on all fours then crawled under the window towards the greenhouse. I turned the handle. It was open. Keeping low, I pushed the screen-door then slipped inside. I paused for a few moments to catch my breath. My heart was beating fast, more from fear than exertion.

With a quick glance over my shoulder to confirm that I was alone, I switched on the torch.

Wow! I'd never seen anything like it. I didn't recognise any of the plants other than a flowering cactus in the corner. I could have been on Mars, for all I knew. There were certainly no missing dwarf conifers, pink azaleas, tea roses or geraniums; nothing that dull. Strange plants cast even stranger shadows across the concrete floor. I shivered.

Two fighting toms screamed; the bigger chasing the smaller across the yard. My torch turned them into raging lions, staking their claim on a jungle kingdom. Nancy Drew became Jungle Jane surrounded by poisonous plants and man-eating flowers.

Remembering my mission, I tried to document the exonerating evidence; but didn't have enough adjectives to describe the bizarre flora. I took out the camera and snapped away instead. Jungle Jane, daredevil photojournalist; I became one with the camera; whirling and turning, selecting and framing.

"What are you doing here?" A tartan dressing gown filled the lens. I screamed, dropping the camera.

"I said what are you doing here?"

I looked up into a dark face, frowning behind thick glasses. "I –I – was looking at your plants."

"I can see that, *'ntombazan*, but the question is why?"

For one mad moment I thought of escape, but my tormentor blocked the only exit. I decided to come clean; I had heard somewhere that one should always make a full confession if death was imminent. It was good for the soul. "I was looking for the stolen plants," I blurted.

"What stolen plants?"

"The ones that have been going missing from all the gardens."

The man looked surprised. "So, other people have lost plants too. I thought I was the only one."

"You've lost plants?" I looked around the greenhouse trying to spot the gaps.

"No, not here *'ntombazan*, from the front. I have an English garden there, just like your *mkhulu*."

"My what?"

"Your *mkhulu*, your grandmother. You are Mrs Porter's little one, aren't you?"

So, he knew who I was. Name, rank and serial number didn't matter anymore. "Yes, I am. My name's Natalie and I'm sorry I came here without your permission."

"So am I. But now that you're here, why don't I show you around. Then we can talk some more about those missing plants." He reached up and turned on the overhead light. The jungle came to life around us. Smiling, he reached out his hand and shook mine. "Professor Gladwin Nkulu at your service. Welcome to my home-from-home."

His eyes were animated as he took me from plant to plant, delighting in his role as tour guide to a foreigner. All the plants came from South Africa. I presumed Professor Nkulu to have the same origin. He had a deep rich voice that should have been sad, but wasn't. His English was clear, but his vowels were quite different. His *a's* sounded like *e's* and his *o's* were very round. His *u's* too were longer than usual. But after having lived in as many places as I had, my ear tuned quickly to the peculiarities of accent.

The little kingdom in exile was in full bloom. In the corner was the brazen aloe with its phallic (Mary Beth McKenzie had taught me that word) orange flower. This was the cactus-like plant I had seen from my spy-spot in the Storey's tree. Then we did a rapid tour from the alternately blue and white football heads of the agapanthus to the heady scents of the frangipanis. The lilies were regal: arums, tigers and kings. Next were the Ericas with the woody velvet proteas taking pride of place. The clivias shouldered out the freesias, but nothing could suppress the perfume of the bright little flowers.

"Why do you keep them in here?" I asked.

"They don't really belong in England. If I planted them outside, they might die. In here, I keep conditions similar to what they would be like in South Africa."

"Will you ever return?"

I thought I saw a shadow pass over his face, or perhaps it was just a frond from the giant fern. "Ah, *'ntombazan*, that is a question that can wait for another day. Why don't we talk about that plant thief over some hot chocolate and biscuits?"

I nodded then picked up my camera; it didn't look damaged. He switched off the light then led the way from the greenhouse towards the kitchen door. "I'll just phone your grandmother to let her know you're here."

"Oh please, Professor Nkulu, don't do that!"

He chuckled as we entered his clean, bright kitchen. "Ah, I see we have a subversive on our hands. You would have done well in the ANC Youth League."

"What's a subversive?" I asked, watching him put the kettle on and take out three mugs.

"Someone who doesn't just accept the way things are because someone older or stronger than them has told them that's the way it should be." He put hot chocolate in one mug then tea in the second. He paused, his spoon poised over the third. He called out into the house: "Thabo, do you want some hot chocolate?"

"No thank you *Tata*." Came the reply. It sounded like a teenage boy.

"Then come and meet our visitor, *bhuti*."

"In a while *Tata*, I'm talking to someone on the Net."

Gladwin turned to me; a frown perched on the bridge of his nose. "That's my son. He came to live with me six weeks ago from South Africa. He's a little shy, so it looks like we're on our own. Please sit down, *'ntombazan*."

He pulled out a red plastic chair and eased himself into it. I pulled out the one nearest the door from the kitchen to the living room. If the layout of the house was the same as ours, I would be able to see through the living room to one of the three bedrooms. Perhaps I'd be lucky. Taking my mug of chocolate, I took a quick peak and was rewarded with a glimpse of a fourteen-year-old boy working on a computer. He looked at me, then pushed the door to, but not quite shut. I turned to the father.

"What's that name you call me, *'ntombazan*?" I pulled down my hood and allowed my red hair to spring out.

He smiled; the frown disappearing from his eyes. "It is *isiXhosa* for 'little girl', but with that hair, and long white neck, perhaps I should call you *Khandlela*: 'little candle'."

I laughed at the thought, secretly preferring the image of a burning flame to a little girl. "Is Kosa your language?"

"Xhosa" he corrected with a click of his tongue, as if he were calling a horse. "Yes, it is my mother tongue"

"Where are you from?" I asked.

"Well, my ancestors are from the Transkei near Umtata. But I was born in Soweto, near Johannesburg."

"Is Johannesburg the capital of South Africa?"

"No. But it's the biggest and richest city in the country. We call it *eGoli*, the Place of Gold."

"Why did you come to England?" I asked.

I came here in 1976. I lecture in Political Science at Newcastle University. Now, tell me what you know about that plant thief."

For the next fifteen minutes we spoke about the missing plants. I showed him my Nancy Drew notebook and he asked me to add some foxgloves and fuchsias to the list. He seemed to be just as puzzled as I was. He offered me a biscuit but didn't take one himself. He poured himself a second cup of tea without sugar.

"Don't you like sweet things?" I asked him.

"Oh yes, I do. But I have diabetes. Do you know what that is?" I nodded. Mary Jane Rosing, a schoolmate of mine from Washington, had to give herself insulin injections every day. She was enterprising enough to demand ten cents from anyone who wanted to watch.

"Well, *Khandlela*, I think it's time you went home; before your *mkhulu* notices that you've gone." I looked at my watch, realising that I had ten minutes to get home before the end of Ruth Rendell.

"May I visit you again, Professor Nkulu?"

"It would be a pleasure. But perhaps next time you can ask."

I flushed. "I'm sorry. It won't happen again. Please, say goodbye to your son."

He nodded, showing me to the front door. Walking through the flower garden to the high gate covering the driveway, I had to agree with him: it was just as English as Grandma's.

Chapter Five

THE NEXT MORNING over breakfast I rehearsed my confession between spoonfuls of shredded wheat. Like most children, and some adults who never learn that most essential of life-skills, the quenched conscience, I saw my grandma as a quasi-divine figure, whose omniscience was sure to find me out; but the goddess was otherwise occupied. If she knew about my late-night jaunt she didn't say so. The competition was the focus of conversation.

"I don't know if the weather's going to hold, pet. Some gardens just aren't their best in the rain. Say a prayer to the Man Upstairs, will ya?" Grandma often called on the Man Upstairs in times of need but could manage without him when the weather was fine.

Straight after breakfast we went on a final inspection of the garden. Despite attempts to fill the holes, Grandma was still concerned that the judge would spot the damage caused by the thief. "Who would do this pet?" I wasn't sure, but at least I knew that it wasn't Gladwin Nkulu.

Auntie Rose was also in her garden. She waved me over. "Hello, pet. Is your grandma ready for the competition?"

"Yes," I said. "Are you?"

She picked a dead head off a rose bush. "As ready as I'll ever be, I suppose."

For some reason Auntie Rose was only entering her front garden into this year's competition. "There are some things a person would like to keep to themselves," was her only explanation. But the front garden was more than ready for the contest, I thought. She had replaced the two missing tea roses yesterday morning, and only a trained eye would know the difference. But that was the problem; the judge was a trained eye.

Not surprisingly, Auntie Rose's speciality was roses, the one thing absent from her sister Iris' display. The focal point of her garden was a trellised tunnel arching over the full-length of the driveway. It supported an awesome display of climbing and rambling roses. The white rambling rose had smaller flowers than its climbing cousin and only flowered in early to mid-summer. The larger pink climbing rose had a much longer flowering season, but at this time in mid-July, complemented the rambler like a bridesmaid to a bride.

The rest of my aunt's garden was a formally laid out blend of modern hybrid teas grafted to form high-standing trees; neat little bushes with exotic names like *Jacques Cartier* and *Robert le Diable*, and free-standing stems which made up for lack of volume with the most beautiful single heads in the whole garden. The main theme was pink and white, but Rose had managed to tastefully blend lilacs, purples and reds as well.

"Why do you only plant roses, Auntie Rose?"

"Well, in the front I do. The back's another story."

"But why?"

"Well, pet, any rose lover will tell you that they're like a jealous mistress. They demand special treatment that can't be given when there are other plants around. They're also quite fragile. If you plant them too near other large plants there'll be a battle for moisture and food that the rose might lose. Sometimes it's just safer to be on your own." She bowed her head: dove-white hair shrouded her face while her little pink mouth was tight as a spring bud.

"You were out late." A knifepoint in my heart. What to do? Come clean or play along? I wasn't sure how long my mental health could sustain the latter.

"I was out looking for the missing plants."

"At night?"

"Yes, well, I thought …"

She smiled; the bud blooming into full flower. "You don't have to explain yourself to me, pet, sometimes a person needs to do things on their own. As long as you're safe; that's all."

"Don't worry; I don't think I was in any danger." Relieved, I said goodbye then headed across to the Rashid's to check on their competition readiness.

Mr Rashid was out front with Gazza and the twins. The boys, Aktar and Abdullah, (Dullah for short), were thirteen and a great deal of fun to be around. We had played together a lot the previous summer, and I was looking forward to a few more games of street football or cricket. What I liked most about them was that they didn't treat me like a girl. They assumed that I could run as fast and climb as high, and, I was proud to say, I hadn't let them down.

They were in complete contrast to the very feminine Fatima, their twelve-year-old sister who just loved helping her mother in the kitchen and embroidering cushion covers. Now, don't get me wrong, I got on well with Fatima too, but I was much more at home romping with her brothers than helping her unpick cross-stitch.

But that year I thought we might have something else to talk about. Six months before, I started my monthly period and everything that goes with it: sprouting hair in all sorts of inconvenient places and crying at the drop of an egg. I wondered if Fatima had done the same. Apart from the physical changes, (not least my mismatched breasts), there was a lot of other stuff going on as well. Take boys for instance. The year before, Jack Mason was just an irritating boy in my class. But then, I discovered to my dismay, I actually enjoyed it when he teased me, and felt rejected when he hadn't done it for a while. I blushed, wondering if Aktar and Dullah noticed the change.

I needn't have worried. "Hi Nattie, wanna play cricket later?" Aktar smiled, revealing metal braces, just like mine.

"No time for that today, son," said Mr Rashid. "I need your help in the garden. Then don't forget you have to take Gazza for a long walk before twelve, I don't want him jumping all over the judge with his muddy paws."

"Maybe tomorrow, then," said Dullah.

"That'll be great," I agreed, turning to his father. "Are you ready for the contest, Mr Rashid?"

"I hope so, Natalie. The rhododendrons out front are looking fine, but the thief messed up Mrs Rashid's herb garden in the back."

Like Auntie Rose, Mr Rashid chose to specialise in one plant only. Bravely, I asked him why, even though I knew I would be in for a long lecture. I was at an age when I craved knowledge like some children crave sweets; Mr Rashid was a source of both. But I'm embarrassed to say that in later years I avoided him, averting my eyes from his pedantic gaze. He never took it personally though, and was as warm to me as his three children, who sadly treated him the same.

Offering me a polo mint, he started to teach: "Rhodos are very strong plants, Natalie, I've tried planting other things with them, but they just dominate any garden. They like to stick together, that's why they grow in forests back home."

"Where's that, Mr Rashid?"

"Well you can find them all over the world now, but they were first discovered in the Himalayas. They're very common in China, Pakistan, Northern India and Nepal. When the European explorers first found them, they thought they were a new kind of rose, so they called them *Rhododendrons* which is Greek for Rose Tree. They soon discovered that they weren't related, but by that time they were so popular in Europe that they kept importing new species from the East. There are now over eight hundred known species in the world.

"When my family first came to England in the 1950's they were surprised to see that our plants were already here. They were the first victims of colonialism. But we weren't complaining; it was encouraging to see how well they adapted; it gave us hope."

He lost me there. I asked him if Fatima was home. "Yes, she's helping her mother in the kitchen. They're preparing an early lunch."

"What are they making? Curry?"

He laughed. "No, I think it's fish 'n chips."

I walked down the side of the house to the back garden. Mr Rashid was right; the thief had done a lot of damage here: it was a shadow of what it had been last year. I remembered how Mrs Rashid had shown me around, like a scientist in a lab. Every plant had a purpose, whether for food, medicine or housekeeping.

Around the outside were various fruit trees: quince, apple, pear and mulberry. These were turned into the most aromatic jams, jellies and pies. Then there was an assortment of rosebushes in yellow, orange, white, pink, red, lilac and mauve. This sweet-scented rainbow was used to make pot-pourri that freshened the house and brought in a little extra cash when sold at the home industry shop. The rose hips were also used to make jam and syrup. Lavender freshened laundry and rosemary made therapeutic oil. Mrs Rashid said that if you had any aches and pains you could add it to your bath, or inhale it to fight off a cold. Mint was used for tea and basil, bay, garlic, cilantro and dill for cooking. In addition there was a substantial vegetable patch that supplemented the meagre fare offered by the local supermarket.

I was in awe of Mrs Rashid. None of my friends had a mother like her. Mine, although we were great friends, was as different from her as east from west. Mrs Rashid was straight out of a period novel: kind and softly spoken, living for her husband and children. My mother said she was repressed, that the feminist movement hadn't reached Pakistan yet; that she wasn't aware that there was another way to live. The thought that Salima Rashid might be more fulfilled in her family circle than in the boardroom, never crossed my mother's mind.

I remembered what she looked like the last time I saw her in the garden: her soft silk skirt brushed lavender, coaxing a gentle scent onto the breeze. Her glossy black hair was partially covered by a white scarf, a few strands pulled loose around her neck. Oval eyes smiled at me from an olive face. I had drunk in her spirit like a parched traveller.

Then, remembering why I was there, I turned from the raped garden and knocked on the kitchen door.

"Come in," called a gentle voice. It was Mrs Rashid. I pushed open the door and walked into the kitchen, welcomed by warm tones of yellow and bronze. Dried flowers hung from the ceiling and vegetables overflowed from tiers of wicker baskets. Fatima was peeling potatoes at the wooden table while her mother whipped up a batter for the fish.

"Hi Nattie," said Fatima with a smile; her perfect white teeth not needing the discipline of a wire retainer.

"Yes, hello Natalie," said her mother. "It's wonderful to see you again."

"You too Mrs Rashid, I hope you're well."

Fatima laughed. "You've got more of an American accent than you had last year."

"Yes, but I can still hear the French," her mother teased. "You should stay with a good Pakistani family and learn to speak proper English!"

I laughed then asked her how she felt about her garden being damaged so near to the contest. "Well, my dear, there's nothing I can do about it now. Whoever it was who stole them must have had a very good reason for doing so, now that we're in the age of VCR's and stereos. I'd be interested to find out what he's doing with them."

"Or she," corrected Fatima.

"Or she," said her mother. "Will you be staying for lunch, Natalie? We're going to eat at eleven so that it's over and done with when the judge comes."

"Thanks, but I think Grandma's already made something for when the judge has gone. I think she's on a fast until then; she thinks it might influence the divine favour."

Mrs Rashid smiled, knowingly. "Well another time then. Are you finished with those potatoes, Fatima?"

"Yep, can Natalie come with me to my room?"

"Of course. But lunch will be ready in twenty minutes."

We left the kitchen and went to Fatima's candy-striped room. The back of her door was covered with posters of *Take That* and *Jason Donovan*. "I like your hair," she said as she threw herself onto the bed. "I'm thinking of getting a perm, but Mam says it wouldn't look natural. It's still up to me though."

"I think she's right," I said, flopping into a rocking chair next to one of Fatima's hand-stitched dolls. "Your hair's so thick it would be top heavy. Why don't you just layer it a bit to give it some shape?"

"I'll think about it." A white dressing table drawer was slightly open; I spotted the tell-tale packaging of sanitary pads. So, we were in the same boat. I wasn't sure how to broach the subject and felt strangely awkward. I heard Mrs Rashid call her husband and sons to come and wash up. The boys ran past the window with Gazza at their heels. I wished I could be with them.

"Perhaps I should go," I said, as casually as possible. "I think Grandma needs a bit of moral support."

"Okay, I'll see you later then. Perhaps we can go to the new Metro Centre. They say it's the biggest shopping complex in Europe."

Now that excited me. "Oh, yeah! I'll ask Grandma. Will it be okay with your mum?"

"I think so. As long as we catch the bus back before it gets too dark."

I got up to leave. "Turrah!"

Fatima grinned. "That's more like it! Ya'll be sounding like a real Geordie before too long. Turrah!" Laughing, I shouted a goodbye to the rest of the family then walked the short distance to my grandma's house.

The next hour was painfully slow. Grandma was picking, prodding and sighing while hoeing and re-hoeing already perfect beds. Auntie Rose across the road kept popping out her front door and checking her mother-of-pearl watch. Mrs Storey was repeatedly dusting her containers, cigarette in hand, while her husband swept the driveway. After their early lunch, the Rashid boys took an elated Gazza for a long walk to the common, while Mr Rashid wiped the glossy leaves of his rhododendrons with a damp cloth. The clock struck twelve.

At exactly two minutes past, an Evening Chronicle van came around the corner. It drove to the end of the cul-de-sac, turned around in front of the Nkulu house, then parked on the left-hand-side of the street in front of Auntie Rose's driveway. Rather selfish, I thought if she had to leave in an emergency. But Rose didn't look as if she was going anywhere in a hurry. She came out of her house with consummate grace, as if surprised to see her two guests climbing out of the van. She shook hands with a short, portly gentleman with spectacles and a receding hairline then reached out her hand to the tallest, skinniest woman I had ever seen. Her dark hair was streaked with grey and draped across a long, sunken face like a prayer-shroud in a synagogue. The head was perched on the wafer-like body by means of a very snappable neck. I wondered if the ribbon around her straw hat, tied under the chin, was just added insurance.

I followed the pair, a transvestite Laurel and Hardy, from house to house, plot to plot, gardener to gardener. They didn't say much, making notes or taking the odd photo; from Auntie Rose to Pam and Bert Storey to the Nkulus. They stopped at Gladwin's gate, consulted their list then passed over like the Angel of Death. A fiercely benign Abe Rashid greeted them then introduced them to Salima who emerged with some iced-mint tea. The other contestants, standing with their praise offerings, raised their eyebrows as if to say: "Trust the Pakistanis." Then brows came down, colliding with each other, as Ollie Hardy said "I love rhododendrons too." But the Rashids' hope was quickly dashed when the judges emerged from the vegetable and herb garden shaking their heads.

Next was Grandma Iris. Nine-nine-nine. Nine-nine-nine. I repeated the emergency dialling code in case the septuagenarian quivered herself to shreds. "Ah Mrs Porter, we've been looking forward to your offering after your previous successes". Iris tossed a quick glance at Rose who was pretending not to listen. "Pity about the gaps though." She wilted.

"We've had a thief in the cul-de-sac," she mumbled.

"Oh," said the judges, "pity." They climbed into the van then noticed that the road was filled with supplicants. They looked at each other then nodded. Stan Laurel rolled down her window. "Sorry, we'll have to look somewhere else for a winner this year. I hope you catch the thief." The window rolled up, the van pulled off, and the gardeners stood watching as it drove out of sight.

No one spoke. As one body they turned and stared at the Nkulu house. They didn't see the Toyota pull up behind them. "Excuse me, could I get past?" It was Gladwin. Thabo was sitting next to him. "Oh, by the way, how did the competition go?"

"Ya know very well how it went," Bert Storey lurched towards the car.

"How could ya do this to us?" cried Grandma.

"Is this any way to treat your neighbours?" spat Auntie Rose

The Peace Garden

with as much venom as she could muster.

The Rashids said nothing, but were clearly wondering if he was the one.

"Why don't ya just push off back to Africa?" said a recently broken voice. It was Roger.

"Now hold on there Roger," said Mr Rashid with a worried tone.

Standing next to her son Pam didn't know whether to be proud or ashamed, "The lad's entitled to his own opinion."

Thabo said something to his father in *isiXhosa*. The elder Nkulu snapped back, his knuckles pale on the wheel. Thabo tossed his head in disgust. Why wasn't he defending himself? I wondered. As the car edged forward, his guilt was confirmed. The man needed an attorney. "It wasn't Professor Nkulu. He's not the thief!"

The car stopped, the crowd whipped round. I stepped forward. "I was in his garden the other day," I looked at Grandma; her face was ashen, "Okay, last night. I was looking for the plants. They're not there. I checked. Professsor Nkulu isn't the thief."

Gladwin's knuckles turned brown, the mob backed off, Thabo stared ahead. "I took photos if you want to see them!"

"That won't be necessary, Natalie." Abe Rashid reached his hand through the window. "We owe you an apology, Professor Nkulu."

"Yes, you do," said Gladwin, ignoring the hand and staring at his persecutors one by one. They dropped their eyes. He drove off without a word.

Chapter Six

THE NEXT DAY at Jasmine Close was deathly quiet. The Rashids piled into their station wagon at about half past eight, leaving Gazza to mourn alone. There was no sign of life from the other four houses, other than Roger Storey kicking a ball against the garage wall. At ten o'clock I took pity on Gazza and decided to take him for a walk. I asked my grandma if it was okay, and she didn't seem to mind. After doing her housework Grandma Iris had retired to her room where she was poring over old photographs and tidying up her scrapbooks. I had a glimpse of a photo of her and Granddad George in happier days while visiting Kew Gardens in Kent.

Gazza was thrilled to see me as I opened the chicken-wire gate that kept him in the back garden. I fetched his leash that Dullah had told me hung outside the kitchen door. "Come on then, let's go for a walk." I loved dogs and had always wanted a puppy of my own. Unfortunately our roving life-style didn't allow for the luxury of having a pet. I spent a few minutes going over the basics with Gazza, showing him who was boss. It took a while for him to get the message that he wouldn't choke if he didn't pull on the chain. Eventually, we came to an understanding and started out on our adventure.

It was a lovely, clear day. Saturday's threat of rain had never materialised, and the sun shone bright and hot. I wore my play-jeans and a loose checked shirt. My hair had calmed down a little from yesterday and lay obediently around my face. I turned right out of Jasmine Close then headed slowly up the hill towards the common. The road curved until I was almost behind the Nkulu house.

This area on the outskirts of Gosforth was less developed than the estates closer to Newcastle. Despite having been zoned for residential development in the early 'seventies, there was some controversy over a nearby heath, and conservationists had pushed through a moratorium on development until further notice. Thus, the street behind Jasmine Close which housed a small Co-op suparette, was the last sign of civilisation before the wilds of the common; all except a hedged-off area about the size of two football fields. It was popularly known as the Wasteland and had been about to be developed before the conservationists put a stop to it.

I bought a coke and crisps from the Co-op then decided to share them with Gazza in the privacy of the Wasteland. I remembered from the exploration of previous years that there was a gap in the hedge, that, as long as you didn't mind getting your knees dirty, and watched out for some strands of barbed wire, gave you access to the fenced-off area. I found the hole and with Gazza snuffling at my heels, started to crawl through.

The ground was recently scuffed and twigs freshly snapped: someone had passed this way not too long before. I thought of backing out and going to a safer place for my picnic, but decided that it would be too much trouble to reverse proceedings. Besides, who would hurt a girl with a dog? I pushed the last branch aside then pulled back. There was someone else in the Wasteland and that someone was Thabo Nkulu.

He was bending under a large oak tree in the bottom right-hand corner, about fifty feet from my tunnel. He was digging. Gazza began to whine, wondering I suppose why we were stuck in this stupid hedge. I emptied my crisps on the ground to placate him. What was Thabo doing? The boy had his shirt off and his dark torso glistened over faded blue jeans. Something stirred in my lower abdomen, and it wasn't for want of food. At fourteen, Thabo was on the brink of manhood, a firm layer of muscle over his boyish ribs. His back was turned, but I remembered the high cheekbones and wide-set eyes that had stared through the windscreen of his father's Toyota.

The boy straightened, flexing his lower back, muscles rippling. He stepped aside, spade in hand, and revealed a newly planted pink azalea that looked suspiciously like the one that had disappeared from my grandma's garden.

Suddenly the pieces fell into place. There were Auntie Rose's yellow and white tea-hybrids and a large patch of lavender from Mrs Rashid's herb garden. A tree house had been built in the oak with a ladder leading up to it. Mrs Storey's dwarf conifers, pots and all, stood sentry on either side. A flagstone path led from the tree towards the tunnel in the hedge where I was hiding with beds of recently planted geraniums, fuchsias and foxgloves on either side. Further back were gladioli flanked by sunflowers and irises. Honeysuckle cascaded from a hanging basket attached to the tree. I looked at Gazza incredulously: "Thabo's made himself a garden. He's the thief!" The dog just chewed a stick.

Thabo looked at his watch then pulled on his shirt; it was clear that he was packing up for the day. I decided that I should get out of there before I was discovered. To Gazza's relief we backed out of the hedge then hurried home, checking every few minutes to see if Thabo was following us. What should I do? Like any child I resisted the idea of telling grown-ups who would take the whole thing out of my hands. Knowledge was power, I decided, and I was in control. Oh, I wasn't planning on blackmailing the boy – that wasn't in my nature – but I wanted to keep the secret until I had investigated the whole thing thoroughly. There were too many unanswered questions to let it slip out of my hands so soon.

As I turned into Jasmine Close I resolved to follow Thabo at the next opportunity, and perhaps take a closer look at the intriguing garden. Confrontation was not an option as the mysterious South African boy scared me as much as he thrilled me.

Gazza tugged viciously at my arm, breaking free and running to meet Aktar. The Rashid children were back, playing cricket in the street. I apologised to the Pakistani boys for taking their dog without permission.

"Oh, that's fine, Nattie, I'm sure Gazza didn't mind," said Dullah.

"Where'd ya take him?" his brother asked.

"To the common," I lied, only skipping a couple of beats.

"Wanna play cricket? Fats has gone to ask Roger too."

"Okay," I said, wondering how the boys could let their delicate little sister speak to the terrifying Roger on her own. Besides, I didn't think he'd come.

"I'm gonna bat first, and if ya don't like it ya can get stuffed!" Roger announced his arrival; a blushing Fatima close behind. There was something going on here that I didn't want to know about. The twins didn't object. Dullah took the ball; Aktar stepped behind the wicket. That left Fatima and I to field. Before long, it became clear that Roger should stick to football. He was clean-bowled twice then caught behind. He refused to budge, accusing everyone else of cheating. I was surprised at how readily the twins gave him "one last chance." Then, at last, a miracle happened: bat connected with ball and it flew over our heads, destined for a six.

"You're out!" Thabo walked up behind me, ball in hand.

"You can't catch me out; yer not even playing!" Roger snarled.

"Okay," said Thabo, "then catch!" He threw the hard ball directly at Roger; the skinhead ducked, just in time.

"Ya black bastard!" Roger ran towards the newcomer, thrashing the air with his bat. The Rashid boys grabbed him from behind, trying to pry the bat handle out of his thick fingers. Roger roared as Thabo calmly stood his ground. Aktar finally managed to liberate the bat, but as his grip slackened on the raging boy, Dullah couldn't hold him on his own. Thabo and Roger collided like freight trains.

Now, I didn't know much about boxing, but I'd heard that you get allocated points for the number of clean blows you inflicted upon your opponent. If I were a judge, Thabo would have three and Roger two. Beyond that, there wasn't enough space between them to get a clear shot. They tumbled to the ground, tearing their flesh against the tarmac. I reckoned that round one had almost come to an end, when the fight was stopped by Mr Rashid. But I wasn't sure how long the slightly-built referee could keep them apart, and was glad to see their respective fathers arrive on the scene.

"What's going on 'ere," asked a red-faced Bert Storey.

"He nearly took me head off with that bloody cricket ball, Dad!"

Bert turned on Thabo: "Keep your filthy hands off my son!"

Gladwin squared up to Bert, chest to chest, "You will not talk to my son like that!"

But before Bert could respond, Thabo pulled his father back. "I don't need you to fight for me, *Tata*, mother and I have fought many battles without you." Gladwin winced then watched as his son walked away.

"I hope this won't stop everyone from coming to the barbecue tonight." It was Mrs Rashid. She touched Gladwin's shoulder. "I think this shows us once again that we need to work out our differences in a peaceful way."

Gladwin and Bert stared at each other. "Well, I don't know about him, but I'll be there, Salima," said Bert.

"So will I," said Gladwin. "I will not cheapen your hospitality, Mrs Rashid."

I was confused. "What barbecue?" I whispered to Fatima. The two of us were standing at the back of the growing crowd of neighbours.

"My mam thought that she would try to bring us all together after yesterday's flare-up. She said the reason these things happen is that we don't talk to each other. So she asked everyone to a barbecue while you were away with Gazza. Will you come?"

"I'll see what my grandma has to say." The crowd began to disperse. I noticed my Auntie Rose watching through a lace net curtain. Grandma was nowhere to be seen.

When I got inside, Grandma was on the phone. It looked like she'd been crying. "It's yer dad, pet," she said, offering me the handset, and retreating to her room.

I took the receiver, "Hi Dad!"

"Hello darlin', how are things at Grandma's?"

"Oh, very exciting. There's just been a fight outside, and there's been someone stealing plants. And I know who it is!"

"You be careful Nancy Drew! And I was worried that you might be in danger if you went with your mother to Rwanda!"

"How is she?" I asked.

"Fine. I spoke to her last night. She sends her love. She said she'll be flying out on Wednesday. Do you want to come home for the rest of the summer and see her?

"That depends. Will the two of you be together?"

"I don't know darlin', that might be difficult."

"Why?"

"You know why. I've got my work, she's got hers. I'm going to a conference in Manila and …"

"It's all right, I'll stay here. Maybe Mum can pop over?"

"Maybe, but don't get your hopes up. You know that she doesn't get on well with your grandmother."

"Is that what's wrong with her?"

"Who?"

"Grandma, something's wrong with her. She can't be so upset about losing the garden competition, can she?"

"Well, with your Grandma, I wouldn't be surprised. But not this time."

"Why, what is it?"

"It's the 17th July. The day Grandad George died. That's why I called."

"But I thought Grandma didn't really love Grandad, so why would she be so upset?"

"Who told you that?"

"Mum did." I regretted it as soon as I said it, realising that it could be used as ammunition in a future parental battle.

"Well, that's not true, pet. No matter what Grandma says, she loved him. She could just never forgive him for who he was."

"Oh," I said, struggling to understand.

"Well, I've got to go. I'm missing you."

"I'm missing you too, Dad." We said our goodbyes then put down the phone.

"Want some tea pet?" It was Grandma. She'd splashed some water on her face and was looking much better.

"Yes please," I said, ignoring the ill feeling I had about the future of our so-called family unit. Instead, we chatted about the barbecue and decided that it would probably be a good idea to go. Grandma felt surprisingly bad about accusing Professor Nkulu of stealing the plants, admitting that if she had taken the trouble to get to know him earlier, she would have known the truth, and perhaps saved the plants.

"Ya see I didn't want to go to the police if it was a neighbour. It would have caused a whole lot of unpleasantness in the street, not to mention bringing down the tone of the neighbourhood. We don't want to become like those council house people, being carted off to prison every other week, now do we? But now, I think I'll speak to the others and see if we should report it."

I sipped my tea, imagining Thabo being bundled into the back of a police van, much to the embarrassment of Grandma, and the delight of Roger. It was up to me to make sure it didn't happen. But how could I do it without telling the grown-ups? I decided that I should try and warn him.

Chapter Seven

IT WAS A BEAUTIFUL evening for a barbecue: mid-July in the North East of England, with long summer days, and short starry nights. The sun was still shining at eight o'clock when Grandma and I walked next-door to the Rashid house. Roger and the twins were playing one-bounce football on the front lawn. Gazza was trying to join in, producing the occasional header to impress his human team-mates. Around the back, Pam and Fatima were sitting on deckchairs discussing potential hairstyles, while Salima walked to and from the kitchen with a variety of delectable snacks.

Bert and Abe stood at the grill, tongs in hand, sharing tips on how to produce the best barbecue. According to Abe, the secret was in the preparation of the meat: the best cuts soaked overnight in marinade. Bert believed that it was in allowing the coals to settle and glow before putting the meat on and how long it was marinated made no difference at all. Auntie Rose sat nearby with one ear on the conversation and one eye on the meat. She suggested they were both right, but since her perspective didn't produce an outright winner, the duellists refused to compromise.

Grandma and I sat in the two available chairs between the hairdressing and barbecue special interest groups. As Mrs Rashid emerged from the kitchen with a tray of veggie sticks and dip, Gladwin popped his head around the corner. He stood there for a moment, unsure of what to do. Salima put him at ease: "Professor Nkulu, how delightful that you could come. Please sit down!"

"Thank you Mrs Rashid, it is an honour to visit your home."

Salima put down her tray and took him by the arm, leading him like a chaperone at a coming-out party. Abe, noticing the newcomer, hung up his tongs, wiped his hands on his apron then pulled out a chair.

"Please, Professor Nkulu, take a seat."

"Thank you Mr Rashid," said Gladwin stretching out his hand. The men shook firmly, lingering for a moment, savouring their first contact as neighbours.

Gladwin nodded to the rest of us: "Good evening, ladies." The ladies acknowledged his greeting then carried on with their conversation. Gladwin sat down. Suddenly, Bert Storey approached the South African with two beer cans under his arm. All conversation stopped.

"Would ya like a beer, Professor Nkulu? It's the world famous brew, Newcastle Brown Ale."

Gladwin stood then reached out his hand. "I would indeed, Mr Storey." He took the beer in his left hand, leaving his right outstretched. "And please, call me Gladwin."

Bert smiled, took the hand then said, "And I'm Bert. There should be no airs and graces between neighbours." Gladwin joined the other men at the grill and added his tuppence-worth to the gathering body of evidence on how to have the perfect barbecue.

Where was Thabo? I had expected him to come with his father and told Gladwin as much. "Ah, *Khandlela*, my son did not want to come. He said that peace between parents is not peace between children. Perhaps you could persuade him otherwise. Why don't you go and see him; the house is open."

I turned to ask Grandma, but she was embroiled in the hairstyle discussion group, asserting that perms were the only cure for terminally straight hair.

I left without asking; assuming that if she noticed she would think I was playing with the boys on the lawn. Skirting the cup final, I headed towards the Nkulu house. Roger called after me, asking where I was going.

"I'm going to ask Thabo to come to the party."

"Why bother? That black bastard's better off not comin'."

"I wish you wouldn't call him a black bastard, Roger," Aktar said quietly.

"Why not?"

The dark-skinned boy caught the football, holding it as he answered. "Well, we're black too."

"Don't be daft, it's not the same. Yer one of us. He's a foreigner.

The Peace Garden 49

'ere, chuck us the ball." The twins looked at each other then shrugged, continuing with their game.

I opened the Nkulu gate, walked through the pretty English garden and knocked on the door. There was no answer. I knocked again: still no response. I turned the knob. Gladwin was right, it was open. I walked through the hall and into the living room, taking in the wooden and soapstone sculptures of people and animals. The walls were adorned with vibrant paintings of African ghettos.

I could see Thabo sitting at the computer through his open doorway. I called out, not wanting to surprise him. He addressed me without taking his eyes off the screen. "What are you doing here?"

I walked towards the doorway. "I came to invite you to the party."

His fingers moved ceaselessly on the keyboard. "Thanks, but I've already been invited."

"Then why didn't you come?"

"I've got better things to do than pretend that everything's okay."

"Like pretending we don't exist?" By this time I was in the room, standing next to his desk. There was a poster of Malcolm X on the wall as well as of another man I'd never heard of. The blurb said: *Steve Biko*.

"No; like talking to my real friends on the Internet." His eyes were fixed, his fingers mobile.

"What's the Internet?"

For the first time his eyes left the screen and looked into mine. They were a rich chocolate brown, laced with glossy black lashes. He motioned for me to sit on his bed. I was surprised to see that he had a Newcastle United duvet cover: just like an ordinary boy. A wry smile partially lit up his face. "You've never heard of the Internet?" I shook my head.

He swivelled in his chair to face me. It was a small room and his knees nearly touched mine. I tried to disguise my shallow breathing. "It's not that surprising, I suppose," he said, almost to himself, "I only got connected because my dad's at the university."

"But what is it?" I asked, not really sure if I cared, but wanting to keep him talking; acutely aware of his body so close to mine.

"It's a way of talking to anyone in the world as long as they're linked up along phone lines with their computer. It's cheap and very effective. Not only can you talk person to person via the keyboard, but you can find out stuff about almost anything; it's like the biggest library in the world."

"That sounds amazing," I said, "but if it's so hot, why doesn't everyone know about it?"

"Don't worry, they will. In five years, everyone will have heard of it, and in ten years it will only be weirdos who don't use it. Soon, people won't need books, and in perhaps twenty years, people won't need to go to school or work, they can just connect from home."

I liked the idea about not having to go to school but I was reluctant to accept that I wouldn't be able to curl up under the covers with my favourite Nancy Drew and a cup of hot chocolate. I decided that I would sign a petition against this phenomenon that threatened to take over the world – if anyone asked me to. But for now, I would keep my subversive (my latest word) beliefs to myself, and use it to keep the channels of communication open with this enigmatic boy.

He turned back to the keyboard and started typing. "Are you talking to someone now?"

"Yes, and you're interrupting me."

"Well, I'm here and they're not. Doesn't that make me a little more important?"

Thabo kept his attention on his computer friend. "At least these friends don't come into your home uninvited. I speak to them only when I want to." I noticed that he signed himself as *Ché*.

"You don't use your real name?"

"No one does. Well, those who know what they're doing don't. You see that's the beauty of meeting people on the Net. You can be whoever you want to be."

"You mean you can lie?"

He signed off then exited the programme. He was irritated. "Why did you come here, again?"

"Your dad asked me to try to get you to come to the party."

The Peace Garden

"Hah! That's just like him, getting a girl to do his work."

"What do you mean?"

The boy looked out of the window as if straining to see beyond the garden wall. "He left South Africa when my mother was pregnant with me. He should have stayed to help with the Struggle but he ran away. My mother didn't have that luxury. She was pregnant and they still arrested her. They only released her after she nearly died giving birth to me."

"Is this the struggle against apartheid?" I asked.

He looked at me scornfully, "What other Struggle is there?"

I didn't know what to say. He carried on, regardless of whether I was listening or not. "A lot of people left the country after the '76 riots but most of them went into training to become freedom fighters. My father wasn't one of them. Others went to university in places like England to learn stuff to bring back to the country."

"Isn't that what your father did?"

"So he says. But I know he won't go back. He's too comfortable where he is."

"Did he tell you that?"

"No. My mother did."

"How do you know she's telling the truth?"

He was silent for a while, staring out of the window. I thought he'd forgotten the question. I was just about to rephrase it when he turned to me and said: "Because I've known my mother for fourteen years and my father for six weeks. Who would you believe?"

Did he really want me to answer that? I didn't think so. I tried to change the subject. "So why did you come to England?"

"With my father living here, I was able to get a visa to come and study. Education for black people in South Africa is very poor."

"But you seem well educated enough. You know all about computers and speak English very well."

"Thank you *madam*," he said. I noted the sarcasm, but didn't understand why. I think he realised this and took pity on me. "Look, South Africa is a very difficult place to understand if you haven't lived there; particularly for a child like you." I bristled. He noticed, but carried on anyway. "My grandmother is a domestic servant for a wealthy white family in Johannesburg. They're good people. They helped get my father out of the country when he got into trouble. Then they paid for me to go to a private school that accepts black and white students together. The government doesn't like it, but I think they've just given up trying to shut it down. Now that Mandela has been released, it looks like things might change, but not quick enough for kids my age. Anyway, this white family arranged for me to come here. I'm going to finish high school, then go to university."

"What are you going to study?"

"Horticulture. You know, all about flowers and trees and things. Then I want to go home and plant gardens. Where I come from not many black people have gardens – they don't have enough land. The whiteys have got it all."

He looked at me then laughed. "You haven't understood a thing I've said, have you?"

"Of course I ..."

"Look, you're just a little kid, why don't you go back to the party?"

I started to object, but he turned his back and started typing on the computer. "They're going to call the police, you know."

"Who?"

"Everyone in the street. They're going to call the police and catch the thief. He won't get away with it forever!" Hah! I'd said it! He shouldn't mess with this kid! I turned to make my grand exit but as I reached the front door I heard him call after me: "And so they should! Stealing plants is such a terrible crime; it's right up there with apartheid!"

I slammed the door on his sarcastic laughter. What a horrible boy! I never wanted to see him again.

Chapter Eight

THE NEXT TWO days poured with rain. The long days and short nights weren't half as appealing when you couldn't go outside to play. I watched the water forming patterns on the front window and looked to see if any of the neighbours were out and about. But there was no sign of life. Only Gazza, who stuck his nose out once to do his business, then hurried back inside.

I had heard Mr Rashid's station wagon and Mr Storey's van leave early for work that morning, but Professor Nkulu's Toyota hadn't left the driveway. Grandma said that he had told everyone at the barbecue that he had taken leave during the university vacation so that he could work from home. "Cushy job," she commented. "And I bet he gets paid more than the other poor fools who really work for their money."

None of the children were around either. I didn't care about Roger, and I was more than happy not to see Thabo, but I wouldn't have minded spending some time with the Rashids. I phoned to see if I could go and visit. Mrs Rashid answered. "I'm sorry Natalie, but Fatima has a temperature and I'm keeping her in bed. If it's the 'flu, the boys will already have been infected, but I don't think you should take the chance with further exposure." Frankly, I wouldn't have minded a bit of 'flu, at least it would have given me something to do. I didn't confess my sickly fantasy.

So the next two days were spent chatting to Grandma about the not-so-good-old-days and reading all of my Nancy Drews twice over. Grandma said that when the rain stopped I could use her library card to get some new books. I wouldn't need it when the rain stopped! For once, Nancy Drew was not as distracting as usual. A new character kept butting into my mental landscape: he was dark and good looking. The more I reminded myself that he was a horrible boy who didn't deserve to be given the time of day, the more he kept demanding to take centre stage. It was quite irritating.

Fortunately by Wednesday morning the sun had chased away the rain. Soon after breakfast, Auntie Rose called and asked if I would like to spend the morning at her house. I asked Grandma if it was okay; she just raised her eyebrows and said: "I'll not stop ya if ya want to go." I did want to go.

Auntie Rose was in her back garden, the one that she didn't enter for the competition. It was exactly the kind of garden that Grandma Iris despised: the free-growing cottage style. I thought it was beautiful. When I was younger I imagined I saw fairies playing hide and seek amongst the foxgloves, gathering mistletoe for their druid masters. It was a secret world, suggesting depths to Auntie Rose that she kept hidden from ordinary mortals.

In direct contrast to the manicured precision of the front, the back was a haphazard mix of flowers and shrubs, as if it had just sprung up that way long ago. A narrow cinder path, fortified with stepping stones, wound its way through fairytale arches covered with clematis, sweet pea and golden hop leading to a circular lawn around a rustic old apple tree. Under the tree was a weathered bench a short distance from a pewter bird-bath.

Auntie Rose was sitting on the bench with a tray of tea things beside her. She was wearing a pretty pink dress, the skirt flowing loosely from an embroidered bodice. She smelt of musk, subtle yet distinct from the other fragrances in the garden. Her dove-coloured hair was tied back into a ponytail with a soft chiffon scarf, the same dusky colour as her dress. She put her finger to her mouth and indicated a pair of bathing starlings with a lift of a brow. I perched myself on the solid oak swing that my dad had put up four summers ago. The thick rope creaked, alerting the starlings to an alien presence.

"Don't worry pet, they'll be back. It just takes them a while to get used to visitors. Here, throw some of these crumbs on the lawn, they won't be able to resist for long." Auntie Rose passed me a saucer of bread pieces then poured us both a cup of tea. I noticed with pleasure that she also had some Spotty Dick on the tray, ready buttered and jam-packed with raisins.

The Peace Garden 55

"You disappeared for a long time on Sunday night." It was a statement, not a question, as was usual with Auntie Rose who invited but didn't demand confidences. I decided to treat it as the latter and get some things off my chest.

"Yes," I said, "Professor Nkulu asked me to call his son to the party."

"Well, you obviously didn't succeed," said Auntie Rose, passing me the Spotty Dick. "You came back on your own with a very red face."

"Oh did I? Do you think anyone noticed?"

"You mean your red face?" I nodded. "No, I don't think so. It's just that I know that look, I've seen it many times in the mirror."

"What look's that?" I asked suspiciously.

"The look that says if this boy wasn't so irritating I would fall in love with him." I could feel myself glowing as red as my hair. How did this sorceress know? She laughed gently then closed her eyes so she could see more clearly. I started to swing, backwards and forwards, to and fro. It was as hypnotic as the old lady's voice.

"When I went to Durham University in the 1930's I was so scared that no one would like me. There were so many beautiful young people from wealthy families who didn't speak with working class accents like I did. I didn't know how to make friends with them. Oh, I envied Iris so much. She spoke so easily with people, and everyone admired her. After Dad died, I wanted to help her in the shop, but Mother said I would just be in her way. I waited for her to go to university so that I could take over in the business, but she never did.

"I did well in school, particularly in English and Art, so I enrolled for a Bachelor's degree at Durham University. One evening in my second year I went to see *Romeo and Juliet*. There was a bit of a mix-up at the ticket office and somehow I was given a seat two rows back from my friends. I didn't mind, as I've said I was used to being on my own. But the strange thing was I wasn't. Alone I mean. Sitting right next to me was the most beautiful boy I had ever seen. He was about nineteen, the same age as me, with soft blonde hair, and the bluest of eyes.

"I was very aware of him throughout the first act and apparently the feeling was mutual. At interval he introduced himself as Richard Worthington and asked me if I would join him at the bar. In the best English I could muster I said that I would love to. We had a wonderful time, sipping martinis and laughing about Mercutio's Scottish accent. Before the end of interval I had discovered that he was a law student in his second year, and that his late father was Lord Worthington of Worthington Hall near Carlisle. He must have noticed something in my expression because he said: 'Don't worry, we're just minor aristocrats, and I'm the younger of two brothers. That's why I've been forced to get a qualification. It's either that or becoming a tour guide in our ancestral home.'

"'Oh, that's all right then,' I said rather stupidly. He laughed but I was saved further embarrassment by the foyer bell.

"After the show, he asked me if he could walk me back to my digs. Of course I agreed and I all but floated the two blocks home. He kissed me goodnight then said he'd call. But I waited two weeks and he didn't. I was furious! How dare he take advantage of me like that! How could I have let him kiss me? He probably thought I was a working class trollop. To top it all I saw him coming out of the Marks and Spencer's tea room with an ice-blonde on his arm.

"After that I decided to forget about him but somehow he wouldn't let me. Every time I tried to concentrate on a set work he arrived on the page. I even found myself sketching him during art class; most irritating. But it was on a Student Union outing to Corbridge that things came to a head.

"Our group had stopped off for a pub lunch at the Wheatsheaf. We had just finished starters when Richard Worthington and another young man came in. They didn't come with the SU group but Richard's friend seemed to know most of the crowd. The young man sitting next to me went off to the bar to order another round and Richard took the opportunity to steal his seat. I was cold and refused to even acknowledge his presence. He tried to make small talk then gave up after a while.

It was a long, painful meal. As soon as I could I excused myself saying I was going to the ladies' room; but sneaked out the back door instead. As I walked down the alley, squeezing past a shiny new sports car, I came face to face with Richard who had come out the front door.

"I couldn't get past him as the car was parked so close to the wall, but I certainly wasn't going to back out. Neither was he. We stood there, braced, neither giving nor taking. I was just about to say something about him not being a gentleman, when I saw the Student Union bus pull off from in front of the pub. I called out but it left without me. I was furious. I glared at Richard who just leaned against the bonnet, smiling, so I backed out from behind the car.

"'Where are you going? The bus has gone!'

"'I noticed. I'm going to the train station.' Then to myself: 'How could they forget me?'

"By this time he had run around to the other side of the car, again blocking my path. He opened the door, indicating that I should get in. 'Because I told them that Frank would take your place and you would come with me.'

"'How dare you! What makes you think I will go anywhere with you?'

"'Because you're interested to find out if I'll apologise for not calling you after that night at the theatre.'

"I crossed my arms, ignoring his gesturing towards the car seat. 'Well I'm not. Frankly, I've never given it a second thought.'

"'Well, I have,' he said softly, 'and I am sorry. Please, get in. I'll drive you to the station.' Then it started to rain, making my protestations ridiculous. We sat in silence, watching the wipers sweep from side to side.

"'To the station please,' I said.

"We drove through the village then over the old bridge on the Tyne to the railway station on the other side. But when we got there, getting wet between the car and the platform, the station master came up to us and said that there wouldn't be any trains for the rest of the day because of a derailment near Prudhoe.

"'To the car then,' he said.

"I looked at the empty platform and pouring rain then nodded. 'To the car then.' We were quiet for a while, but when I realised that we were heading north instead of south-east back to Durham, I asked him where he was going.

"'I just want to show you something; by way of explaining my bad behaviour.'

"'Oh, so you are going to explain it then?'

"'I thought you didn't care,' he said. I blushed, becoming extremely interested in the passing fields of daffodils. We stopped about a ten-minute drive north of Corbridge at a ruined manor house. Well, I don't really know if you could call it a house anymore as all that was left was a crumbling tower raised above the scattered rubble. By now the rain had stopped and Richard took my hand and led me up the steps to the top of the turret. The view was amazing: to the north were the Scottish lowlands, to the south, the Tyne Valley, to the west, the Pennine Mountains and in the east I thought I could glimpse the sea.

"'My family used to own this land, you know?'

"'I thought your land was over Carlisle way,' I said.

"He sat beside me, too close for comfort. 'It is; what's left of it. But at one time we owned land all across the North.'

"'What happened to it all?'

"'Well, like this place, it fell into ruin and we couldn't afford to keep it up. This one fell to a Jacobite raid in 1745. My ancestor withdrew to Carlisle but somehow never got around to rebuilding it. We may still own the land, I'm not sure, but it's been common ground for so long that it would do no good to claim it now.'

"'Why are you telling me all this?' I asked.

"'To explain what happened after that night at the theatre. As we were talking at the bar I realised that you were the type of woman that I would like to marry.' I blushed, allowing him to put his arm around me. 'The only problem was you were so obviously working class no matter how much you tried to hide the accent.' I started to pull away from him, embarrassed at being exposed, but he held me tight, carrying on with his explanation. 'I thought what it would be like to marry a girl like you and expose her to the likes of my mother. She would tear you apart. She's like many of my kind, refusing to accept that things are changing; she's like a dinosaur, I suppose. She was devastated when Edward chose Wallis over the

The Peace Garden 59

monarchy last year. I saw it as a sign of the times.'

"I finally found enough strength to pull away from him. 'Look, if you're going to insult me,' I said, standing up, 'then you can just …'

"He grabbed my hand, looking up at me, 'No, you don't understand, I'm not insulting you. I love you.' I stood there, confused. He got up, putting his hands on my shoulders. His blue eyes were earnest as he looked into mine: 'I didn't want to hurt you, I should have called, but I needed some space to work out what I was feeling. I finally realised when I saw you today in the pub that if I didn't listen to my heart, I would become a dinosaur too. What I'm trying to say … to ask … is, Rosemary Ludlow, will you marry me?'

"I don't know if I looked like I was going to faint but he quickly moved his hands from my shoulders to under my elbows. You may think I was stupid, Natalie, but as I stood there I felt like Guinevere in Camelot. Somehow this knight had asked Merlin to put a spell on me, a love spell, and it was working. If I was more practical I would have said no; but I wasn't.

"We were married a few months later; to his mother's disgust and my mother's rapture. Unfortunately Iris felt the same as the Worthingtons. I've never understood your grandmother, Natalie, you're either too rich or too poor; you can't win.

"Anyway, we lived in my digs in Durham until we both graduated in '38 then moved to Carlisle. We had a lovely little flat in town and I got a teaching post and Richard joined a firm of solicitors. But when Hitler invaded Poland the following year our honeymoon came to an end.

"Richard was called up to the army. As Captain Worthington he was sent first to France, then after Dunkirk, to North Africa under Montgomery. His elder brother, Christopher, was also there but was killed at El Alamein in 1942. How ironic: there was Richard, stuck in a desert on a mad crusade; now, officially, Lord Worthington. I saw him for a brief period in October '42 when he came home for his brother's funeral. We spent a blissful week at a hotel in the Lake District where I fell pregnant with our first child.

"But three months later Richard was seriously injured in a grenade attack in Egypt. He lost half his leg, and almost all his nerves. I went to visit him at the veteran hospital, but he didn't recognise me. I lost our baby a week later and never conceived again.

When he was released from hospital the doctors suggested that we go to live in Worthington Hall; they thought childhood memories might restore his equilibrium. They never did. In time he did improve: he remembered who I was and sometimes made sense. But the old Richard who had proposed to me on the tower of Camelot never returned. He finally died in 1968 when we were both fifty. The doctors said that his heart just stopped.

"As soon as he died I left Worthington Hall. Even though I was officially Lady Worthington, Richard's mother and sister never accepted me. At the reading of the will I discovered that they had somehow managed to get Richard to sign a document denying me the right to use the title after his death and bequeathing the bulk of the estate to his sister's eldest son. I could have contested it, I would probably have won, but I had enough money in my name to leave that place and start again somewhere new. So I decided to come here, near Iris; she's the only family I have now. I still have a few friends from my days as Lady Worthington, those people in the Audi for instance, but otherwise I don't socialise much and just keep to myself. Just like the old days."

She opened her eyes and smiled through welling tears. "Be careful not to fall in love with someone from another world Natalie; not all the dinosaurs have died."

Just then it started to rain; just like that day in Corbridge so long ago. I picked up the tray and ran inside, followed by my beautiful, sad, elderly aunt.

Chapter Nine

THE NEXT DAY, a Thursday, was hot and dry. My play-jeans were in the wash so I put on a pair of candy-striped Bermuda shorts. I wanted to wear a matching sleeveless sun-top, but it showed off my breast deformity without shame. I chose instead a loose, white T-shirt, which matched my shorts but disguised my chest. My hair was wild again so I used an Alice Band to pull it back from my face.

Grandma had a phone-call that morning from her solicitor: some urgent business required her to go to London for the next two days. She quickly arranged for me to spend the night at the Rashids'. Fatima's flu had progressed from the bed to the couch but Mrs Rashid said that it would probably be wise if I spent as much time outside as possible.

I spent the morning in town window-shopping then caught the bus back to Gosforth in time for lunch. Then I decided to take a walk up to the Co-op. Gazza looked at me expectantly from behind his chicken-wire fence but I decided to go on my own. As I entered the Co-op street my eye was drawn to the hole in the hedge. It wouldn't hurt to have a peek, now would it? Besides, the small car-park was full, implying long queues at the tills. It would be wise to wait a while.

Thus, fully justified, I got down on my knees and crawled through the hedge. And there was Thabo weeding his garden. It wasn't my fault he was there, now was it? After all, he didn't own the Wasteland, although you would think he did the way he behaved.

Suddenly I felt something cold and wet on my leg then panting warm breath on my neck. A lolling tongue slurped across my cheek as Gazza muscled his way into my not-so-secret place. The dog was thrilled to see me; chuffed, no doubt, that he'd outwitted the chicken wire and hunted me down. Leaving him behind must have been an oversight, he thought, but he'd forgive me anyway. He decided to bark to let me know his decision, alerting Thabo at the same time.

"Sssshhh," I said, probably interpreted in doggy-language as, "Glad you're here, let's play." He barked again. Thabo walked purposefully towards the hedge. I backed out as quickly as I could, hoping to get away before I was discovered. But, in my haste, I forgot to avoid the strands of barbed wire running through the hedge. One of them caught in my shorts. I tried to unhook it but Thabo was almost at the hedge. Gazza bought me a few seconds by jumping up at him and treating him to a tongue-lashing. I lurched backwards, my shorts, then my flesh, tearing in one long jagged line.

I must have cried out, I don't remember, I was only aware of the searing pain in my leg and the gushing blood darkening my shorts. Gazza was on me again, licking and snuffling, his hairy tan face blending with green leaves, red blood then numbing black.

"Leave, boy, leave." A firm voice. Gazza backed off, subdued. Arms under mine, pulling. The wire cut deeper. I think I cried again. "Here, let me see." Thabo was beside me, unhooking the barb from my flesh. He tugged, gently, pulling me free of the hedge. We were on the street side, an electricity generator hiding us from the supermarket car-park.

"Does it hurt?" I nodded. I looked down and saw a long jagged gouge from half way down my left thigh to just above the knee. "You'll definitely need stitches." He untied his shirt from his waist and used it to bandage my thigh. It only took a moment for white to turn to red. I started to get up. "What're you doing?" He asked.

"I'm going home," I said.

"Not on your own, you're not." He stood up then helped me to my feet. I leaned heavily against him, swaying. My foot felt squishy; a bloody reservoir filled my shoe. I swayed again, almost falling over. Without a word the boy picked me up. I think I protested, but as my cheek fell against him I felt his warmth, his strength. I closed my eyes.

The Peace Garden 63

The next hour was a blur. With Grandma not in Thabo took me to Mrs Rashid. She had one look at my leg and announced that I needed to get to a hospital as soon as possible. They only had one car and Mr Rashid had taken it to work. She told Thabo to go and get his father. So Thabo, Gladwin, Salima and I all headed off to the hospital, while the twins tried to get Gazza under control.

Twenty stitches and one tetanus shot later, I was released from the emergency wing and sent home with Mrs Rashid. The flu-ridden Fatima was demoted from the couch to the bed and I was settled in the living room. I was surprised to see Thabo agreeing to stay with his father for tea, which Mrs Rashid insisted was just what we needed for the shock. As she came through with the tray she turned to Thabo. "Oh, Thabo, I don't think I asked you where you found Natalie."

I was beginning to succumb to the painkillers but fought against my drowsiness to hear his answer. *I may have to save him*, I thought.

"She was caught in the hedge near the Co-op," he said.

"What was she doing there?" asked Mrs Rashid.

"I don't know."

"Where were you?" asked his father.

Thabo was silent then started to say, "I was ..."

"On the way to the Co-op," I answered. "So was I when I saw Gazza in the hedge. His collar was caught. He must have followed me." I felt guilty about lying, but soon forgot it as I drifted into a drug-induced sleep.

I woke later that afternoon when Mr Rashid came home from work. He was a pharmacist and Mrs Rashid had asked him to bring home some fresh dressing for my wound. She said I would need it in a day or two. The Nkulus had left and Fatima was sitting in an armchair wrapped up in a duvet. The boys brought out the Monopoly and the four of us had a game before supper. Fatima won, ruthlessly.

"So what were you doing in the hedge, Nattie?" she asked.

Now that the drugs were wearing off I felt bad about lying again. "I can't really tell you. It's a secret."

"A secret? Oh please tell us!" It was Dullah. I thought the boys were out of earshot but they had stashed the Monopoly and heard my confession in one go.

"Not yet. I'll have to speak to someone else first."

"You mean Thabo." Fatima's eyes were old.

"You got the hots for him?" teased Dullah.

"Leave her alone, Dud!" Fatima flashed as she defended me.

"You're only taking her side because you've got the hots for Roger the Dodger!" said Aktar.

"I do not!"

"Yes you do!"

The siblings continued to squabble until their father came in and put a stop to it. My little 'secret' was overlooked in the chaos. Supper was served around the coffee table instead of in the dining room to accommodate the couch-bound guest. With the twins sitting cross-legged on cushions, it appeared more comfortingly eastern than the usual straight-backed dining ensemble. The food was eastern too: a spicy ginger chicken dish with rice.

Aktar was asked to give thanks for the food. "Dear Lord, thank you that Natalie is safe and that Fatima is getting better. Please bless this food, in Jesus' name, amen."

In Jesus' name? Something wasn't right here. This was a Pakistani family. Did they say it just for me? I decided to correct their misunderstanding. "Don't worry, I'm not a practising Christian," I said.

Mr Rashid looked surprised, "It's all right, Natalie, we are. Didn't you know?"

"But you're Muslim!" I protested.

"No, we're Pakistani," said Mrs Rashid. "It's not the same thing."

I looked at her, puzzled, but she just smiled her earth-mother smile and asked the boys to help her clear the table.

I wasn't prepared to leave it like that and turned to Mr Rashid: "But I thought only Europeans were Christians and other people were forced to accept the Bible, like in the Crusades."

It was now Mr Rashid's turn to smile. I hated it when grown-ups smiled like that, but I really wanted to know. "Mr Rashid?"

"Christianity isn't just a European religion, Natalie. It may have taken root here more than anywhere else in the world until this century, and there have been forced conversions, but there were Christians in Africa, Asia and the Middle East from the first century onwards. Did you know that the Apostle Thomas reached as far as India on his missionary journey and that when the English missionaries arrived there were already Christians there?"

I didn't. Mr Rashid was pleased. Warming to his subject he sipped his coffee and continued to re-educate me on what he considered to be my warped view of Christianity, Islam and religious imperialism. An hour passed before Mrs Rashid interrupted her husband. "Don't you think that's enough Abe?" Fatima was asleep in her chair. Her father smiled at me, picked up his daughter and carried her to bed. The boys switched on the television and together we watched *Mr Bean*.

Chapter Ten

I WAS HOUSEBOUND for five days. Grandma kept the kettle on the boil to accommodate all my well-wishers. Pam Storey came to visit and gave my fringe a trim. Auntie Rose brought me some flowers: roses, naturally. The Rashids were regulars, including Fatima since she had recovered from her flu. Even Gladwin came out from behind his wall to bring me some *Time* magazines. Their glossy covers and colourful maps eventually lured me away from my latest supply of Nancy Drews.

Most of the magazines were dated 1989, but one of them, the one with Nelson Mandela on the cover, was from February 1990. There were about twenty pages of background information regarding the so-called 'South African scenario', most of which I had heard a little of at school and on the news. So, this was the home of Gladwin and Thabo. It was hard to believe that over ninety per cent of the population was told where and how they could live by a small group of paranoid whites. But according to *Time* things were going to change: *'After twenty-seven years in prison a man has been released and on his shoulders rest the hopes and dreams of an entire nation.'* *Time* wondered how long it would be until they tried to crucify him.

I then turned to the older issues. Wow! A lot had happened last year while I was reading Nancy Drew. The bi-centenary of the French Revolution had been celebrated in style with a score of Eastern Bloc nations breaking away from the old order, demanding the right to make it on their own. On 2nd May, Hungary began to roll up the Iron Curtain and on 10th September Czechoslovakia followed suit. Then Poland, East Germany and Romania all turned their backs on the Soviet Union.

Two images stood out. The first: excited people tearing down the Berlin Wall; the second: a lone Chinese student standing before a long line of tanks in a sun-bloodied Tiananmen Square.

How much of it I took into my twelve-year-old mind I don't know, but I look back on that day as my first step towards awareness that my little world was part of something bigger. But it wasn't just the *Time* magazines; so many roads were leading me in that direction. School, puberty, my parents leading separate lives, my world travels, Mr Rashid, Gladwin, Thabo ... yes, Thabo. He was only two years older than I was but he lived in a totally different world: an adult world; the world of *Time* magazines.

On the fifth day after my accident Grandma asked Professor Nkulu if he would take us to the hospital to have my stitches removed. He said he would be glad to. When I came back with a ten-inch scar on my leg, Thabo was waiting to see me. Grandma said he could keep me company while she went to the shop.

"So how's the leg feeling?" he asked.

"Much better, thanks. I can walk around without a problem."

"That's good."

"Yes."

He sat in the armchair; I was on the couch. "Tea?"

"Juice, if you have any."

"I think we've got some lemonade." It was definitely cooler in the kitchen. I carried the two glasses back into the living room.

"Thanks."

"Pleasure."

"No, I mean thanks. For last week."

"For what?" I asked.

"For not telling about the garden."

"Oh that. No problem." He was looking at me, expecting more. "I suppose I should thank you as well," I conceded.

"For what?"

"For helping me with my leg."

"I couldn't leave you bleeding in the bush, now could I?"

"I suppose not. But thanks anyway." He nodded. We drank our lemonade. "So why did you do it?"

"What?"

"Create the garden with stolen plants."

He smiled. "I knew you wouldn't be able to resist that one."

I scowled then said: "Well if I'm going to keep the secret I'd like to know what it's all about. Lying doesn't come easily to me, you know?"

"Well thank you for lowering yourself to my level!" I thought I'd blown it when he thumped down his glass. But then he surprised me. Thabo always surprised me. "I stole the plants because I didn't have money to buy any myself."

"But they didn't belong to you and you ruined everyone's chances of winning the garden competition."

"I didn't know about the garden competition; but anyway, I don't think it's fair for people to be entering their gardens for contests when most people in the world don't have any land of their own."

"But you have a garden; your dad's."

"No, that isn't mine, it's his. Nothing that he has is mine, except his name. I wanted something of my own and no one was using the Wasteland."

"But it's owned by the Council. You can't just claim it."

"Why not? At least I'm doing something constructive with it."

There was something vaguely socialist about what the young South African was saying, but after only five days of reading *Time* magazines I wasn't sure what it was. But he was making sense. "Yes, I suppose you are. Can I help?"

"With the garden, you mean?"

"Yes, I'd like to."

He was quiet again, toying with his glass. "But it's mine. I made it. No one else."

"Yes, I know. But don't you think it will be more fun if you share it? Then other people can enjoy it too."

"Like who?"

"Well, me and maybe the Rashids. They're nice kids; you should get to know them then maybe you won't be so lonely."

"I'm not lonely."

"Oh really?"

"No, I'm not!" He got up, stomping towards the door. But as he turned the handle he said: "You can come if you want. It's a free world after all." I smiled as the door closed, knowing it would soon be open again.

Chapter Eleven

I THOUGHT IT WOULD only be polite if I waited a few days before taking him up on the invitation. It wouldn't help to appear too eager, now would it? It was Thursday, a week after my last visit, when I decided to have a go. I had spent the morning looking out of the window to see when Thabo walked by. Grandma wanted to know what I was doing. "Oh, nothing, just looking."

"Why don't ya go outside then; yer leg's much better."

Just then, Thabo walked past. "All right then, if you insist." I jumped up, put on my trainers and followed the boy from a distance. Soon he was out of sight. My leg ached; it was not quite as fit as I thought it would be. Five minutes later I arrived at the hedge then smiled as I saw the barbed wire newly cut and tied back. I crawled through. Thabo was waiting on the other side, pliers in hand.

"It's about time. I thought you might chicken out."

"Me? Never!" We walked down the flower-lined path towards the oak tree.

"You can clean out the tree house if you like, I'm going to separate this daisy bush." I balked at the idea of being assigned 'woman's work' but decided to let it slip as I wanted to see inside the tree house. I climbed the ladder between the conifers, aware that Thabo watched me all the way. I wondered if he was admiring the way my jeans hugged my rear or whether he was just concerned that my leg would hold up to the exertion. I fear it was the latter.

The tree house was rather dull: four walls, a floor and a roof. Up until then Thabo had used it as a tool shed. My mind redecorated as I swept with the hand brush. A lick of paint, a few posters and cushions and this would be a great meeting place for the neighbourhood kids. That's if Thabo would agree. I looked through a crack in the wall at the lonely gardener, bending and flexing as one bush became two then multiplied again.

A while later Thabo called me down for lunch. Either he ate an awful lot or he had packed for two that morning. I wisely held my tongue. We munched on ham and cheese sandwiches in silent companionship.

Then he spoke. "I hope one day I can plant a garden like this in my own country, when every person there has the right to own land wherever they want to. My garden will be the most beautiful of all. I'll have *braais* there in the summer, and the whole community can come."

"What's a *braai*?"

"A barbecue. It's what we call it in South Africa."

I wondered why he hadn't come to our community *braai* but then realised that it was because he didn't feel he belonged. Did I belong? At the time I thought so. For me a community, a family, could be as small as two people eating ham and cheese sandwiches no matter what was happening in the rest of the world.

But back then, in that glorious summer, I doubt I was thinking anything that deep. We were just a boy and a girl eating sandwiches. I started to pack up the lunch things and heard shouting from the other side of the hedge. Thabo put his finger to his mouth. I wasn't going to say anything anyway but I stopped packing in deference. Suddenly Gazza exploded through the hedge followed by Aktar and Dullah. Thabo's finger came down as his brows collided with his broad nose. "Oh great!" he said.

Dullah pulled Gazza off my leg but couldn't stop him scoffing down the last of the crusts. Aktar was looking around. "So, this is your secret, Nattie."

"It's not hers, it's mine. What are you doing here?" asked Thabo, getting up. He was a head taller than the Pakistani boy who was only a year younger. Aktar wasn't intimidated; his open nature not used to labelling strangers as enemies.

"Gazza got out again. We ran after him and he led us straight here. We weren't out to get you or anything."

Thabo clearly didn't know whether to believe him or not, but I did. "It doesn't really matter, does it? You won't tell, will you?"

"Of course not," said Aktar. "Will we Dud?"

"Why should we?" said Dullah. "The ground's not being used for anything, anyway."

Thabo softened a little. "My point exactly." I held my breath, waiting for the wall to be dismantled from both sides but nothing happened. The boys just collected their dog and left the way they had come. I waited for Thabo to say something; he didn't.

"Hey, wait up!" I shouted then followed my friends through the hedge.

Chapter Twelve

THE NEXT MORNING I planned to help my Grandma with the baking but changed my mind when Thabo knocked on the door. "Want to come to the garden?" he asked.

"I don't think so," I said. He looked disappointed.

"You can bring the twins," he said. You could have bowled me over. I just didn't understand this boy. But not wanting to appear too grateful, I replied nonchalantly, "Okay, if you want. I'll join you there."

"They'll have to bring their own lunch though," he tossed back as he walked out the door. I was just about to snap that he could keep his stupid garden – and his lunch – when I saw Dullah and Aktar come out of their house.

"Hey," said Thabo. "You can meet us at the place we met yesterday if you like."

"Yes, but he says you have to bring your own lunch," I said petulantly.

"That's all right," said Aktar, "we'll see you there." Then they turned excitedly and went back into the house.

Thabo looked down on me with the adult smile I hated so much and asked: "Well are you coming, or do I have to make friends with those two on my own?"

"No, I'll come. Thank you." The last bit stuck in my throat.

"It's a pleasure," he said, with no such problems of the larynx.

So Thabo's garden became ours: his, mine and the twins'. But he didn't give up dominion that easily. For the first few days it was Thabo who dictated when we arrived and when we left, what we did and when we did it. But after a while he forgot to be in charge, particularly when he was engrossed in conversation with one or other of the twins. Sometimes I would arrive late and the boys would already be there, talking about football or looking at a magazine that they would hurriedly hide behind their backs thinking I hadn't seen.

"What's that?" I asked one day.

"Oh nothing," Thabo said casually, but by the red flush on Dullah's cheeks I knew it wasn't just nothing.

"Tell me!"

"No," said Thabo. "It's just boys' stuff."

"What kind of boys' stuff?"

"None of your business. Do I ask you what you're talking about with Fatima?"

He touched a nerve there. What had he heard? "I don't talk with Fatima!"

"Why not?" asked Aktar, concerned that I might be sleighting his sister. "What's wrong with her?"

"Nothing, nothing," I said quickly. "It's just that I don't see her much now that we spend all our time here."

"Yes," said Dullah. "She has been left out, and we don't like lying to her, Thabo. Can she come too?"

"Why are you asking me? It's your place too. If you want her to come you can ask her." Then before anyone could comment on his spectacular about turn: "Hey, anyone for footie?"

The next day Fatima arrived with her brothers and Thabo didn't protest. She took over the decorating of the tree house and I helped the boys plant vegetables down below. I couldn't bring myself to be alone with her. I didn't really know why at the time but I see now that her femininity threatened me. She was so comfortable with it and I wasn't. I was scared that the blood both of us shed every month bound us together in some kind of eternal pact that set us apart from boys forever. I didn't want to be set apart. I didn't want there to be boys and girls. Why couldn't we all just be the same? But then, when I looked at Thabo, I was glad we weren't all the same. I wanted to be different; I wanted him to notice me. But I don't think he did. Not in that way. The way a boy looks at a girl. The way Roger looked at Fatima; the way Thabo looked at Fatima. I wished she'd never come.

I couldn't face her anymore, particularly when I had my period. The boys wouldn't know, but she would. I didn't want her to know.

So when the blood came I stayed at home for one day and then another. I told the boys I was sick. On the third day there was a knock at the door. It was Fatima.

"Hi Nattie. Are you feeling better?"

"No," I said, reluctant to let her in.

"What's wrong?"

"Nothing. I just have a cold."

"My mam thinks it's something else. Do you want to talk to her?"

"No, just leave me alone!" Fatima looked hurt. She started to turn away. "I'm sorry Fats, it's just, it's just …"

"Your period?"

"Yes, my period," I confessed.

She smiled, relieved. "Oh good, I thought I was the only one. I've been really scared to tell you, in case you wouldn't want to be friends with me anymore."

"Really?" I said, surprised. "Why?"

"Oh I don't know. I thought you would think that I thought I was better than you. But I don't Nattie, I don't. I don't know what's gone wrong this year but we used to be such good friends. What's happened?" She was starting to cry.

"Nothing Fats, it's just me. I'm a bit confused, that's all. Don't cry. I still want to be your friend if you'll have me."

"Of course I'll have you," she said and gave me a hug.

I didn't quite relax into it but she had definitely broken the ice. I agreed to two things that day: going back to the garden and talking to Fatima's mother. I tried unsuccessfully to get out of the latter but when I did I felt a whole lot better and wondered what all the fuss was about in the first place. Yes, I was part of a special club, but it wasn't such a bad thing, was it? Millions of women had been through this, Mrs Rashid assured me, and they all survived it. My depression lifted and I was back to my old self.

The next day I went back to the garden but Fatima wasn't there. I was disappointed, particularly now that we'd renewed our friendship. Where was she? I didn't have to wait long as Fatima came through the hedge followed by Roger. What did she think she was doing? What would Thabo say? The two boys had nearly

The Peace Garden

killed each other the last time they clashed.

The African boy thrust his spade into the ground and walked to the edge of his territory. Yes it was his territory again; we all knew that. The twins and I watched and waited for the inevitable explosion.

"What are you doing here?" Thabo demanded.

Fatima looked up at the South African and stared him straight in the eye: "I asked him; he's my friend."

Roger rose to his full height and thrust out his chest. Thabo didn't back down. But then, surprisingly, Roger did. "Look Fats, I told ya this would happen. If he doesn't want me I'm not sticking around." The skinhead started towards the fence. The pretty Pakistani girl grabbed his hand, pulling him firmly towards Thabo. She reached out her other one, feminine and soft, and invited the South African with a wistful 'please'. But instead of taking her hand, Thabo walked back to the tree house and returned with a pot of paint. He gave it to Roger, saying, "We need all the help we can get."

So, encouraged by Fatima, Roger swallowed his pride and spent the next hour painting the tree house. Eventually Thabo picked up a brush and the two of them worked side-by-side. Soon, they started talking and finally, laughing. The hours became days, the days weeks, and the stolen plants that once brought division bonded us together in our Peace Garden.

Chapter Thirteen

"WHEN ARE YOU leaving, Nattie?" asked Fatima.

"In two days time. I'll be meeting my dad in London then flying out to Washington."

"To meet your mam?"

"Maybe. I don't know."

We were all sitting in the tree house on Fatima's hand-stitched cushions. Roger and Thabo were playing cards in the corner while the Rashids and I just lay about talking. "We'll be sorry to see you go," said Aktar. "Can't you ask your mam and dad to come and live here?"

"What, with my Grandma and Auntie Rose? I think that would start World War Three! Besides, my parents' jobs take them all over the world. Don't worry; I'll be back again next year. And we'll always have this place."

"No we won't." It was Roger, speaking above a loud rumbling noise coming from the other side of the hedge.

"Whadya mean?" asked Thabo, putting down his cards, and looking out of the doorway.

"Me mam and dad have been talking about opening a hairdressing shop in a new complex that they're planning on building here. Well me mam has anyway, Dad doesn't think it's such a good idea."

"How do they know about it?" I asked, vaguely remembering something from the day I had my hair cut.

"They read about it in the Chronicle. Apparently it's just a matter of time."

"How much time?" I asked.

"Not much," said Thabo, climbing down the steps. The rumbling was getting louder. Puzzled, I followed him, with Roger and the

The Peace Garden

Rashids close behind.

Thabo was walking purposefully across the Wasteland, towards the corner diagonally opposite the oak tree. He filled my vision as the rumbling filled his ears. He was wearing black jeans and a green sweatshirt. His sleeves were rolled up revealing strong brown arms. His hair had recently been trimmed, exposing the nape of his neck. I could see his veins swelling with anger as his pace quickened. Suddenly, a large yellow bulldozer broke through the hedge with four others following close behind. They trundled towards the garden like tanks. Halfway across the square they stopped, Thabo blocking their path.

"Here, lad, get out of the road." Thabo didn't move. The driver shouted again. "Move it, we've got a job to do!" Thabo just stood there.

"What's goin' on Horace?" One of the drivers shouted from behind.

"Some lad won't let us past."

"Well go around him then." But as the heavy machines tried to change direction, Roger moved to block their path. They tried again, but there was Aktar. And again, but Dullah was in the way. Fatima and I took up the next two positions. The cat and mouse game went on for a few minutes then escalated into a screaming match. The drivers told us to bugger off and we told them much the same. It was our garden, we said. No it wasn't, they replied.

Eventually, one of the drivers got down and dragged Fatima and I away. A second one took on Aktar then the third grabbed at Dullah. The fourth, a little reluctantly, started to tussle with the thickset Roger, but the fifth remained in the cab of his machine. Slowly, the beast edged forward; Thabo stood his ground.

By now the rest of us were subdued; angry but resigned to our fate. "Get out of the way, Thabo," said Fatima. "There's nothing we can do."

"Maybe not, but at least I'm going to try."

And die doing it, I thought. His veins were pumping strong, his eyes blazing with a fire much too strong for this small piece of earth in Newcastle. His fists were clenched, stretching to white. One of the bulldozer drivers armed himself with a spanner. Things were about to get ugly.

Fatima ran off as the driver who had accosted us loosened his grip to call the police on his radio. With the first sound of the siren Roger ducked out, the only one of us with a police warning against his name; the portly driver who had challenged him looked relieved. Thabo remained firm. But it wasn't long before the flowers in the little garden were trampled by site managers, police officers and parents. Fatima had told her mother.

Salima spoke to the senior police officer then reasoned with her boys. Grandma Iris just looked at me and I knew I was beaten. But Thabo refused to move. Eventually Gladwin arrived and spoke to his son in *isiXhosa*. I don't know what was said, but tears were streaming down both their cheeks. Defeated, Gladwin approached the police officer giving him permission to remove his son. It took four officers to drag away the screaming boy as his father stood by and did nothing. But then, to no one in particular, he said: "My son is more of a freedom fighter than I will ever be."

Part Two:

"Old Enemies"

"Segregation is the tradition of gardeners: not into ecological but into horticultural niches. The plants that behave in such a way and like such a soil are grown together with as little competition as possible, protected from diseases, bugs, other plants and each other. When their protector goes on holiday their artificial world is immediately under threat. Instead of the stability of a hard-won Darwinian niche they occupy a pampered place which will be usurped by the quickest, most aggressive, coarsest plants – which are the ones we have come to know as weeds."

(Hugh Johnson, The Principles of Gardening)

Chapter Fourteen

July 2001: present day

ONE WOULD LIKE to think that friendships last forever, especially childhood ones. When I was eight and lived in Canberra I had a friend whom I liked to refer to as 'my best'. We were inseparable; skipping together around the playground, sharing secrets that we thought would bind us together for eternity. I can't remember her name.

Sitting in that tree house nearly eleven years ago was as good as it would ever get for me. I never had friendships like that again. It cost too much. I would like to say that we remained friends and kept in touch over the years, but we didn't. It was mainly my fault; or my parents' anyway. The following summer I was desperate to get back and had told all my friends the same thing in my weekly letters. But my mum and dad's inevitable divorce stopped me. I was put into boarding school in New York and spent alternate summer holidays between my two guilt-ridden parents. The first summer was with my mother's family in Paris, the next with my dad and his new girlfriend in Bali. It was four years before I got back to Jasmine Close, at Christmas, and the Rashids were away on holiday visiting family in Pakistan. Two years later I was there again, but once again the Rashids were away. Thabo was gone too; on a college trip, Grandma told me. There was always Roger, but after a day with him at the Metro Centre, hanging around while he smoked with his footie friends, I decided not to renew our friendship.

Within two years the letters had stopped; even from Fatima who was the only one who wrote regularly. It's a girls' thing, my dad said, boys just aren't very good at writing. But just when I thought all my friendships in Jasmine Close had died, I received a card from Gladwin and Thabo on my eighteenth birthday.

24 March 1996: five years ago

Dear Natalie,

We were so sorry to have missed you at Christmas. Thabo was away with friends in Scotland and I was at a conference in Leeds. Your grandmother tells me you are well. We hope you have a very happy birthday Khandlela. Do you remember what that means? If not, have a look at your cake – there should be eighteen of them.

Yours sincerely,
Gladwin and Thabo Nkulu
PS I am going to South Africa in July and will send you a post card if you like.

I was thrilled, even though I knew it was really from Gladwin and not Thabo. I wrote back immediately.

Dear Prof Nkulu (and Thabo),

Thank you so much for your very kind birthday greetings. Yes, I had a lovely day and I went shopping with my mum at Macey's. Have you ever been to New York? I haven't been to South Africa. I would love a post card. I'm going out to dinner tonight with my dad so I had better get ready. I'll write again later.

Love,
Natalie Candle!

As promised, I received a post card from South Africa; it was a nightscape of Johannesburg.

Dear Natalie,

I've just arrived in Johannesburg. Everything is so different from what I remember. I left here when I was 19 – a year younger than Thabo is now – I don't know if I told you that. No, I didn't, I didn't tell you anything. But I need to. I need to tell you what happened to me 20 years ago – and what's happening to me now. If anything

bad happens to me, please pass these on to Thabo. He needs to understand. If nothing does, then keep them to yourself – please. I'll write again soon.
Gladwin

Gladwin. Not Professor Nkulu. Not Gladwin Nkulu. Not Gladwin and Thabo. That was the first letter of many. Sometimes they didn't even have 'Dear Natalie' at the beginning – they just started; and no longer on a post card, but reams and reams of A4 paper. I wondered if he realised whom he was writing to. His son's friend? His neighbour's granddaughter? A stranger in America? I wondered if it mattered. I was just an excuse for putting pen to paper, for opening his heart and letting it all come out. This, as much as I could tell, was his story:

June 1996

Gladwin was sitting on a plane on his way to South Africa.

"Another drink sir?" Gladwin looked up and was surprised to see a pretty Afrikaans stewardess pushing a drinks trolley.

"*Nee dankie, een drankie is genoeg vir my,*" he answered in Afrikaans. No thanks, one drink is enough for me. It felt strange on his tongue, this language of white South Africa, this language of power and privilege. He hadn't spoken it in twenty years. Not since his schooldays in Soweto when it was forced into the curriculum and sparked a riot.

But it wasn't just the words that were strange. It was the fact that this young white girl spoke to him, a black man, with deference, the same as she would to any other businessman in the first class cabin. Twenty years was a long time. And clearly a lot had changed if this South African Airways flight was anything to go by: attractive young stewardesses (black, white, mixed-race and Indian), smiling at each other and the multi-racial passengers: a rainbow nation, just as Tutu had promised.

Or had it? A 'mixed' couple sat two rows in front of him: a white man and a 'coloured' woman. The other passengers were trying to avoid staring at the social anomaly and the stewardess' smile was a

The Peace Garden

little brighter than usual as she served them chilled white wine.

Then there was the twenty-something youngster sitting to his right. Gladwin chatted with the English-speaking, white South African (I was surprised at how quickly he slipped into the compulsive categorisation) and was interested to hear that the young man had just come back from a job interview in London.

"I'm planning on moving there as soon as possible." He was blonde and tanned and clearly spent a lot of time at the beach; a surfer, maybe.

"Why?" asked Gladwin. "Are you unhappy with the changes in South Africa?"

The young man appeared to feel awkward telling the truth to this older black man, when it was *his* kind who were the main reason for the move abroad. But after a couple of drinks, Anton, (that was his name) began to explain.

"Look, it's not that I supported apartheid or anything, I didn't. I was a member of NUSAS at varsity, and even went to see Mandela when he was released from prison. It's just that I've been out of university for almost two years now and I can't get a job. I've got a master's degree in commerce, but they're only hiring blacks or women. They say that if I had more experience they'd take me on. But how am I supposed to get experience if no one will hire me?"

Gladwin didn't think he really wanted an answer so he just waited for the young man to continue. He didn't wait long.

"If you're white you're expected to have experience, but not if you're black. I know they're just trying to make up for all the years of injustice, but unfortunately it's at my expense. I never thought I was a racist before, but now …"

"So you don't think it's fair, then?" Gladwin asked.

The young man flushed red. "Oh please don't tell me about how unfair it was in your day. I know all about it. We whites were bad. You blacks were victims. It's time you got your place in the sun. But you know something? Two wrongs don't make a right."

Neither of them knew what to say after that. Anton sipped his beer and Gladwin read his paper. At the end of the flight they would shake hands, embarrassed, and go away thinking of all the things they should have said.

The birth pangs of a nation: that's all Gladwin could think of as he turned the pages of *The Star* newspaper; either that, or a rapid descent into hell. Gladwin preferred the former. White families murdered on farms. Black commuters caught in the crossfire between rival taxi associations. A family of eighteen massacred in kwaZulu-Natal; two Swedish tourists gang-raped and murdered on the Wild Coast; gang warfare on the Cape Flats claiming the life of a toddler; a bomb blast at a Cape Town restaurant tied to a militant Muslim group; right-wing Christians beating a black vagrant to death for urinating outside their church; a world-renowned sociologist announcing that South Africa has the highest crime rate outside of a war zone; the minister of safety and security denying that the police force has lost control; Miss South Africa flying off to Atlanta: Gladwin was still surprised she was black.

"Please fasten your seatbelts ladies and gentlemen. We are approaching Johannesburg International Airport and it's a mild winter's day at twenty one degrees. We'll be landing in ten minutes. Thank you for flying SAA."

Gladwin looked out of the window as the Boeing 747 banked right over Kempton Park, lining up for a landing at South Africa's biggest airport. He'd never seen the city from the air before as the last time he left it was in the boot of a car.

It seemed as if he were looking at a child's giant sandpit: flat-top mine dumps that might have popped out from a sand-filled ice-cream container, intersecting at awkward angles; trees clinging desperately to the sharply-graded sides. They were the legacy of the millions of tons of earth dug up in search of *eGoli*'s hidden treasure over the last hundred years, leaving a pseudo-mountainous landscape across the scarred reef. He'd read somewhere that companies were now buying the rights to reclaim the gold from the dumps with advanced new technology, unavailable to the mining magnates of old. Hopefully one day the area's indigenous landscape would be restored.

He was struck by the black and brown patchwork of the Highveld winter with not much green in sight. No rain could be expected until the following spring. Nature was in survival mode; life hoarded in roots. The black was from the prolific *veld* fires that savaged the landscape; the result of the harsh winter sun on parched grass. Quite unfortunate for the plants whose fate it was to live at that time. But that was to be expected from martyrs: the sacrifice of the few for the good of the many.

But at least it was beautiful in summer. The charcoaled fields brought new life as unwanted competition was destroyed and carbon fed into the earth. In a few months, with the first September rains, green shoots would demand attention and the hilly Johannesburg landscape would have its day.

The plane straightened up and began its rapid descent.

Chapter Fifteen

IT WAS TWO weeks before I received the next letter from Gladwin. I wondered how things were going in South Africa. He'd never quite explained why he was there. Was it to see Thabo's mother? Just when I thought he'd forgotten me in the busyness of his homecoming, I received a letter. But this one was far more disturbing than the last. It was rambling and at times incoherent. It jumped around in time between 1996 and 1976, so, rather than subjecting you to the same confusion, I'll just try to tell you the story as I understand it.

The car had been behind him since he left the airport in his rented Corolla. People drove like maniacs on the N12 highway between Springs and Johannesburg, so it was unusual to see a new Camry staying behind him at only 100 km/h. The actual limit was 120, but you were considered to be dawdling unless you pushed 150. He'd never driven in South Africa, only getting his licence in the relatively peaceful roads of Newcastle, so he decided to take it easy on the twenty-minute drive from Kempton Park to Parktown. But what was this guy's excuse? A forty-something white man with ears that could only have been born in a rugby scrum; call him prejudiced if you will, but it didn't fit the profile.

His passenger was younger. Twenty-five perhaps; well built with a stylish haircut and a brown leather jacket. A cop? Five years ago maybe, but these days it was fashionable to have mixed-race partnerships to prove the un-provable: that 'transformation' was taking place in the South African Police Force. Besides, he'd already had a run-in with the police today.

He'd just got through customs when he was approached by another white man in a brown leather jacket. "Mr Gladwin

Nkulu?"

"Yes?"

"I'm Inspector Nel of the Johannesburg CID. Would you come with me please, we have some papers for you to sign."

Polite and to the point but Gladwin was sure it was an order and not a request. They walked through the VIP lounge into a private suite. A snappily dressed black man was seated at a table.

"Detective Sergeant Khumalo," Nel explained. The two newcomers sat down.

Khumalo glanced at an open file then spoke without meeting his eyes. "You understand, Mr Nkulu, that there is an outstanding warrant for your arrest dating from 1976, for the murder of..."

"Inspector Fritz Labuschagne," Gladwin offered.

Khumalo twitched, straightened his glasses, and continued.

"At the request of the Truth and Reconciliation Commission's Amnesty Committee, this warrant has been suspended for two months to allow you to testify at the hearings. If your amnesty application is unsuccessful it will once again become valid and you will be arrested immediately. Do you understand?"

Gladwin nodded.

"Please vocalise your response," said Nel, gesturing to a tape deck.

"Yes, I understand."

"During these two months you will be restricted to the magisterial district of Johannesburg, and must check in at John Vorster Square once a week. Do you understand?"

"Yes, but I was hoping to visit my son's mother in Cape Town."

"I'm sorry but ..."

"We'll see what we can do," interrupted Nel. Khumalo looked at him for an instant then turned back to the papers in front of him.

"Will you sign this please?" Gladwin made his mark.

The super shopping complex of Eastgate was on his left; Thabo had told him about it. He indicated to turn right at the statue of the colonial miner. The Camry was two cars behind. Right into Bez Valley, past Brumer Lake then on into Observatory. He turned right again at the giant Ponte tower – reputedly the home of thousands of illegal African immigrants – and up the hill towards Parktown. Soon Johannesburg General Hospital was on his left and he was passing the old Baptist Theological College. A few more turns and he was in the tree-lined Parktown street that he'd dreamt about for twenty years.

The houses were old by South African standards, dating back to the 1880's when British mining magnates staked their claim and built their mansions; first with gold, then wrought iron and stone.

He checked his mirror. There was the Camry, parking under a Jacaranda, not even trying to hide its presence. He turned into number 17, set back from the road, behind an alternating line of Jacaranda and Oak. In summer the street was purple, in autumn, bronze; South American and European trees guarding the entrance to an African Jewish home. *Cohenville* was the name on the bronze-plaqued gatepost. He drove up the gravel drive.

The lawns were lush and green hugged by variegated shrubbery and roses. The Cohens had a borehole, he remembered, so like Persephone they were able to cheat death until the following spring. He remembered as a child coming to the Cohen house and showering in his mother's two-roomed flat when emergency water restrictions elsewhere in Johannesburg limited the residents to two buckets of water a day. Ah, the privilege of wealth.

He parked his Corolla behind a 1970 Jag and a new Mercedes Benz: Mr and Mrs Cohen respectively. People were approaching from the double-storey house. Mrs Cohen was first: grey-blonde bouffant and cashmere pant suit. Mr Cohen was next: balding and showing all of his seventy years. And then, almost afraid to step out of the shadow of the bougainvillea, was his mother, Sophie Nkulu. She'd looked sixty since she was forty, but now just looked her age. The Cohens stepped aside and allowed her through; the madam pushing gently at her domestic's back.

"My son, my son," was all she could say as she fell to her knees on the gravel path. Gladwin knelt too, taking her two clasped hands in his.

"*Mama*." Tears welled in his eyes and ran down her cheeks.

She took off his glasses and ran her hand over his face, as if blind. "My son, my son." Gravel cut through her pantyhose and scuffed his glossy shoes. The Cohens were afraid they would stay there all day in full view of the neighbours, so they ushered them inside and offered cocktails.

Chapter Sixteen

THAT EVENING AT dinner, Gladwin wrote, the Cohens showed their liberal roots: Sophie was allowed to sit at the table. He remembered an old joke that attempted to explain the subtle differences in white South African left-wing politics. What's the difference between a progressive and a liberal? A progressive lets the maid watch Dallas when she's doing the ironing and a liberal does the ironing while the maid watches Dallas.

They had hired a young woman to help in the kitchen so that Sophie could sit with her son, but from the taste of the traditional Cape Malay *babotie* (a curried mince with stewed fruit and white sauce), sweet pumpkin, rice and salad, Sophie had still supervised.

"On Mondays we usually have beef," explained Mrs Cohen, "but we thought we'd have something a little bit more African to welcome you home."

"That's very kind of you," said Gladwin, knowing that his grandfather would have slaughtered a cow for him when he visited the Transkei homestead. But his grandfather was dead and these white people had made untold sacrifices to help people like him.

"How's Bryan?" he asked.

"Wonderful," said Mr Cohen.

"He's with Stan in the firm now. Isn't that right Stan?"

"Yes dear," said Mr Cohen.

"So they didn't break him then," said Gladwin, half asking, half musing. Bryan was the Cohens' youngest son. When he fled the country in '76 the boy was still at school. He'd heard via one of the rare un-intercepted letters that he had gone on to study law at university, just like his father. When he graduated he refused to do his national service. As a conscientious objector he wasn't allowed to practice his trade and had to perform menial government-approved labour – if anyone would take him. But because the majority of white South Africans considered him a traitor, a *Kaffirboetie* (lover of blacks), no one would take him on. Most objectors either left the country or retreated into academia, swelling the ranks of liberal universities with Peter Pans. But Bryan was never happy in academia and would never leave the country. "I won't allow them to defeat me, not after what they did to Wayne," he once wrote.

"More *babotie*, Gladwin?" asked Mrs Cohen.

"Yes thank you".

Mrs Cohen reached for the bell, about to call for the stand-in, when Sophie said: "Please, madam, let me."

"No Sophie, tonight you're a guest," said the madam. "It's not everyday you have your son visiting you."

"No madam, and it's not everyday I have the honour of serving him," said the mother, standing up and walking towards the kitchen with more purpose than she had shown all night. Gladwin watched her go, seeing her pause to straighten Wayne's photo on the sideboard.

A young private, proudly wearing his national defence force uniform: the Cohens' eldest son. Wayne's decision to join the army with the rest of his matriculating class in 1975 wasn't an unusual one. Joining an army established largely to maintain white privilege by holding back the *swart gevaar* (black danger) at the borders, and maintaining 'public order' in the townships, did not automatically mean a man supported apartheid; he just hadn't thought through the alternatives, if he had thought about it at all. And besides, it was compulsory, and if there was one thing white South Africans were good at, it's doing what they were told.

Gladwin remembered Wayne fondly. They were the same age and would play football and cricket on the sleek Cohen lawns when the black boy came to visit his mother. Wayne may not have understood the ins and outs of apartheid like his brother, but he never lived it. Not in his heart anyway. And besides, he had saved Gladwin's life, and Gladwin, like Wayne's family, suspected that that was the real reason the boy came back from the border in a coffin.

Sophie returned from the kitchen with a steaming plate of

babotie. She placed it in front of her son then announced that she was going to bed. "But you can't!" said Mrs Cohen. "You've hardly seen Gladwin."

Sophie stood for a moment, trying to decide whether or not to force her way out of tonight's miscast role by standing up to the madam. Mr Cohen, seeing her dilemma, intervened. "Let her go Rochelle; there'll be plenty of time to catch up tomorrow. Hey Sophie?"

"Yes master, thank you," said the mother; and to Gladwin: "Goodnight my son." Then the dark woman slipped back into the shadows.

The rest of the evening was uneventful. Mr Cohen outlined his strategy for Gladwin's representation to the Truth Commission. He saw no reason for the exile not to get amnesty for his role in the '76 Soweto riots, although the murder of Labuschagne may be a bit more problematic.

"It's that photo you see. It looks like you did it in cold blood. Opposing council will argue that your motive was revenge, not political, as the terms of amnesty require. But we'll talk about it in the morning, you look tired."

"Yes I am. It was a long flight."

"*Ja*, of course it was. Let me show you to your room," said Mrs Cohen. She led the way upstairs into a part of the house that Gladwin had only seen when he helped his mother turn the mattresses when he was a child. He had marvelled at all the space back then, how one white person could take up as much room as ten black people in the township. And those sheets! The crisp, clean, just-ironed smell; he closed his eyes and was nineteen.

He curled up, tight as a ball, hoping that no part of him peeked out of the pile of sheets waiting for ironing. He heard a voice: white, male, Afrikaans: "'Waar's die pikkinin, kaffir? Where's the little one?"

"I don't know master; I haven't seen him since the trouble started." It was his mother, soft and frightened.

"Jy lieg!"

"I'm not lying master." Higher, sharper. Lying in the laundry basket he heard a hard slap on a soft cheek. He was just about to jump out and defend his mother when he heard Mrs Cohen's voice.

"How dare you strike my maid! What are you doing here?"

"We're looking for Gladwin Nkulu. Do you know him?"

"Yes, of course. But he isn't here." Mrs Cohen summoned every ounce of superiority her family's eighty years of acquired wealth could give her, and surprisingly the policeman backed down.

"I would think twice about harbouring a fugitive if he comes here Mrs Cohen. He's not playing revolutionary games anymore; he's a murderer. He killed an officer in cold blood. He picked up a brick and smashed in his skull. We've got a photo. It was completely unprovoked. Murder Mrs Cohen, surely not even a Jew could defend that."

Neither woman spoke for a few minutes, waiting until the stench of racism left the house. Then Mrs Cohen pulled back the sheets.

"I hope the bed's firm enough for you. You mentioned in your last letter that you'd been seeing a chiropractor in Newcastle."

"I'm sure it's fine Mrs Cohen, thank you, and good night."

"Goodnight Gladwin." And then, just as she was leaving: "It's a pity Wayne couldn't be here."

"Yes it is." He waited until the elderly Jewish woman closed the door, then undressed and climbed into bed. But he couldn't sleep. Something didn't feel right.

He lay awake for over an hour, listening to the gradually diminishing noises of the Cohen household. Eventually there was silence. That was Gladwin's cue. In slippers and gown he stole down the stairs, through the kitchen and out the back door. It was a short walk through the vegetable garden until he reached the servant's quarters, coyly called 'Sophie's flat' by her employers. He scratched under a flowerpot and was rewarded with the spare key that she left there for her occasional visitors. Twenty years hadn't changed a thing. It was dark in the two-roomed flat, but no light was needed for the son to find his mother. He lay down on the floor near her bed. The years curled back; he was home.

Chapter Seventeen

January 1976

"MAMA, I'M HERE!"

Sophie Nkulu stepped out of the kitchen, wiped her hands on her apron, and greeted her son. "*Hau*, Gladwin, how did your new shirt get so dirty and torn? You're in matric now my boy, and you need to smarten up."

"I'm sorry *Mama*; I had some trouble after school."

"Was it that Gugile Sithole again? I've told you that boy is nothing but trouble. He and his comrade friends."

"Yes *Mama*, it was Gugs, but it wasn't his fault."

"Whose fault was it then?"

"Labuschagne."

The Xhosa woman's eyes grew wide, fearful, but her voice was scolding: "*Hau*, Gladwin, you must stay away from that Gugile; his face is known to Labuschagne and the other *boere* in the security police. I don't want to pick you up from the pavement of John Vorster Square."

John Vorster Square police station, and particularly the tenth floor, was notorious for the large number of questionable suicides that took place within its walls. Revolutionary instigators, ANC members and other ordinary folk suspected of complicity in 'the struggle', were taken there for questioning by the security police – a special branch with the brief to investigate 'political crimes' and activities deigned to threaten the security of the state.

Legislation that allowed for detention without trial for indefinite periods was introduced in 1967, giving commissioned officers *carte blanche* to question detainees. The aim was to elicit any information that could help them quell opposition to white

The Peace Garden 95

minority rule. More often than not, the questioning took the form of torture that sometimes led to death.

Death in detention was an embarrassment that needed to be covered up at all costs, particularly in a 'Christian' country that considered itself on a moral par with other western nations. The most expedient method (according to rumour) was throwing the bodies out of the tenth floor window of John Vorster Square and claiming suicide. Sometimes, it was alleged, the detainees weren't even dead at the time, but this was remedied when they hit the pavement below.

Others 'slipped in the shower', as in the case of Steve Biko in September 1977. It was widely believed, and later proved in an amnesty hearing of policemen involved in his death, that a bar of soap had nothing to do with it. He was actually beaten about the head and died after being transported naked in a police van for 1200 km.

I remembered when I read this that Steve Biko was one of the dead saints on Thabo's wall in Jasmine Close, along with Ché Guevera and Malcolm X. But in the early days of 1976 Steve Biko was still alive and Gladwin's school friends were ardent fans. Biko was one of the founding members of the South African Student Organisation that was affiliated to the Pan Africanist Congress (a rival organisation of the more famous ANC). The PAC (as it was known) was an enthusiastic advocate of Black Consciousness, and Biko was particularly evangelistic in spreading the message.

So in January 1976 Gladwin found himself sitting in the rundown assembly hall of his Soweto high school being addressed by a charismatic Steve Biko.

"Comrades," said the handsome, youthful Biko, "do not let the will of the white man be your life. You are men, you are women; you are African. All over Africa our brothers and sisters are rising up and saying 'no more!' Are you going to join them or do you believe the lies of the *boere*? Do you believe what Strijdom says? Do you believe that Africans cannot think for themselves?"

"No!" cried the high school seniors in unison. Biko stepped back from the podium, lifted his spectacles and wiped the sweat from his forehead with a pure white handkerchief. "No!" the crowd cried again, just in case their hero hadn't heard them. The trained lawyer allowed a faint smile to play on his well-formed mouth; then put his hands on his hips.

"You're lying," he whispered. Only the kids in the first row heard him, and they looked at each other confused. "You're lying," he said again, this time louder. "You're lying!" he shouted, noting with satisfaction the shock rippling through the crowd.

He continued at full volume: "You are letting them rule you. You are letting them train you to be servants. Why do you think they want you to learn in Afrikaans? Who else in the world speaks Afrikaans except the *boere*? How can Africans stand tall amongst the nations if they cannot learn in English?"

"He's right, you know," said the young man standing next to Gladwin. It was Gugile Sithole who had recently been transferred to the Soweto school from Mamelodi near Pretoria.

"*Ja*, I suppose," said Gladwin. Gugs, as the Sithole boy was known, continued to comment on Biko's rhetoric, but Gladwin wasn't listening, he had another agenda.

The younger boy hadn't really taken much notice of Gugs until a few weeks ago when he first realised that the beautiful Poppy Fakile, the unattainable dream of every boy at the school, had started to hang out with him. So Gladwin was sitting next to Gugs in the hope of having a word with the alluring Poppy, rather than being spurred on to political action by the enigmatic Biko. There was a faint smell of roast *mealies* in the air, and a trace of sweat. Gladwin hoped that Poppy would realise it was Gugs and not him who smelt so bad. In fact, he was hoping that Poppy would simply notice him.

But Biko's words kept distracting him from his primary purpose.

"Women of Africa, do you want to clean up after white women for the rest of your lives? Men of Africa, do you want to be gardeners or work down a mine for whatever crumbs the white man chooses to give you?"

"No!" came the cry, and Gladwin heard himself declare it too. Thoughts of his mother looking after the white people's children while he slept alone in a township shack lured his thoughts away from Poppy for a while.

"Do you want to be doctors? Do you want to be lawyers? Do you want to earn money and own a nice house?"

"Yes!" came the cry.

"Then you need to throw off the shackles the white men are trying to put on you. You need to refuse the Afrikaans!"

Just as Biko thrust his fist into the air in the characteristic Black Consciousness salute and exhorted the group of seniors to join him in his mission to scupper the government's plans, all hell broke loose. Security policemen burst through the doors and leapt onto the podium, dragging Biko to the floor. A group of khaki-clad white men and their darker sidekicks formed a circle around their prisoner: eyes steeled, necks stiff – goading the youngsters to try and rescue him.

Responding to the invitation, a group of angry youths surged forward only to be greeted by rifle butts. One or two fell; then their comrades rallied and surged again. But there was never a chance that the police would lose this battle. A white man with a megaphone climbed onto the podium and ordered the crowd to disperse. He didn't wait long, and after a few moments of non co-operation, ordered tear gas to be thrown into the hall.

That was Gladwin's cue to get out of there; he'd been caught one too many times in the lung-searing mist before. He scrambled out of an open window, scooted along a gutter then crawled through a hole in the fence. He ran and didn't stop until he reached the Chinaman's shop over two kilometres away. Suddenly, there was Gugs, laughing, offering him a coke. Behind him was Poppy.

"Thanks for the escape route, comrade. No one was watching you, the *boere* don't know you yet, and I was wearing a cap. We got away!"

"Yes, thanks Gladwin. I didn't know you were so fit?" said Poppy, unashamedly assessing the boy's physique.

"I think she likes you, comrade!" laughed Gugs.

Gladwin blushed which made Gugs laugh even more. Poppy laughed too, quickening Gladwin's heart, but then rose on her tiptoes and kissed Gugs on the cheek. The older boy pulled her close and smiled at his new friend over her shoulder.

Chapter Eighteen

GLADWIN SPENT MORE and more time with Gugs after that, and not just because of Poppy. The few friends he had were studious types who tried to keep their noses clean and out of trouble. Sometimes, Gladwin feared, that made him and them collaborators with the white oppressors. Besides, if Biko was right, soon even a good education wouldn't get you anywhere in black South Africa; maybe Gugs and his friends had the answer. Gladwin wanted to find out.

The older boy was involved in student politics and invited Gladwin to a number of clandestine meetings at break times and before school. There was talk of standing up to the *boere* concerning the Afrikaans issue, but Gladwin didn't hear anything particularly revolutionary. In fact, Gladwin feared, most of the 'comrades' were more interested in the odd joint that was passed around than the smuggled pamphlets from the banned revolutionary groups. It was all very low-key, yet it was the most politicised Gladwin had ever been. His mother was fearful of his new friendship as everyone knew that Gugs had had run-ins with the notorious Labuschagne.

For Gladwin, Inspector Fritz Labuschagne of the security police, epitomised the worst in white South Africa, just as his friend Wayne epitomised the best. An Afrikaner of Afrikaners, who believed what his family had been taught for generations: that South Africa was their nation's inheritance from God. He was thirty-five-years-old, born and raised in a conservative farming community, the seventh generation of Labuschagnes since 1838 when his family first claimed the land near the Vaal River. His people had fought long and hard to win their independence from the British whose grandiose illusions of Empire and lust for wealth

The Peace Garden

prompted them to fight the Anglo-Boer war. That war, which has long been forgotten by the British, still eats away at the collective memory of the Afrikaner as a symbol of injustice.

Like most frontiersmen, they had worked hard to be where they were and would defend their rights fiercely. Not all fit the stereotype of the Calvinist racist. Some of the most forward-thinking people in the New South Africa are Afrikaans. However, back in 1976 many of them fit the stereotype perfectly, and Fritz Labuschagne was one of them.

He, like many of his kind, had been taught from an early age that the stories of the Old Testament, of Israel's return from Egypt and God's command to wipe out the inhabitants of Canaan, was a direct word to them in South Africa. But like the Israelites, Labuschagne's people didn't kill off the locals (no more than other colonials did, that is) but instead committed themselves to living apart, giving the English dictionary a new word: *apartheid*.

Unfortunately for black South Africans demographics were against them; there were simply too many of them. It was feared that their superior numbers would not allow European culture to survive and so, logically, they needed to be suppressed. Then of course there was the spectre of communism – another threat to the Afrikaner culture and religion – that took on satanic proportions during the Cold War. *Die Swart Gevaar* and *Die Rooi Gevaar* were interchangeable – the black and the red danger.

So Fritz Labuschagne was a God-fearing, black-fearing, communist-fearing and English-fearing Afrikaner. As a result, Gugile Sithole, Poppy Fakile and Gladwin Nkulu, could not be seen as three youngsters trying to live a normal life, they were communist-inspired revolutionaries who threatened the very existence of Labuschagne's family and state. Thus, it was perfectly reasonable that they were 'neutralised'; it fell well within the law of self-defence – which even the Bible condoned.

But it was Gugs, with his sharp-dressing and quick-talking ways that irked Labuschagne the most. Most of the time it was just harassment, like the time when Gladwin came home to his mother with a torn shirt after running away from a laughing, gun-wielding Labuschagne. But sometimes it was more serious.

Gugs and Gladwin were walking home from school one day when Labuschagne pulled up in an unmarked police car. In the front seat was a white boy, his son perhaps, about six years old. In the back was a black policeman by the name of Koto. Koto and his kind were hated in the townships, but in 1976 it hadn't reached the point where he and his colleagues had to fear for their lives, and where their families were in danger of being burnt alive in their homes, which was to happen in the Eighties.

"Is this the one, Koto?" asked Labuschagne pointing to Gladwin.

"No *baas*, it's the other one, Sithole." Gugs and Gladwin kept on walking.

"You telling me Koto, that this is the boy you saw let down the tyres of a state vehicle?

"Yes *baas*, that's him. And when he did he said 'Free Mandela and the other comrades'".

"But that's revolutionary talk!"

"Yes *baas*, he was talking about a revolution."

"And that makes him a terrorist, making trouble for black people like you who know your place and want to live in peace with us whites. Isn't that right Koto?"

"Yes *baas*."

Gugs stopped. Gladwin grabbed him by the arm. "Not now, brother, keep moving." Gugs shrugged him off.

"Yes *baas*, no *baas*," he mimicked Koto. "We want to live in peace with you whites, just like dogs. We want you to spit on us and treat us like filth. We want our children to go to school to learn to be servants, and maybe if they're very good they can become traitors and join a white man's police force to keep our own people down. We want to let you pay us slave wages and force us to live in starving homelands and crime-ridden slums. We want you to…"

Koto leapt out of the car and shoved the barrel of his gun into Gugs' mouth. Gladwin pressed himself against a wall, terrified. Labuschagne laughed. He turned to his son and asked: "What do we do with cheeky *kaffirs, seuntjie*?"

The boy smiled at his father, but his eyes were like Gladwin's. "We shoot them pa?" he said, half asking. Labuschagne laughed

The Peace Garden

again, tousling his offspring's hair.

"That's my boy, but no, not usually, that would be against the law, now wouldn't it? No son, we take them to the police station. Koto! Get that boy in the car."

Koto took the gun out of Gugs' mouth and used the butt to beat him over the head. As he fell to the ground, blood pouring from a gaping wound, Koto dragged him to the vehicle. Gladwin ran away and jumped on the first bus to Jeppe.

Stanley Cohen, his mother's employer, had a law practice in Jeppe and already had a reputation for taking on 'apartheid cases'. Cohen was an activist. He worked within the law, exploiting the fact that the state, at least on the surface, was still subject to the judiciary, and if you were lucky to get a sympathetic judge, and you presented your case convincingly, you could beat them at their own game.

So Gladwin arrived at Stan Cohen's office and told his secretary to tell him that 'Gladwin the gardener' was there, and needed his help. Cohen called him in after five minutes and heard his story. He was particularly interested in the fact that Labuschagne had his son in the car with him, which suggested he was off duty and therefore acting outside his jurisdiction.

Cohen bundled Gladwin into his Mercedes and sped off to John Vorster Square. Gladwin was too scared to go in, so he waited in the car. He got a few suspicious looks from passers by, particularly the white folk, and one of them, most likely a plainclothes policeman, stuck his head in the window and asked him where he had stolen the car.

"It belongs to my employer," said Gladwin.

"Oh your *employer*," said the man in a plummy mock accent. "Don't you mean your *master*?"

Gladwin didn't answer.

"Don't ignore me *kaffir*!" said the man. "Who does the car belong to?"

Gladwin sighed, not wanting to provoke the man anymore. "It belongs to Stanley Cohen, a lawyer, my mother works for him ... yes, he's her *baas*," he said wearily.

"Oh a lawyer," said the man, moving away from the car. "A

Jewish lawyer." He laughed then walked into the police station. After that Gladwin climbed into the back seat – the appropriate position for a black person in a white man's car – and waited. He waited for a long time.

Four hours later Stan Cohen came out, half-carrying Gugs. Gladwin had expected him to be a mess, but wasn't prepared for this. His head was bandaged with his own shirt, bloodied and dirty from the beating he received from Koto's gun. His eyes were swollen shut, his lips ballooning into a mass of blisters, his nose splayed; his cheeks raw and peeling.

"He said they used a clothes iron on him," said Mr Cohen as he helped his client into the car. Gladwin didn't bother asking whether or not the police denied it. He climbed in the back with his friend and held him all the way to Johannesburg General Hospital.

Gugs didn't talk much on the way but Gladwin gleaned that in the time it took Mr Cohen to wield some legal clout, the boy was taken to the tenth floor and 'questioned' – with the aid of an electric clothes iron – about his connections to the banned ANC and PAC organisations. He was also asked to name names and whether or not Poppy Fakile and Gladwin Nkulu were active in student politics.

"Of course I denied it, don't worry my brother, I would never betray you," Gugs whispered, before drifting into unconsciousness.

Chapter Nineteen

GUGS SPENT FIVE days in the black wing of Johannesburg General Hospital before being discharged. No questions were asked about his appalling injuries; he was just treated and sent on his way. Stan Cohen offered to lay formal charges on Gugs' behalf, but the boy declined. On the day of his friend's release Gladwin skipped school to pick him up and helped him onto the bus from Parktown to Soweto.

"Hell!" said Gugs, grimacing through his swollen face, "I forgot about Nelspruit."

"What about Nelspruit?" Gladwin asked.

"I promised I'd go with Poppy. She's got a pass to go and see her old man."

"When?"

"This weekend."

"You can't go, Gugs. You need to recover; besides, if Labuschagne hears you're visiting a known activist, he'll have your balls!"

"I'm not going to let that pit bull get the better of me!" said the battered boy loudly, who was already drawing attention to himself on the bus simply by the way he looked. The other commuters, mainly women, lowered their eyes not wanting to appear too interested. But they all knew what had happened to him and if they weren't careful it might happen to them too; there were informers everywhere.

"Hey Gugs, live to fight another day brother."

"But what about Poppy? She won't want to go on her own."

"I'll go with her," said Gladwin, trying to sound nonchalant.

"*Hau* Gladwin," said Gugs. "Why do you kick a man when he's down?"

"What do you mean?" asked Gladwin, refusing to look his friend in the eye.

"You want her man! Don't try to hide it."

"No Gugs, that's not true."

"Like hell it isn't!"

"It's not, I promise you; I would never do that to you Gugs."

"Yes you would," said Gugs. "And if you wouldn't, you're stupid. I'd do it to you. I'd take her if she was yours."

Gladwin was just about to say something, anything, when Gugs started to laugh: a rasping, smoky laugh. "Man, that hurts!" Gugs wheezed then laughed again. Gladwin started to laugh too, at the top of his voice, not caring that the *mamas* on the bus were looking at them with disapproval.

"Well, I can promise you one thing, Gugs," said Gladwin.

"And what's that?" asked his friend, placing a cigarette between his bruised lips.

"I won't kiss her unless she wants to."

"Then there's no hope for you Gladwin; you're too soft to make a real revolutionary, too soft."

Gladwin didn't know whether he was joking or not. There was a side of Gugs he didn't want to see; one he feared might come out if enough pressure was applied.

The bus dropped them off at the Chinaman's shop. Gugs started walking in the opposite direction from his home. "Hey Gugs, where're you going?" asked Gladwin.

"To see some comrades." Gladwin kept pace with him. Gugs started to slow down. He looked at Gladwin, first in his eyes then over his shoulder. "Why don't you go and see Poppy? Tell her that I can't go with her, but that I'm sending you. Tell her I'll see her tonight." He flicked away his cigarette and walked away. Gladwin knew that he'd been dismissed. He shrugged and headed over to Poppy's house.

Poppy Fakile lived with her mother in one of the better parts of Soweto. She was a stunning seventeen-year-old; young to be in the final year of school. It meant that her family had enough money so she could start school at six and they were able to pay for her school fees each year without interruption. So if all went well, Poppy would leave school at the end of the year, the same age as the white children of the country, two years younger than Gladwin. Her mother was a teacher at a nearby primary school. Her father, a doctor, used to run a thriving practice in Soweto, but as a political activist, was under banning orders in Nelspruit.

Banning was one of the unique punishments inflicted by the state on political troublemakers. The idea was to isolate the individual from their place of influence in a rural location and limit the number of people who could visit them. It was essentially house arrest, but not in the prisoner's own home. After the incident at Gladwin's school Biko was banned to King William's Town, but was notorious for violating his sentence and popping up all over the place, earning him the nickname the Black Pimpernel.

Gladwin arrived at Poppy's house. He opened the chicken-wire gate and walked up a cement path. Being a part-time gardener, he couldn't help noticing the neglected lawn, patchy in too many places, and the bone-dry flowerbeds. Only a few mangy marigolds had managed to survive the recent drought, but even they looked as if they wouldn't live long. Unlike the Cohen house, there was no borehole to water the garden and the precious water there was, was used for human consumption. But at least Poppy's house had running water and water-borne sewage, unlike many of the houses in Soweto, including the shack Gladwin shared with his mother's sister and her six children. That reminded him, he needed to get home; the sewage truck was coming for its weekly visit tonight and it was his turn to empty the night soil buckets into the steaming tanker and get fresh ones for the coming week.

But first things first, he needed to speak to Poppy. He was just about to knock on the front door of the neat two-bedroom house when he heard a voice behind him.

"Hello Gladwin, I thought that was you."

He turned to see Poppy walking up the dusty path carrying a bucket of water on her head. Her neck was tense, her eyes staring straight ahead. One beautifully formed arm was holding the bucket and the other rested lightly on her waist. Her hips strained against the faded black cotton of her school skirt. The scrap of material stopped well above her knees, allowing her long brown legs an uninterrupted flow to the ground. She wasn't wearing shoes, and her feet took on the red hue of the earth.

"Well, aren't you going to help me?" She said, chidingly.

"Ah, of course, I'm sorry." He reached out to take the two-gallon bucket from her head. It was heavy and as he took the weight, some water spilled, splashing Poppy's feet.

"Be careful, I've just stood for half an hour to get that water," she said, rubbing the back of her stiff neck. She was clearly unaccustomed to this household chore.

"I thought you had running water in your house," said Gladwin, not judgingly, as his house didn't have any.

"We did. But since papa has been placed under banning orders, he hasn't been able to work much and we have to pay for two houses now; this one and the one in Nelspruit."

"Did they cut off your water?"

"Yes, after we didn't pay for three months. *Mama* won't go to the street tap, she's too proud, but apparently I'm not," said Poppy bitterly.

"Don't worry Poppy, we all have to do it."

"Not *all* of us, Gladwin. I didn't see too many men in the queue."

"That's because it's woman's work," said Gladwin teasingly.

Poppy was in no mood. "*Woman's work? Woman's work?*" She tried to grab the bucket from him, but he held it tight.

"Give it to me, Gladwin," she said, choking back tears.

He was surprised. He had never seen her like this before. So feminine; so vulnerable. "Hey, it's okay," he said soothingly. "I was only joking."

"Well it's not a joke!"

"I know; I'm sorry."

She reached out for the bucket again. This time he didn't stop her.

"So what do you want?" she asked, suddenly composed.

"I – I – I have a message from Gugs," he said, suddenly shy.

"Gugs?" she asked, not as excitedly as Gladwin had expected.

"Yes, he came out of hospital today. He will be coming to see you tonight."

"Oh, will he?" Irritation was creeping into her voice again. "And you came all the way over here to tell me that?"

The Peace Garden

"No, Poppy. I came to tell you ... to *ask* you ... if you would like me to come to Nelspruit with you. Gugs can't, so I thought you would like some company."

He waited, half closing his eyes, fearing the explosion that was to come. But it didn't. She smiled, softly, waiting for it to spread from her eyes to her mouth before speaking. "That would be nice Gladwin. I would like that very much."

"You would?" he asked, reaching out his hand to touch hers on the bucket handle.

"Yes," she said, covering his hand with her other one and stepping towards him. There was nothing between them now except a bucket, and even that didn't seem like much of an obstacle. He decided to kiss her, but as he bent his head down towards her, another voice interrupted him.

"Poppy Fakile! What are you doing kissing boys on the doorstep?" It was Mrs Fakile, Poppy's mother.

"I wasn't kissing him, *Mama*," said Poppy sharply.

"Well it certainly looked like it. Now get inside, we don't want everyone to see you with that bucket."

"But everyone has already seen me at the tap."

"Yes, but not *our* neighbours," said Mrs Fakile, clutching her briefcase tightly. "Goodbye young man, and next time you want to kiss my daughter, you should ask."

Gladwin blushed, smiled a goodbye to Poppy and ran out of the garden gate. Two blocks away, as the houses became shabbier, he passed a queue of people at the communal tap. He saw his aunt patiently waiting to get water with a shopping trolley filled with bottles and buckets. She had a large family, and like the other residents of Soweto who could not afford indoor plumbing, she was collecting water to cook an evening meal and wash her children before putting them to bed.

"Do you need any help auntie?"

"No thank you Gladwin, but hurry home, the sewage truck will be here soon."

The sewage truck! He had nearly forgotten.

Chapter Twenty

GLADWIN WAITED ON the platform of Johannesburg Central Station with the other black commuters. There was no barrier between him and the part of the platform reserved for whites; there didn't need to be. There was a sign in the two white languages of the country: *Blankes alleenlik / Whites only* and even though many of his fellow black Africans could not read they knew what it meant. They would not have access to the more comfortable waiting rooms, the better-kept lavatories and the carriages with the soft seats. Instead, they would be crammed into hard-benched third class coaches with sweating people, over-laden with bags of maize and second-hand clothes, given to them by their white employers in the hope that they could be sold to neighbours and friends.

But when the train arrived Gladwin did not get on with the others. He didn't know how she came up with the cash, but Poppy had managed to get them a second-class coupé which gave them privacy from the masses of people crushed into the third-class carriages, but still separated them from the whites in first class. He wasn't complaining: he was going to spend the next four hours alone in a cabin with a beautiful girl and a very small bed.

Where was she? Had she changed her mind? It wasn't like her to be late. Then, just as the conductor called out for the last boarding, he saw Poppy running towards him. Her braided hair was flying, her chest heaving, and a weekend bag was slung over her shoulder. She didn't stop, but leapt onto the second-class coach in front of him. Gladwin jumped in behind her.

"What happened to you?" He asked.

"I'll tell you in a minute," she said, handing their tickets to the conductor. He checked them, looked at the young people with a smirk and said sarcastically: "Mr and Mrs Nkulu?"

"Er, what?" asked Gladwin, puzzled.

"Yes, that's right," said Poppy confidently. "We've just got married."

"Mmm," said the guard, unconvinced, but showed them to their coupé anyway.

"What was that about?" asked Gladwin as they closed the cabin door behind them.

"The last time I travelled with Gugs and we gave separate names, they refused to give us a coupé because we weren't married. Can you believe it?"

Gladwin could. His mother had wanted to know how they were travelling and he had lied to her, saying they would be in third class with plenty of other passengers to chaperone them.

"And when you get to Nelspruit?" his mother asked suspiciously.

"I'm sure Mr Fakile will have a spare bed for me," he said.

He told Poppy what his mother had said, and asked her what she had told hers.

"That it was none of her business," said the girl throwing herself down on the bunk. Gladwin wondered if that was true, but didn't really care. He was finally alone with Poppy and he would relish every moment of it. He sat down on the bed beside her and asked again why she was late.

"It was Labuschagne," she said, spitting his name out like a piece of gristle.

"Why? Did you see him? Did he hurt you?" asked Gladwin, concerned.

"No, he didn't hurt me. But he did call me Gugs' black whore and wanted to know where he was. I told him I didn't know and that I was going on a trip. And you know what? He knew already. '*O, ja, Nelspruit, né?*' he said."

Gladwin smiled at Poppy's mock Afrikaans accent.

"Then he said: 'say hello to your terrorist father. Tell him I'll come and visit him one night.'"

"So what did you say?" asked Gladwin.

"Nothing. What could I say? If I told him to screw himself like I wanted to, he would have hit me or arrested me or something. If I had shown him I was scared he would have won anyway. So I just walked away."

"And he let you?"

"Yes. Koto was with him and he grabbed my arm, but Labuschagne told him to let me go. He said 'Better not get too close to the bitch, you don't know what you'll catch'." Poppy slammed her hand against the wall of the cabin. It stung. Gladwin took it gently; it was red and swollen.

"Don't let him get to you, he's not worth it."

"I know, but he makes me so angry. They all make me so bloody angry!"

"I know, I know, but he's not here now. I am, and I don't want to share you with him." He kissed her hand, softly at first, then with more intent. She sat, motionless, still fretting about Labuschagne.

He sensed it. "Hey, they may think they can run our lives, but they can't tell us how to feel, and right now I feel like kissing you."

Gladwin was surprised at his boldness. So was Poppy. But instead of saying something about it, she took his hand and placed it over her chest. He felt her heart beating strongly. She looked at him and moistened her lips; that was all the permission he needed. He drew her towards him and kissed her. For the rest of the journey they forgot all about Labuschagne and Biko and Gugs and her father. Revolutionaries one moment, a boy and a girl alone on a train, the next: at another time in another country that's all they ever would have been.

Chapter Twenty-one

June 1996

EARLY IN THE morning Gladwin snuck out of his mother's flat, back through the vegetable garden and into the Cohen house. He didn't want to embarrass his hosts with what they couldn't understand. Although his mother was asleep when he left, the blanket over his shoulders told him that she had been awake enough to know that he had come home. Decades of sacrifice had prepared her for the day her son would come and the day her son would go. Education, like many of her generation, was lacking, but a discerning spirit was portion enough. Gladwin, she knew, straddled two worlds, and she was grateful for the time he came into hers.

After breakfast, Bryan, the younger Cohen son, came around and spent time with Gladwin and Stan going over the TRC testimony for the following week. Bryan, like his father, felt that the trump card for those opposing amnesty, that is the Labuschagne family, would be the twenty-year-old press photograph that appeared on the front page of a major Johannesburg newspaper on 17 June 1976, the day after Gladwin had killed Fritz Labuschagne.

"Have you been able to trace Viljoen, the photographer?" asked Gladwin.

"Yes," said Bryan. "We found him a few years ago in a Hillbrow flat. He could barely remember his name, let alone the Soweto riots."

"Or so he claimed," said Stan. "When we asked him what he remembered about '76, his hand shook when he poured his Johnny Walker. Then he kept licking his lips, looking over his shoulder."

"Yeah, he was scared," agreed Bryan. "The man was in the wrong place at the wrong time. If what you say is true, which of course it is, that spool he shot revealed scenes of police brutality that would have shocked the world even more than the Hector Petersen picture."

"But what happened to the rest of that film?" mused Gladwin.

The only photo that was ever published was taken completely out of context and appeared to show Gladwin killing a helpless Labuschagne by crushing his skull with a brick. Labuschagne's back was to him, and also to the photographer, with his body and a lamppost blocking the mitigating evidence: Gugs on his knees with the policeman's gun against his head and a twitching finger on the trigger. The frames before and after would have shown the climax and denouement of the tragedy, but they disappeared along with Koto and the gun soon afterwards. Gugs also disappeared but popped up ever so often like a reincarnation of the Black Pimpernel. Although not in the last seven years, and no one had seen him since 1989. But Gladwin was sure he was still alive – he could feel him.

"Well at least we have one live witness, if we can get Viljoen to talk. Maybe he will, if he's offered protection," said Gladwin.

Bryan shook his head. "No go. He was found hanged earlier this year."

"Suicide?" asked Gladwin.

"Maybe. They never found a note."

"Well, it's down to my word then. I heard that Koto was necklaced in 1985."

Bryan nodded. Gladwin didn't consider himself a vengeful man but he didn't shed a tear when he heard the black policeman was the victim of the gruesome method of execution that became popular in South Africa in the 1980s – necklacing. A suspected collaborator was caught by a mob, his hands tied behind his back, then set alight with a petrol-drenched car tyre (the necklace) draped around his neck. Mob justice. Gladwin felt sick when he considered the depths to which both sides had sunk in the struggle for and against apartheid. He needed some air.

He excused himself and walked through the open French

The Peace Garden

windows into the Cohens' well-kept garden. Scalloped flowerbeds filled with a mixture of indigenous and alien shrubs edged the large, spacious lawns, big enough for a game of football or cricket. Brazilian bougainvillea mixed with aloes, cycads, poinsettias and roses: a fiery array of the best of both worlds. The foreign flowers had adapted well, with deep roots and a sense of permanence that blurred the distinction between old and new. Stan Cohen's mother, back in the 1930's, had tried to plant herbaceous beds with cottage flowers. But the rain-free Highveld winters and the rain-scarce Highveld summers proved too much for the delicate blooms. One could only import so much luxury, and then one had to make do.

Although it didn't belong to him, this piece of earth had deep roots in Gladwin's spirit. He took his first steps on the rolling lawns back in 1957 in the shadow of his father, Nelson Nkulu, who had worked in the Cohens' garden since 1946. Nelson had replaced his father George after he failed to come back from North Africa, defending one imperial power against another. Sophie told Gladwin that *Tata* George had believed he would be given his own plot of land if he fought for the white government. But all he got was a bicycle; the only inheritance he could leave to his son. And that was stolen two years after he died.

So Nelson became a gardener in a white man's garden, just like his father before him. But it could have been worse. He could have died down a mine like his brother Sipho or nearly starved to death in a rural village like the rest of his family. And then of course, there was Sophie. Sophie, who claimed that the famous freehold township of Sophiatown was named after her, had taken a job in old Mrs Cohen's kitchen in 1948, when she was fourteen, just in case her jazz career didn't take off. She had told Gladwin once that Miriam Makeba had been asked to fill in for her when she went into labour with him in 1956.

Whether the Miriam Makeba story was true or not, Sophie and Nelson Nkulu had lived unremarkable lives. Unremarkable, that is, until Nelson decided to join a group of men led by PAC president Robert Sobukwe in 1960 who turned in their passes at a police station in protest against the latest influx control laws.

Gladwin explained to me in one of his letters that the infamous pass laws were designed to uphold the Group Areas Act that separated South Africa's racial groups into their 'own' areas. But someone high up wasn't very good at maths because eighty percent of the population was supposed to squeeze into twenty percent of the land.

In order for a black person to 'visit' a white area, he or she needed a pass. Gladwin's father Nelson had a pass, as did his mother Sophie, but Nelson's only allowed him into Parktown during daylight hours to work as a gardener. Sophie, whose domestic duties sometimes took place at night, was allowed to sleep over in the white area. If she wanted to spend the night with her husband, she would have to travel to Soweto where he lived with her sister's family: seven people squeezed into a two-roomed shack. Occasionally he took the chance and stayed overnight in Parktown, knowing that the Cohens wouldn't turn him in, but the same couldn't be said of their neighbours.

So on 21 March 1960 Nelson Nkulu marched to the nearest police station without carrying his pass and demanded to be arrested. The PAC, as organisers of the protest, hoped to swell the jails and courts with minor pass offenders, thereby preventing the processing of genuine criminal cases and showing the ridiculousness of the system. The result was the massacre of over sixty people outside the Sharpeville police station and the declaring of a state of emergency.

Nelson Nkulu, because of his association with Robert Sobukwe, was labelled an instigator and sent to jail at Modder B prison near Springs. He was only sentenced to three months, but as he told Sophie during a short visit, he didn't trust the *boere* to let him out, and so tried to escape. He was hunted down by police dogs in a mealie field near Daveyton and sentenced to five years on Robben Island. He died there of tuberculosis in 1965, two days before he was due to be released.

Gladwin lay back on the sun-scorched grass, watching a beetle push a dung ball up a slope, refusing to give up, even when the ball rolled back down and knocked the insect off its feet.

"I knew I'd find you here." Gladwin looked up and saw his mother.

"Do you remember when you planted this tree?" She gestured to an avocado tree that was providing shade for a host of other plants. "You were four years old and you asked when *Tata* was coming home. I said that I didn't know, but if you planted the avocado seed that your father left on his plate after his last meal you would have something to show him when he came home. You watered that seed everyday then ran to the gate to see if he would come."

"And he didn't," said Gladwin.

"No he didn't. But the tree is big and your tears weren't wasted. I look at that tree and remember the sacrifice he made, and how what our people planted so long ago, has finally grown fruit." Sophie wiped away a welling tear.

"*Mama...*" Gladwin reached out his hand and grasped her shoulder. He watched as she teetered like a baby starting to walk; on the border between breakdown and composure. Years of discipline paid off and she pulled herself back from the edge.

"Come my son, no time to weep, this is the new South Africa and I have to go shopping side by side with all the white people. Will you drive me to Eastgate? I want to buy something for you to take home to Thabo."

"Yes *Mama*, I'd be proud to," he said, taking her arm and leading her to his rented Corolla. As he opened the door for her, he half regretted that she hadn't given in and released the pent-up grief of thirty six years. God knows he needed to, even if she didn't. But the lady wanted to go to Eastgate, to live and shop in the present; and that's where she would go.

Wearing her best hat and second-hand shoes, Sophie Nkulu proudly walked with her exiled son through the air-conditioned corridors of the Eastgate shopping mall. On advice from Gladwin, she bought a book on indigenous South African plants to send back to Thabo. Then they had lunch, along with some of the best of Johannesburg's white folk, in a once-forbidden restaurant. The white waitress called Sophie 'madam' and the white manager thanked her for coming and asked her to come again. Sophie was right, thought Gladwin: the victory was here in the present.

But while the mother and son walked to their car, basking in the freedom of the new South Africa, they didn't see the white Camry driven by a young man in a brown leather jacket and his middle-aged passenger with the rugby-scrum ears. The car came off the circular ramp from the upper car park at break-neck speed. Gladwin, hearing a commotion behind him, turned and saw the vehicle just in time. He shoved his mother behind a snake of shopping trolleys winding its way across the tarmac. He dived after her but only managed to get himself behind a stop sign before the Camry rammed it. Miraculously the sign bent double over his body, half impaling the low-slung chassis of the Camry.

Uninjured but unable to move, Gladwin looked into the headlights of the lurching car. He closed his eyes, preparing for the worst. But the car pulled into reverse as a crowd gathered, and with Inspectors Nel and Khumalo of John Vorster Square pushing their way to the front, it made its getaway.

Chapter Twenty-two

IN THE WEEK leading up to Gladwin's appearance before the TRC, he told me that the police presence after the Eastgate incident became more visible. A yellow van replaced the white Camry under the Jacaranda tree outside *Cohenville*, which, while it brought back unpleasant memories of police harassment during the Sixties and Seventies, was strangely comforting. Gladwin, who had memorised the Camry's registration number, demanded that the police do something to apprehend the men. Nel told him that it would be nearly impossible to trace the car, and besides, someone with his history should expect to have enemies.

The thought of police complicity in the incident crossed Gladwin's mind but would be impossible to prove. The Cohens, however, resorted to good old-fashioned bribery; ensuring the occupants of the yellow van remained vigilant by sending Sophie out with *vetkoeke*, *koeksusters* and other delicacies on an unashamedly regular basis.

Gladwin had been following the Truth and Reconciliation Commission hearings with interest for the past few months. The commission, made up of government appointees from across the political, religious and racial spectrum was set up to try and address South Africa's past so that the country could move on into a multi-coloured future. The commission was given powers to subpoena people to appear before it and encourage them, if not force them, to tell the truth about their past. Although how clear the road appeared through cracked rear view mirrors, is still a question of debate. Well, at least that's what Time says.

A lot still remains a mystery about South Africa's history, particularly because thousands of documents pertaining to police, army, government and secret service activities during the apartheid era mysteriously disappeared before the Commission could see them; the victim, it seems, of a passionately dedicated recycler. An acre or two of rain forest may have been saved thanks to the diligence of the environmentally friendly cop, but much still came to light during the hearings, mainly because of individual testimony.

Criticised by both sides as either going too far or not far enough, the TRC, whilst being far from perfect, had at least made an attempt to uncover the truth about South Africa's problems. And if, as in many cases, the stories told by those testifying just made the past even more confusing, at least the victims of apartheid, both black and white, had a chance to tell the world how they felt about what happened to them.

Gladwin decided to participate in the process when he heard TRC chairperson Archbishop Desmond Tutu speak on television. He said: "the wounds of the past must not be allowed to fester. They must be opened. They must be cleansed. And balm must be poured on them so they can heal. This is not to be obsessed with the past. It is to take care that the past is properly dealt with for the sake of the future." I vaguely remember seeing the portly old priest declaring this on American TV, but at the time I didn't realise that his words were so important, so I turned back to *Bay Watch*.

But not so Gladwin. It was for the sake of the future that he had come to South Africa: Thabo's future. As I well knew, the boy didn't understand why his father couldn't (wouldn't, he believed) return to the land of his birth. It was time to bring the past to light, to finally tell his story, for the first time in twenty years. Ever since the day when Thabo stood alone against the bulldozers, and called his father a coward in *isiXhosa*, Gladwin knew that he must turn around and look behind him, for the sake of his son. It was time to face the truth, because he, like his son, believed he had failed as a freedom fighter. Now he was leaving it to a nation to judge.

As Gladwin went over his prepared testimony in the car outside the conference centre, he wept. He wept for the boy he had been and the games he had never played. He wept for his mother and the singing career that drowned in a sink-load of dishes. He wept for his father who decided he wanted to be an archaeologist when his own father wrote to him about the wonders of the pyramids in World War II, but only managed a Grade Three education and a life as a white man's servant. He wept for Thabo who hated him for leaving his mother when she was three months pregnant, and for Poppy and the life they never had.

Poppy. He'd heard that she had been arrested then exiled to the Eastern Cape after he left for Zambia in 1976. He hated to think that she had to go through the pregnancy on her own; although he had heard that Gugs came in and out of hiding to help her during and after that difficult time. After her banning orders expired, she left Thabo with her mother in Soweto and went to study law at Fort Hare University. She was now a legal advisor to the ANC based in Cape Town. He would go and see her as soon as this ordeal was over; which reminded him, he should get inside.

Brushing away his tears, Gladwin filed the papers back in his briefcase and secured the gear lock. Looking up he realised with horror that he was being watched by two men in the car next to him. It was the leather-clad youngster and the rugby-eared one. They were sitting in a mid-Eighties gold BMW. Maybe the Camry was in for repairs. Gladwin quickly opened his door to get out but the BMW passenger door was flung open and rammed into his. The doors scraped against one another, going head to head, until Gladwin backed down. He was contemplating whether or not climbing out the passenger side was the cowardly thing to do when Inspector Nel opened the driver's door for him. The BMW men just waited, staring at him like a housewife at a cockroach with a can of Doom in hand.

"Thank goodness you're here, Inspector Nel. These men are…"

"Yes I know," interrupted Nel. "This is Riaan Labuschagne and his uncle Kobus. They're Fritz Labuschagne's son and brother."

Gladwin was just about to demand that Nel arrest them for trying to kill him at Eastgate, when the Labuschagnes climbed out of the car and walked towards the conference centre.

"Well, aren't you going to arrest them?"

"For what?"

"Attempted murder!"

"Oh, you're talking about the Eastgate incident. That was a white

Camry not a gold BMW. Besides, it might have been an accident."

Gladwin was just about to reply when Stan and Bryan Cohen arrived. They summed up the situation and hurriedly ushered their client away.

Chapter Twenty-three

THE AUDITORIUM WAS packed. Members of the press jostled for seats near the back, oblivious to the centre-aisle division between black and white that separated the other South Africans as naturally as oil and water. Gladwin's was not the only case being heard that day: there were dozens of Soweto Riot-related hearings scheduled to run successively over the next two weeks. Family members and their lawyers huddled together in small groups, representing those applying for and those opposing amnesty.

In some cases amnesty wasn't being sought, as the perpetrators of the various human rights abuses had not been identified. In these cases the survivors were just there to tell their stories, hoping that the commission could provide some answers. One woman, whose son disappeared during the riots, wanted to know if the commission could help her find out if he was dead or alive. If the former, she wanted his body back: she had a plot at Diepkloof cemetery reserved in anticipation of his homecoming. Her case was referred to a sub-committee dealing with apartheid-era disappearances.

An old man wanted to know if he could claim compensation for all of his belongings that were destroyed in a fire set by rioters in 1976, including six potted fruit trees which he said he was keeping for the day he got his farm back. In 1971 he had been forced to leave his orchard and smallholding near Badplaas during a forced removal of black occupants from white-zoned land; carried out as enthusiastically as a teenager tackles his pimples. His claim was forwarded to the reparations committee and the land claims court.

A forty-year-old woman in a wheelchair had to be carried up the stairs to the hall because the new black council hadn't got around to building a ramp yet. She wanted to place on record that she knew the identity of the policeman who had been responsible for crippling her twenty years ago as she marched with her school friends on the first day of the riots. Despite being subpoenaed the policeman had failed to arrive. The chairperson, Archbishop Desmond Tutu, instructed his legal team to petition for the officer's arrest.

Then Gladwin's turn came. He took his place at the table with the Cohens while the Labuschagnes and their lawyer sat across the aisle.

Archbishop Tutu, flanked by two other commissioners, read the application form set before him. He reminded all present that this wasn't a court of law that could legally find Gladwin guilty or innocent nor impose a sentence; it was merely a hearing to try to get at the truth of the events of 1976. However, if Gladwin confessed to killing Labuschagne and applied for amnesty, the commission could grant it. He explained that for amnesty to be granted the commission needed to be convinced that full disclosure had been made and that it be shown that the motivation for the killing or context in which it took place was political and not criminal. If sufficient grounds could not be found for amnesty, which the Labuschagnes would try to show, then Gladwin could be tried for the crime in a court of law if the state decided there were sufficient grounds to prosecute.

So Gladwin finally told his story and the whole country, and potentially the world, could hear him. The proceedings were being televised and broadcast over the Internet. He hoped Thabo would dial up and hear what his old man had to say. I didn't tell Gladwin in later years that Thabo told me that he had attended a football match in Newcastle that day, but he did browse the highlights when he got home.

Gladwin started by telling the commission about the regular harassment that he and Gugs were subjected to by Labuschagne. An affidavit was read out from Poppy about what she had witnessed.

"But honorary chairperson, this is just hearsay. Does Mr Nkulu have any witnesses here today to back his story?" The Labuschagne lawyer whined.

The Peace Garden

Stan Cohen was ready for this: "There were six witnesses to the events. Officer Koto was killed in 1985 and Gugile Sithole could not be traced."

"Yes, the commission has been trying to trace Mr Sithole in connection with a number of other matters before us and we have also been unable to find him. Although our sources believe that he is still alive. But who are the other witnesses?" a commissioner asked.

"I'm the third witness and Riaan Labuschagne, the victim's son, is the fourth," said Stan, well aware of the ripples his pebble-drop had caused in the auditorium. Stan went on to recount the story of when he had helped to get Gugs out of John Vorster Square and what Gugs and Gladwin had told him at the time.

"Hearsay! My learned friend only knows what he was told, how does he know that it's true?"

"No, I'm telling you what I saw as well as what I was told. I may not have seen the incident, but I saw the results," said Stan.

Before Labuschagne's lawyer could object, the commissioner asked: "And the other witnesses. You said there were six?"

"Four witnesses to the initial harassment, and six, including three of the initial four, to Inspector Labuschagne's death."

"Well who are they?" asked the archbishop, slightly impatient.

"The fifth," said Stan, "is also, unfortunately, dead. The press photographer Brian Viljoen was found hanged in his flat a few months ago. I visited him before he died and he told me that there was more on the film he took than just the picture of my client killing Inspector Labuschagne. And if the commission will allow it…"

"Once again, I say, hearsay. If my learned friend could produce this supposed film it would be different. But he can't."

"Mr Cohen?" Archbishop Tutu queried.

"No sir, I can't. The film has disappeared."

"Well then, let's stick with what we do have. Please call your first witness."

"We would like to call Riaan Labuschagne." Another murmur swept the room, swelling to a breaker then rolling back as Archbishop Tutu raised his hand.

Stan Cohen adjusted his tie, pushed back his thinning fringe, and turned to his victim with a surprisingly warm smile. "Mr Labuschagne, how old were you in 1976?"

"I was six."

"And were you with your father on the day of June 16 in Soweto?"

"Yes. I often travelled with him."

"Yes, so we believe. Did you ever witness your father assaulting anyone on his travels?"

"Objection! Honorary chairperson, my learned colleague should stick to the case at hand."

"Yes, but the case at hand is influenced by these other events," said Stan.

"I agree. Go ahead Mr Cohen," the archbishop conceded.

"Thank you your worship. Did you ever see your father assault Mr Nkulu, Mr Sithole or any other people?"

"I don't remember," said Riaan, "that's all very vague. All I remember in any detail was the day my father died."

"And what happened on that day?"

"My pa told me that he would take me to see John Wayne at the bioscope, but first he had to take care of some business in Soweto."

"What business?"

"He didn't tell me, I was only six."

"Yes, of course. When you drove into Soweto did you know that the riots had begun?"

"No, I don't think Pa knew either. He was off duty. But when we were driving someone called him on his radio. I heard him say 'Okay, I'm going that way now'. Then he turned to me and said, 'There may be some *kaffirs* running around and throwing stones, but don't be scared *seuntjie*, papa won't let anyone hurt you. And don't tell your ma where we came'."

"Why did you think your father took you into a riot?"

"I don't think he realised how bad it would get. He would never do anything to hurt me."

"Fair enough, go on."

"Well, I remember driving through the streets and seeing black

The Peace Garden

people, mainly youngsters, running around wildly. I saw some policemen and soldiers too, but Pa didn't take us too close to the action, so I only saw it from a distance.

"We picked up Koto at his house then drove to the Chinaman's shop. My pa usually bought me some liquorice sticks there, but not that day, it was all boarded up. But then the Chinaman came out from behind the shop talking to a young black man."

"Who was the black man? Had you seen him before?"

"I don't know. I don't think so."

"Wasn't the man Gugs Sithole, a man whom your father and Officer Koto had frequently assaulted in your presence?"

Riaan flushed red: "I told you, I don't know; I was only six years old! You're lucky I remember what I've told you already!"

"Yes, I'm sorry. What happened then?"

"My father got out of the car with Officer Koto and started talking to the Chinaman and the black man. Then, when his back was turned, this man," he said, pointing to Gladwin, "jumped out of a bush with a brick in his hand, and hit my father over the head. Pa fell to the ground and I ran to see him. Both the black men ran away and Koto chased after one of them."

"Which one?"

"Him."

"And what about the Chinaman?"

Riaan was silent but his breathing was deep.

"Mr Labuschagne," said the archbishop in the gentlest of voices. "I know this must be terrible for you, having to remember what it was like to see your father beaten to death, but you must try to remember. We need to get a better picture of what really happened on that day."

"Yes, I'm sorry. The Chinaman was kneeling down beside my father. He tried to stop me from getting too close, but I managed to push past him. Pa was already dead. His eyes were fixed, staring, but not at me. There was a lot of blood. The Chinaman's knees were red with it. It was all over my hands. Then ..." Riaan's voice broke as he swallowed a sob. "Then, the Chinaman gave me some liquorice."

"And after that?"

"Koto came back, and called for help. More policemen arrived and an ambulance. They took my pa away."

"Did you see the photographer, Brian Viljoen?"

"I think so, but I'm not sure. He might have been over the road, I thought I saw someone there, but I can't be sure."

"All right. What happened to the Chinaman?"

"I don't know, but I found out when I grew up that his shop was burnt down later that day and his body was found inside. *He* probably did it!" he spat, pointing to Gladwin.

"I object, sir. Honourable chairperson, that is pure speculation; Mr Nkulu has only been accused of one killing, and besides, the medical report on page thirty seven shows that Mr Wong died of a bullet wound and that the bullet was police issue."

"Yes, I see that. Do you dispute that, counsel?" The bishop asked Labuschagne's lawyer.

"No sir. Only that the bullet may have been police issue but there is no evidence that a policeman fired the gun. Many guns were lost or stolen that day and it could have been fired by anyone."

"Agreed," said Stan. "Unfortunately Mrs Wong does not want to bring a submission to the commission regarding her husband's death, so his role in this affair may have to go unexamined."

"I think you're right, Mr Cohen. Do you have any further questions for Mr Labuschagne?"

"No sir, I don't." Labuschagne's lawyer then asked him to clarify a few points, but his testimony remained largely the same.

Then it was Gladwin's turn again. Gladwin's story was significantly different to Riaan's. He told how he and Gugs had been caught up in the turmoil of June 16th even though they weren't in the initial march of the children from Naledi and Thomas Mofolo High Schools a few days before.

However, Gladwin said that he was on the edge of the ten thousand-strong crowd that converged on the Orlando West High School on the morning of the 16th. The march, ostensibly to protest against the use of Afrikaans as a medium of instruction, was to fuel a riot and police repression that resulted in the deaths of five hundred and seventy five people and two thousand three hundred and eighty wounded. But that only became clear a week later, when white South Africa took its first breaths after the uprising was quelled.

Gladwin told the commission that on the morning of June 16th, he had seen police open fire on two schoolboys running to catch up with the marchers and how a teargas canister was thrown into the midst of them. The marchers retaliated by throwing stones, then, said Gladwin, "all hell broke loose. Soweto was on fire and I wanted to get as far away from it all as I could. Then I saw Gugs heading towards the Chinaman's shop so I ran to catch up with him."

"Why was he going to the Chinaman's shop?" Stan asked.

"Leslie Wong was a known police informer. So some student leaders offered him protection on more than one occasion to tell them what he told the police. You could say that he was a double agent. But I see him as a man who walked a fine line to keep himself alive."

"Yes, thank you Mr Nkulu, but could you stick to the events of that day?" one of the commissioners asked.

"Yes, I'm sorry. Gugs had been working closely with some of the leaders from Morris Isaacson School, and he'd been told that if there was ever a spontaneous uprising it was his job to try to find out what the police were going to do; hence his visit to the Chinaman."

"So when did you catch up to Mr Sithole?" Stan asked.

"Only a while later. I have diabetes, although I didn't know it at the time, and running was becoming increasingly difficult for me."

"I see. Please tell us what you saw," the lawyer prompted.

"As I came around the corner I saw Inspector Labuschagne and the Chinaman arguing. Koto was holding onto Gugs. Gugs was bleeding from the mouth so I assumed he had already been hit. The little boy was watching from the back seat of the car and I saw a white man with a camera, I presume Brian Viljoen, standing on the other side of the road."

"Did Inspector Labuschagne see Viljoen?" Stan asked.

"No I don't think so. His back was turned, but I think Koto did."

"What happened next?"

"I heard the Chinaman say 'he's the one. I'm supposed to tell him everything you told me. He said that if I told him everything he would see that I would have a nice shop after the revolution.' The very use of the word revolution inflamed Labuschagne who told Koto to make Gugs kneel down. Then he took out his gun, stuck it in Gugs' mouth, and said: 'There's going to be no *vokken* revolution in my lifetime'."

At this, Gladwin paused and took a sip of water. No one spoke. Even the starlings that nested in the eaves of the community hall stopped twittering while the bespectacled man gathered his thoughts. In his own time, he continued.

"I knew he was going to kill him. He'd threatened to so many times, but this time I knew it was for real. I didn't really think, I just grabbed a brick and hit him. I didn't mean to kill him; I just wanted to stop him killing my friend."

After that, Gladwin's testimony was pretty much the same as Riaan's. With Koto at his heels he ran away. He went to one of the deserted high schools and lay low until nightfall. With Soweto on fire, he made his way out of the township and headed towards Parktown. The next morning he knocked on the Cohens' door with blood on his hands and death in his eyes.

"And Gugile Sithole, what happened to him?"

"I don't know. That was the last time I ever saw him."

Chapter Twenty-four

THE COMMISSION BROKE for lunch after Gladwin's testimony, but when they returned, Labuschagne's lawyer began to question him. Gladwin stuck to his story. Then both lawyers presented their reasons to the commission why amnesty should, or should not be granted. Stan Cohen contended that Gladwin had indeed killed Fritz Labuschagne, however, the fact that it occurred on June 16th 1976 implied a political context. Adding to this that Gladwin associated with known student leaders of the time, Stan argued, the commission had no choice other than to find that the killing was 'political' not 'criminal'. And even if the political context was missing, if this went to a criminal court, Mr Nkulu would be cleared because of his undisputed testimony that he killed Inspector Labuschagne only to save the life of his friend.

"I object," said Labuschagne's lawyer, with a twinkle that suggested he didn't object too much. "Firstly, the mandate of this commission is to determine whether or not the killing of Inspector Labuschagne was politically motivated. Mr Nkulu himself has admitted that he wasn't a political activist at the time. Then when the trouble started, he testified that his first thoughts were to get out of Soweto, not to join the revolt, which was clearly on Mr Sithole's agenda. Secondly, regarding the criminal motivation for this brutal killing, Mr Nkulu's testimony is not undisputed as my learned colleague contends. We have the affidavits of Mr Koto and Mr Viljoen taken at the time, as well as the testimony of Riaan Labuschagne, that things didn't transpire the way Mr Nkulu has testified. This then sheds doubt on the second component necessary for amnesty: a full and truthful disclosure."

Stan Cohen looked as if he was about to interrupt, so Labuschagne's lawyer quickly continued. "And as for these photographs, the only one in evidence is the one which the whole of South Africa saw on 17th June 1976, the one showing Gladwin Nkulu smashing in Fritz Labuschagne's skull."

Once again, Cohen was about to speak, but this time it was the archbishop who interrupted. "Do you have any further evidence relating to the political nature of this act, Mr Cohen?"

"No sir, I don't."

"And you don't have the photographs?"

"No sir, as I have already told you, they have not been found."

"Then the commission will retire for an hour to consider what we have already heard, and to make a recommendation of whether or not we will put Mr Nkulu's name forward for amnesty."

With that, the commission adjourned, and a slightly flustered Stan Cohen turned to his client. "I'm sorry Gladwin; I got a bit too carried away. Maybe Bryan should have presented the case. With my involvement as it was, I found it difficult not to get too emotionally involved."

"That's all right Stan."

"Yes, don't worry Dad; I think we put forward enough evidence to suggest a political context, if not motive. I mean it was the Soweto Riots for goodness sake! What wasn't political at that time? And as for the full disclosure bit – I think Gladwin has held his own against two dead men and a six-year-old-boy."

"I hope you're right," said his father.

Gladwin needed some air. There was a small park outside the community centre, so he decided to take a walk. The park was new, with flowerbeds laid out concentrically around a dismal piece of lawn. Someone had planned this development at the wrong time of year, planting grass just before the winter dry season, and scattering seed that needed more water than was available.

Oh well, at least they tried, thought Gladwin, but it's just like the new South Africa: noble ideas, high ideals, an enthusiastic beginning then the harsh reality of limited resources and the realisation that some things just take time.

He sat down on the paint-bare bench and closed his eyes. He was feeling a little weak, he thought, perhaps he should go and buy a sandwich. But then, he smelt it: roast *mealies* and a little sweat. It was Gugs.

"Don't turn around, my friend, I have a gun. I don't want to use it, but I can't let you see my face; I've made some changes. I don't want anyone who can identify me, not even you."

"Gugs, my friend, where've you been all these years?"

"Maybe I'll tell you when this is all over. But for now, I have a debt to repay. I'll leave it on the edge of the bench. But don't turn around. Count sixty seconds after I say goodbye, take the package and get on with your life. Goodbye Gladwin."

Gladwin wanted with all his being to turn around. He wanted to see his friend again after twenty years. He wanted to hold onto him and drag him inside, to show the world that he was telling the truth. He wanted to ask him about Poppy and thank him for looking after her and young Thabo. He wanted to ask him whether the rumours about him being behind a series of racially motivated murders were true. He wanted to, but he didn't; Gugs was his friend, but he knew he would kill him if he had to. So instead, he counted to sixty, until the *mealies* and sweat were a memory once again, then opened his eyes and looked for the package.

There was a brown folio envelope perched on the edge of the bench. Nothing was written on it. He opened it and wasn't too surprised to see a strip of negatives. He held them up to the light, holding his breath when he saw that one or two of the frames were beginning to perish with age. Then he exhaled slowly as he saw the infamous picture of him killing Labuschagne, and before that, shots of Gugs with a gun in his mouth, and, prior to that, Koto assaulting him, with Labuschagne and the Chinaman standing by and laughing.

Gladwin stuffed the negatives back into the envelope and ran inside the building, his weakness of earlier forgotten. Stan and Bryan were talking in the hall. Both of them looked worried. The Labuschagne clan was on the other side of the room, deep in conversation. Young Riaan looked up as Gladwin came in, his eyes narrowing as he noticed the black man's animated face.

"I've got it, I've got it!" shouted Gladwin, not caring about lawyer-client confidentiality.

"What?" asked Bryan.

"The negatives. The photos that show what really happened!"

"*What?*" said Bryan; this time incredulously. By now the Labuschagnes had turned their full attention to the unravelling events.

"But how? When?" asked Stan.

"Just now. When I was outside. Someone put them on the bench beside me."

"Who?" asked Stan.

"I don't know. I didn't see them. But it doesn't matter, they're here. And they show everything!" This last was directed to the Labuschagnes who turned on their lawyer.

"Well let's see!" Bryan grabbed the envelope from Gladwin and opened it. "Yep, aha, mmm …. I think you're a free man Gladwin!"

"The commission will decide that!" said Labuschagne's lawyer, suddenly beside them.

"You're a murderer!" It was Riaan Labuschagne. The young man looked as if he was going to explode, and it was only the restraining touch of his wife, heavily pregnant, that stopped him. But by now the room was filling up with commissioners back from their break and a swarm of police officers.

"Come Riaan," said his wife. "Let's see what the commission says."

"Yes let's," said Stan, sounding twenty years younger.

Archbishop Tutu took his seat and indicated for everyone to do the same. "Well, ladies and gentlemen, we have come to our decision …"

"Forgive me your worship, but we have new evidence." A rumble ran through the room. Press photographers edged forward and police officers clutched their batons.

"New evidence, Mr Cohen? What is it?"

"The missing photographs from June 16th 1976!"

There was uproar; photographers surrounded Gladwin, the Labuschagne's lawyer physically restrained Riaan and a group of ex-activists at the back of the hall burst into a chorus of *Nkosi Siki'lel iAfrika*.

"Quiet! Quiet!" shouted the archbishop.

"Sit down!" shouted his colleague.

Finally, after two or three minutes, the crowd toned down, anxious to hear what the commissioners would say about the photographs.

"Thank you," said the archbishop. "May we see those photographs, Mr Cohen?"

"They're negatives, your worship."

"Whatever they are we would like to take some time to examine them."

"Of course your worship. How long will you need?"

"As long as it takes."

The negatives were first shown to the Labuschagne's lawyer who visibly went pale when he saw what they depicted, then to the commission. No one in the hall spoke apart from the murmured conference on the bench. Finally, the archbishop signalled they were ready.

"Mr Nkulu, the commission agrees that the negatives appear to show what you said they would. We will of course send them for authentication, but until or unless they prove to be a fake, we accept that they are genuine. And this, added to your lawyer's argument about the political context of the events, has led us to conclude that full and truthful disclosure has been made. We will therefore recommend you for amnesty, pending the outcome of the photographic authentication. Thank you. This case is concluded."

The hall erupted once again. Gladwin, still seated, was dragged to his feet by dozens of well-wishers who did not know him, but knew his kind. Ten minutes later he was still shaking hands, but this time, he noticed that the hand he held was white. He looked up – it was Fritz Labuschagne's brother Kobus. Gladwin swallowed hard. Close up, he could see the resemblance to his brother; the same jaw, the same nose, the same eyes, and yes, the same hatred.

"Watch out *kaffir*," he whispered. "This isn't over yet."

Chapter Twenty-five

I DIDN'T RECEIVE any letters for about three weeks after that. What had happened to Gladwin? Had Kobus Labuschagne carried through with his threat? I felt that I needed to tell someone, but I didn't know who. Besides, I had no evidence that anything *had* happened to him.

I scoured American newspapers and South African news websites to see if what he had told me was true. It was. It was all over the media. I also checked to see what happened with the photographic authentication and was glad to see that the negatives were legitimate. Gladwin was now a free man.

But a week after the hearings, there was no sign of him. He was not reported as 'missing' in the papers; the media had simply got bored with his story and moved on. But that did not account for his silence towards me. Part of me worried he'd moved on and forgotten about me now that his name had been cleared, but another part – the Nancy Drew part – suspected he may have fallen victim to foul play. Given that the letters he sent me took ten to fourteen days to reach me by airmail, I calculated that he had been 'missing' for nearly a month.

Just as I was considering going to the police and taking my pile of correspondence with me, a letter arrived on my doorstep, postmarked Cape Town. It was Gladwin's familiar handwriting.

10 August 1996

Dear Natalie,
Forgive me for not writing for a while, but as you would expect I have been very busy after the TRC hearing – speaking to the press, and so on. It took a week for the negatives to be authenticated, and

it was only then that my amnesty was confirmed. Would you believe it, but even Inspectors Nel and Khumalo wished me well!

My mother was beyond happy. She wants to know whether or not I'll be coming back to South Africa. I told her that depended on whether or not I could get a job here and whether Thabo was ready to come back.

The answer to that is probably no, as he hasn't finished his degree, but I didn't want to tell her that just yet.

There are lots of things to consider, and I'll be able to tell you and her more when I come back from Cape Town.

Things are getting quite complicated – for all sorts of reasons. Let me tell you what has happened here so far ...

Gladwin had parked his rented car under some shady milkwoods. He checked to see that there was nothing in sight that might tempt thieves to try and break into the Corolla, even though a security guard was roaming between the rows of cars. Satisfied that if his car window was smashed it wouldn't be because of his negligence, he locked the door then headed up the paved slope to the entrance of one of Cape Town's most popular tourist traps: Kirstenbosch Botanical Gardens.

He had half an hour before his appointment, so he decided to take a walk around the beautifully maintained grounds, which lounged at the foot of the Constantiaberg. He walked through the sculpture garden, bypassed the spectacular annual flowerbeds, skirted the amphitheatre that was being prepped for a late-afternoon jazz concert, and headed up the slope towards the woodland.

On the lip of the hill he found what he'd been looking for: Van Riebeeck's Hedge. The wild almond hedge was planted in 1660 by the first Dutch governor of the Cape, Jan van Riebeeck, to protect the European settlement from local cattle rustlers. The hedge used to stretch from Wynberg Hill to Kirstenbosch, which in those days was the extent of the frontier.

"Good fences make good neighbours", thought Gladwin, but not in this case.

The hedge may have kept the locals out for a while, but it

certainly didn't keep the invaders in. Pity the Khoi didn't use the arsenic-laden plant to get rid of the aliens before they took root, saving his countrymen three and a half centuries of hell.

Gladwin walked along the red brick path with the hedge on one side and the expansive lawns, littered with mothers and toddlers, on the other. He rounded the bend and entered the woodland. Oh well, it was a *fait accompli*, the European invasion of his homeland, and the aliens were too entrenched to send home again. Indeed, many of them knew nowhere else and even considered themselves African. Integration was the only hope.

He balked at a sign announcing that he was entering the "Enchanted Forest", so Grimm, so European. But he smiled as he noticed the nametags labelling each plant and tree. Many of them, nearly half, not only sported a Latin and common English name, but the indigenous Xhosa or Khoi name too. The Cat's Tail Asparagus was *Cwebe*, the Plectranthus, *Umqoye* and the Clivia Miniata, *Ngoye.*

At last, he thought, a recognition that the landscape existed before European settlement. The white men had come, like Adam and Eve into a new Eden, and named the plants and animals the Lord brought before them. But what they failed to acknowledge was that they had already been named, already been incorporated into the living landscape of the indigenous tribes. For three hundred and fifty years, his people had been cut off from the land; but in this small act of renaming, the land was slowly being reclaimed, or at least, shared. It was an encouraging sign.

Gladwin looked at his watch and realised that he would have to get back to the sculpture garden for his appointment. He decided to take a shortcut through the succulents. Of all the plants in the garden he admired these the most. His greenhouse back in Newcastle was full of them: a testimony to tenacity. Like Gladwin, the plants had highly advanced survival instincts, keeping everything inside, just in case a drought was on the horizon. Neighbours, no matter what their intentions, wouldn't help you when resources were scarce, so the succulents had to look out for number one.

He picked his way through the rockery, taking in the aloes and

The Peace Garden

acacias with their vicious thorns brandished in defence, not malice. The earth was arid, giving nothing freely, so life had to be sucked from the air.

As he reached the first statue, a five-foot granite grandmother knitting a map of Africa, he thanked God that now he had been granted amnesty, he was free to return to the land of his birth. But the murder charge was only one of the things he had come to South Africa to face; the other was winding her way towards him through dozens of statues of mothers and infants. As she passed a soapstone dog suckling two pups, she stepped into a pool of sunlight, and paused for a moment, enjoying the rare warmth on the crisp winter day.

She was still as beautiful as he remembered, only more so. The braided hair was pulled up into a sophisticated French knot, drawing attention to the poised neck and proud jaw. Her shoulders, still slight, gave way to full breasts and her waist, thicker than it had been, slowly swelled to rounded hips, not unlike those of the silent African women bearing witness in stone to the first meeting of these lovers in two decades.

"Poppy," he said softly, then louder when she didn't respond. He stepped out from behind one of the watching women and into her pool of light. She looked, but didn't speak.

"Poppy!" He said, this time slightly pleading. She smiled, but not with her eyes, then took his hand, and led him to a nearby bench. The hand was soft yet cool despite the warming sunshine. They sat together for a long time, Gladwin not knowing what else he could say.

Eventually, she spoke, surprising him with her cultured tones, so different from the singsong lilt of her youth. "How's Thabo?"

"Oh, fine, fine. He said he would write to you."

"He has. I just wanted to know from someone who had seen him. He's doing well at his studies, better than when he was here. Less pressure, I suppose."

"Yes and no. He keeps himself apart, although he did make some friends with the neighbourhood children."

"But he's twenty now. A university student."

"Yes, his horticulture is going well. I'm going to get a job application form from Kirstenbosch to take back to him. I don't know if he'll do anything about it; you know what that child of ours is like."

"That child of *ours*?" Her voice was brittle, as if one of the statuesque single mothers had spoken.

"Yes *ours*: yours and mine, Poppy. I thought you had come to terms with that when you finally told me I had a son."

"But why did I have to tell you? Surely you knew. Those weeks before you left, I was already putting on weight; and the nausea…"

"I was a nineteen-year-old African boy. What did I know of women's things?"

"Yes, what did you know." It was a statement, not a question.

"I couldn't come back, you have to know that Poppy."

"But why didn't you take me with you? One day you were there, the next you weren't. Twenty four hours, not long for a heart to heal."

"I didn't have a choice, when I got to the Cohens' the police were already on my scent. They arrived there minutes later, and if it hadn't been for Mrs Cohen and my mother hiding me in the laundry pile, they would have got me. I had to get out. That night, when Wayne said that he would take me across the Botswana border, I knew it was my only chance to get away. It was the best cover I could have, hiding in the car of a uniformed white South African soldier."

"Yes, but he paid for it later, I believe. Just like everyone who ever tried to help you." Her voice was dead.

"I'm sorry Poppy. I know you suffered; you and the boy. But I didn't know."

"Of course not. You were off playing academic in exile while your son and I had to fight for our lives back home. And I'm sure a British university was a far cry from the King William's Town hovel that I gave birth in. But I suppose you did leave me something."

He looked at her hopefully, but she continued to speak as if his heart had not spoken:

"After I'd been in detention for six weeks, after they'd tortured me, trying to find out where you were, I collapsed and woke up in

The Peace Garden

hospital. They found out I was pregnant and let me go. I suppose they decided that giving birth under house arrest, cut off from friends and family would be a continuation of the torture."

She stopped then, waiting for a young couple carrying a picnic basket to pass by. Hand in hand they were talking excitedly about the jazz concert they were about to see.

"Can't you forgive me Poppy?"

"No." she said simply.

So they just sat there on the wooden bench, with a plaque engraved to someone's loving memory filling the space between them.

"Will you be coming back?" She finally asked, her voice suddenly professional, befitting a woman that had studied law and now worked as a legal adviser for the African National Congress.

"I don't know. I might. I've been making enquiries at the University of Cape Town to see if they have any vacancies in their politics department."

"Well you should. It will be your only redemption. You should work to rebuild the country you abandoned. Maybe then I could forgive you."

"You bitch!" he said, before he could stop himself. Then, embarrassed, got up and walked away, leaving his ex-lover to nurse a heart that had not yet turned entirely from flesh to stone.

Chapter Twenty-six

BY THE TIME he finally got off, Gladwin had been on the train for well over an hour and a half. Ordinarily, a train trip from Cape Town to Muizenberg took fifty minutes, but Gladwin decided not to alight at the old Edwardian station, built the same year the Titanic sank. Instead, he stayed on the graffiti-riddled train as it travelled along the coastal route to Simon's Town, the charming naval village at the end of the line. It was only 10am, and his appointment wasn't until eleven, so he had some time to kill, and some nerves to calm.

The trip was soothing: the *kadunk, kadunk* of wheels on track; the gentle spray from the Atlantic Ocean crashing onto the rocks only metres from the line; the warm sun, massaging his body, which the first class carriage protected from the brisk winter air.

It was a magnificent part of the world, Gladwin had to admit, no wonder some of the first Europeans decided to set up shop here. The picturesque seaside towns of Muizenberg, St James, Kalk Bay, Fish Hoek and Simon's Town clung precariously to the sliver of land between the ocean on one side and the False Bay mountains on the other.

But Gladwin didn't get out at any of the stations. The train stopped at Simon's Town for fifteen minutes, then started on the return journey, with Gladwin taking advantage of his tourist ticket that allowed him to travel up and down the line as many times as he wanted.

As the train picked up speed, he thought back to when he got the message that brought him to this part of Cape Town in the first place. It was the day he met Poppy at Kirstenbosch as he left the gardens, trying to put as much space between him and his embittered ex-lover as possible. As he passed the coffee shop, with its small round tables scattered between pillars and fountains in the brick-face courtyard, a tall blonde man stood up and walked towards him. He was about fifty, with strong Nordic features and a thick hatch of hair. He looked like he might have been an athlete in his youth, but his flesh now hung slack on his big frame, like a loose pair of pyjamas.

"Mr Nkulu?" Gladwin was surprised that the man knew his name.

"Hans Larson," said the Scandinavian, offering his hand. He spoke with a slight American accent, like most Europeans who learnt their English through Hollywood. "I believe we're going to be doing business together soon," he said, inviting a response.

"Oh?" said Gladwin, "but I'm not a businessman."

"So I've been told."

"By whom?"

"A mutual friend, who, incidentally, would like to meet you at the time and place written on this card." On the front were Larson's name and details and his apparent designation as the managing director of the Fjord Corporation; Gladwin hadn't heard of it. On the back was a penned message: "*Rhodes Cottage, 11am, 30 June*". When Gladwin looked up, Larson was gone.

Back on the train the lollipop-coloured bathing boxes of St James were now behind him and Muizenberg station was coming up fast. He checked his watch: 10.35am. He got up and stepped out of the carriage with a bleached surfer, a young mother with two disgruntled children and an elderly Jewish man. "*Jewsenberg*" was the nickname that the town had earned in its heyday in the 1950s, with its twenty-plus hotels brimming over with Jewish holidaymakers. Even now, so he'd been told, many of the buildings in the sadly run-down town were still owned by Jewish families and rented out. No longer the holiday destination of the wealthy, Muizenberg's streets were teeming with refugees from various wars in Africa, and the beach a main attraction for families from the Cape Flats, the wind-swept home of most of Cape Town's 'coloured' people.

Gladwin walked back along the Main Road, parallel to the railway line, in the direction of St James. On his left was the sea, with a few seals sunning themselves on the rocks, and on his right, a series of colonial buildings known as the 'Historic Mile'. First was *Het Posthuys*, originally a Dutch supply depot and along with the Cape Town Castle, the oldest European building in South Africa. It was now a museum, tracing the history of the False Bay area, both colonial and pre-colonial. After that the *Natale Labia*, a regal mansion that used to be the home of the Italian ambassador. It was now a monument to European high society.

About halfway towards the cluster of multi-million rand homes that made up the village of St James, he came across the Rhodes Cottage. It was a poky little place for a great imperialist to spend the last days of his life. But Cecil John Rhodes, with his dreams of stretching British dominion from the Cape to Cairo, with an entire country dedicated to his name, chose to live and die in the two-bedroom cottage, hemmed in by mountains and sea.

A strange place for Gugs to want to meet, thought Gladwin, but then, maybe not. For Gugs, all Europeans were like Rhodes: aggressive expansionists, taking up more room on the planet than God had apportioned them. He remembered how often Gugs had decried the huge houses of the white people and their compulsion to 'have space' even in a supermarket queue.

He checked his watch, there were still ten minutes to go before eleven, and if Gugs were true to form, he would be late anyway. He decided to take a walk around the garden, which was relatively big compared to the small house. Being in the middle of winter, the floral fare was meagre, even more so than usual. However, Gladwin's trained eye soon picked up that the garden was being reconstructed. He saw the tell-tale signs of the beginnings of a bank of hydrangeas along the veranda, and a drastically thinned out plumbago. Stepping out from behind a thriving bushel of lavender was a woman whom he assumed to be the gardener. She was about seventy, though athletically built. She wore khaki work-clothes.

"Hello," she said with an embracing smile. "My name's Emma."

"Hello," he said, warming at once. "I'm Gladwin. Are you the gardener here?"

"Unofficially, yes. I live next door. No one else was doing it, so

I volunteered. It's been sadly neglected, as you can see, and the historical society has been all too happy to let me get on with it. Are you a keen gardener?"

"Oh yes, I can't wait to get back to my place in England; the roses will need some attention soon." Gladwin was surprised. Was he really looking forward to getting back? Wasn't he supposed to be staying in South Africa? His head said yes, but what was his heart saying? And why? Wasn't it his duty to stay and help rebuild the country?

"I'll show you around if you like," said Emma, interrupting his self-examination.

"That would be nice," said Gladwin, relieved. He followed the old lady around the garden, welcoming the distraction. Emma was only too happy to have someone to talk to.

"What I've been trying to do is reconstruct the garden as it might have been when Rhodes lived here a century ago. Oh, excuse me a minute," she said, picking up a tin bowl near a storm water drain. "For Cecil and his family," she explained, then smiled as she saw Gladwin's puzzled look. "They're the resident porcupines who live in the aqueducts. I'm not usually in favour of hand-feeding wild animals, for their own sake, but if I don't, Cecil digs up my bulbs."

By this time they were at the front of the cottage. She pointed to the hydrangea that Gladwin had noticed earlier: it had seen better days: "It's been here since the late 1900s. Original photos and sketches show a bank of them skirting the whole veranda. I've taken shoots from it and planted them all along.

"I've been reading Rhodes' letters and journals and looking at old pictures, to try and figure out what the place would have looked like when he lived here. I want to recreate an original Victorian garden that a man like Rhodes would have been comfortable in. But I also want to make it African."

And so the tour continued. He was so enthralled by Emma's company that he almost forgot why he was there. He looked at his watch: it was 11:15am. Gugs was late; he looked around, in case he had missed him while he was talking to the elderly gardener.

"Are you expecting anyone?" she asked.

"Yes, an old friend. Have you seen anyone?"

"Well, when we were looking at the plumbago, I saw someone – a black man of about forty – on the cottage steps. I was about to call out to him, but when he saw me, he left. Was that him?"

"It might have been," said Gladwin, knowing that it was. He took his leave of Emma, who let him go reluctantly, clearly having enjoyed their conversation. He wished her well with her project, and promised to come back to see how her plans worked out in a few seasons.

Gugs must have seen him and decided not to follow through on their meeting. Perhaps it was because he was talking to the white woman. Oh well, he thought, Gugs could find him again.

He headed back to Muizenberg, hoping to catch the next train to Cape Town. About half way there he spotted a subway that would take him under the railway line and onto the rock-side path. He walked down the steps and around a puddle of seawater. Then he smelt it: *mealies* and sweat. He heard footsteps behind him. "Gugs?" he asked, turning. "Yes," said Gugs, as he hit his friend over the head with the butt of his gun.

Chapter Twenty-seven

16 June 1976

"YOU CAN COME out now Gladwin, the police have gone." It was Mrs Cohen's voice, frightened but still in control. The sheets were pulled back and Gladwin looked up into the strained faces of his mother and her employer.

"*Hau* Gladwin, what have you done? Why is there blood on your shirt? Why are the police after you?"

"It was Labuschagne, *Mama*. He was going to kill Gugs. I stopped him."

"*Aiiiiii*, I knew it! I knew Gugs was trouble! Why didn't you listen to me? Why did you stay friends with him? *Aiiiii*!"

"Shh, Sophie, let the boy get up." Gladwin climbed out of the laundry basket.

"How did you stop him, Gladwin?"

"I killed him, Madam. I didn't mean to. I just wanted to stop him. I picked up a brick and hit him over the head. He was going to shoot my friend, I promise you Madam; I didn't mean to do it. *Mama*, you've got to believe me! *Mama*!"

The blood had drained from Rochelle Cohen's face. "Gugile Sithole? The boy my husband rescued from John Vorster Square?"

"Yes Madam."

"Oh dear Gladwin, what have you done? What have you got us all into?" The Jewish woman started pacing: back and forth, back and forth, her high heels clicking on the tiled kitchen floor. Sophie Nkulu slumped into a chair and buried her creased face in a crisp, starched apron. Gladwin stood next to the pile of rumpled sheets; his shoulders slumped, his blood-stained hands shaking uncontrollably.

They might have stayed like that forever, a tableau in a domestic tragedy, if Wayne Cohen hadn't walked in.

"Hey, Sophie, have you finished ironing my uniform yet?" The nineteen-year-old strode into the kitchen, his bare feet slapping the cool tiles, and headed straight for the fridge. He reached in and grabbed a bottle of milk around the neck. Without thinking he took a slug, spilling some on his Transvaal rugby shirt and jeans.

He suddenly noticed his mother, wiped his mouth and put the bottle back in the fridge. "Hey, Mom, sorry, I know I should've gotta glass, but . . . Mom? Are you okay? Mom?"

"Oh Wayne! Wayne!"

The boy stepped into his mother's path, stopping her compulsive pacing. "Mom, what is it?" he said firmly, taking her by the shoulders.

"It's Gladwin, Wayne."

"Gladwin, what's wrong with him?" The white boy turned to look at the black boy who by now had crumpled to the floor at his weeping mother's feet. "Gladwin? Sophie? What's happened?"

"I've killed someone, Wayne. A policeman."

"You've what? How? Why?"

"It was self-defence. He was going to kill my friend. I stopped him."

"And the police have been here looking for Gladwin. We hid him," said Mrs Cohen. "We're all involved in it. The boy Gladwin saved was a client of your father. We could all be targets now!"

"Oh God, what are we going to do?" said Wayne, starting to pace, just like his mother.

"We are going to get my son out of the country." It was Sophie, her voice firm. She leant on Gladwin's shoulder and pulled herself to her feet.

"How are we going to do that?" asked Mrs Cohen.

"Your son is going to help my son."

"How?"

"He is going to the border tomorrow, is he not?"

"Yes, so?" Mrs Cohen sounded worried.

"He can take Gladwin with him."

"No, Sophie, it's too dangerous. Wayne is going to his army unit.

He can't be seen with a terrorist."

"My son is not a terrorist," said the black woman, stepping between her child and her employer.

"No, no, of course not, I didn't mean that. But he is wanted by the police. It's too dangerous for both of them. I don't think ... "

"I'll do it, Mom."

"But Wayne ..."

"It'll be okay. I'll leave tonight and drop him off before I get to the camp. There's nothing but bush for miles around, no one will see. What do you say, Gladwin?"

"Look Wayne, I don't want to get you into trouble."

"Don't worry, I can handle myself. Besides, it looks like this family is already in trouble. The sooner you leave us, the better it will be for all of us, *boet*." Wayne used the Afrikaans word for brother. It was white slang for mate or buddy. Gladwin had never been referred to as a *boet* before; not by a white boy. He didn't know how to reply.

But Sophie did. She took the young man's hands in hers, the hands that she had washed since he was a baby, and kissed them.

"Are you sure it will be safe, son?" asked Mrs Cohen.

"Yes."

"Then we had better call your father."

Chapter Twenty-eight

"YOU MAY BE in the boot for about two hours. I've loosened the tail light to give you air, and there's food and water in the rucksack. It's not going to be very comfortable Gladwin, but it's the best I can do." Gladwin nodded then turned to his mother to say goodbye.

"*Mama*, I'll write as soon as I can. And I'll come back to visit you when it's safe."

"No my son, do not write. They will catch you. They will send you a letter and blow you up; you know what they do with those parcel bombs. No my son, it is better that I do not hear from you, then I know you will be safe."

"But *Mama* …"

"Your mother's right, Gladwin." It was Stan Cohen, standing with his arm around his weeping wife. Bryan, their younger son, was helping Wayne pack his kit into the Datsun. "I'll do all I can here to clear your name," said Stan, "but until then its best that you don't try to contact us. I'll get word to you when it's safe."

"How?"

"I can't tell you, just trust me. I have connections in the movement."

"Stan …" said his wife reproachfully.

"No Rochelle, it's got to be done. This government's gone too far. After what I saw on the news today, those poor kids fighting for their lives in Soweto, it can't be long before things change. The world can't let this go on for much longer. Don't worry Gladwin; I'm sure it will only be for a couple of years. Now hurry up and get in that boot. Wayne? Are you ready?"

"Yes Dad."

The two young men said goodbye to their mothers and climbed

into the Datsun; the white boy in the driver's seat and the black boy in the boot. Just before the lid closed Gladwin remembered something. "*Mama*, can you say goodbye to Poppy?"

"Poppy? Who is Poppy?"

"Poppy Fakile; the school teacher's daughter."

"Ah yes, yes I will, if I can find her. Now go my son, go with God." The lid closed and the car pulled out of the driveway. A light came on in the neighbour's house, a dog started to bark and the Cohens and Sophie hurried inside.

Two hours later, the car came to a stop and Wayne opened the boot. It was about 2am, the stars were bright, and Wayne's face was a full moon. Gladwin looked around him. "Where are we?"

"Just over the Botswana border. About three hundred Ks south west of Pietersburg where I'm stationed. Here, take my compass. It's army issue. I'll just say I lost it and order another one. According to the map – *ja*, take that too – you're about ten Ks from Gabarone. You should get there by dawn."

"Thanks Wayne, I owe you."

"*Ag*, don't mention it. What will you do when you get there?"

"I don't know. I'll try to get to Zambia I suppose."

"And join MK?" MK was short for *Mkhonto we Sizwe*, or *Spear of the Nation*, the armed wing of the African National Congress in exile.

"*Ja.*"

Wayne was silent. Then, seriously: "Just make sure you don't shoot me if our units come face to face."

"I'll try not to." Gladwin picked up his rucksack, checked his direction on the compass then turned to the white boy in the army uniform. "Look Wayne, from now on we're going to be enemies; that's just the way it is. But in my heart, you'll always be my friend."

"*Ja*, Gladwin I know."

As Gladwin watched Wayne drive away, he didn't realise that it would be the last time he or his family would see him.

Two weeks later Wayne Cohen was killed in a car crash. Forensic evidence suggested that his brakes had been tampered with. The authorities concluded that it was a MK job, but his parents suspected otherwise. Just before he died, Wayne had written a letter to his parents, telling them of a strange meeting that he had with his commanding officer, questioning him about the whereabouts of Gladwin Nkulu. Wayne said he didn't know. The CO just smiled and asked if he'd found his compass yet. "No," said Wayne.

"Well let me know if you do," said the CO before dismissing him. Five days later he was dead.

But Gladwin only found out about it two years afterwards in a letter smuggled to him by one of Stan Cohen's 'connections'. Gladwin felt awful, but what could he do? Wayne was just one of thousands who had died for the Struggle. He was a true comrade, even though he wore an enemy uniform.

Gladwin reached Gabarone without incident.

Word around Soweto was that the leader of the Gabarone MK cell worked at the ticket office in the central train station. A request for a 'one-way ticket to Lusaka' would get you invited into a back room where you would be questioned for at least twelve hours to check that you were a legitimate candidate and not a double agent. Gladwin wasn't sure how these checks were made, but he was eventually given the all-clear and found himself on a train to the Zambian capital.

There were four other young South Africans with him: three of them had been spurred on by the Soweto Riots to join the army in exile, the fourth was a cadre, acting as their guide. He travelled the line from Botswana to Zambia, rounding up all the runaways and delivering them to the MK recruitment camp.

On this trip he discovered that one of the new recruits used to be his next-door-neighbour in Mamelodi near Pretoria. The new boy was pleased to see a familiar face. At one of the stations along the way he asked his old friend if he could use a pay phone. "Who do you want to phone?" asked the guide. "Oh, just my mother to tell her I'm all right," said the neighbour. "No ways," said the cadre, "her line could be tapped."

When the train reached Lusaka, the five young men headed

north out of the city on foot. They came to a petrol station and were told to wait for a pick up truck that would take them further on their journey. The guide said that he was going back to Lusaka. But before he left, he spotted his neighbour heading towards a telephone again. He pulled out a gun and marched purposefully towards the phone booth. Without waiting for him to turn around, he shot his friend in the head as he was talking to his mother.

Gladwin and the other boys were horrified.

"I told him, the lines could be tapped," was all the guide said as he tucked the gun into his belt and headed off back down the road.

In the truck Gladwin started to feel very ill. Perhaps it was the shock of seeing the young man's brains splattered on the inside of the telephone booth; perhaps it was something else, something more serious. He'd been feeling this way a lot lately and his mother had suggested he see a doctor. He'd never got around to it, and now the symptoms were getting worse.

"*Hau* comrade, you look like a ghost," said one of his new friends. "Do you want some water?"

Gladwin nodded. He took the bottle and drank deeply, but it didn't slake his thirst. He started to shake uncontrollably, and then everything went dark.

When he woke up, he was inside a house in a very comfortable bed. A man and a woman were talking anxiously in a corner of the room.

"But why do we have to take him, Peter? These South Africans are nothing but trouble. What if the authorities find out and report us?"

"I don't have a choice, Jessica. I'm a pastor, a man of God. I can't turn anyone away who needs help, you know that. They know that. And besides, this young man is very sick."

"Yes, I know. But I don't like it." With that she walked out of the room to check on the three children who were sleeping in the living room because the stranger had taken their bed.

The pastor saw that Gladwin was awake. "Ah, welcome back! You had us worried there for a while Gladwin, you've been unconscious for four days. I'm Pastor Banda." Gladwin tried to speak, but his tongue seemed glued to his palate. The man of God gave him a glass of water and supported him as he drank.

"Thank you," said Gladwin eventually. "Where am I?"

"You're safe. I can't tell you where, for our security as well as your own, but you're in a safe house in Zambia. Your comrades brought you here on the way to the MK camp when they couldn't wake you up."

"When can I join them?"

"I'm afraid you can't, Gladwin. The village doctor came to see you and he says you have diabetes. You'll be fine if you have regular treatment, but without it, at the MK camp, you might die. I'm afraid your days as a freedom fighter are over."

"But they haven't even begun!"

"Ah my boy," said the pastor. "You have such limited ideas of what it means to be free and to fight for freedom. You can fight wherever you are, and not just with guns. Words too can set people free. If you tell the truth. Tell the truth about what you have seen. Bring it into the light."

Gladwin's head was spinning. He had diabetes, he couldn't join MK, and he couldn't go home. "What must I do?" he asked the kind man sitting next to his bed.

"First, you must rest. You've been very ill. In the meantime I have some friends who can help you."

"How can they help me? Are they doctors?"

"No. They are with the anti-apartheid movement in England. They can arrange for you to go there."

"England? What can I do there? I can't fight in England."

"Yes you can. You're a bright boy. You can get an education and tell people what's really happening in South Africa."

"But I want to be a freedom fighter."

"You will be, just as much as your friends carrying guns. Do you want to do that?" Gladwin didn't know what else to do, so he said yes.

A week later he was on a plane to London. He was met at the airport by a group of South African exiles who looked after him until his claim for asylum was processed. After obtaining refugee status he was awarded a bursary to study political science at Durham University.

When he graduated he got a job at the offices of the anti-apartheid movement in London, lobbying support for the cause from influential business and political figures in Europe.

After ten years he got a position as a junior lecturer at Edinburgh University and studied towards his PhD. His dissertation was on South Africa's freedom struggle but, as he told me, he struggled to finish it because he didn't know how it would end.

In 1989 he was appointed to a senior lecturing position at Newcastle University and moved into Jasmine Close. I met him a year later.

Soon after moving into the Newcastle cul-de-sac he received a letter from Poppy telling him that he had a thirteen-year-old son: no apologies, no explanations, just a demand that he fulfil his fatherly duties and arrange for the boy to be educated in England. It took a year for Thabo's visa to be approved, and he arrived on Gladwin's doorstep with barely a "hello".

So much for speaking the truth, I thought. Gladwin and Thabo had never brought anything into the light. The father was pouring out his heart to an eighteen-year-old girl in America.

And the son? Neither Gladwin nor I knew what he was thinking.

Chapter Twenty-nine

30 August 1996

THERE WAS A faint smell of oil filtering through the darkness. Gladwin, when he regained consciousness, first felt the lump on his head, patted his insulin pack in his pocket then checked that he still had his glasses. They weren't on his face, but his 'attacker' had folded them neatly and placed them in his breast pocket. Gladwin smiled wryly then reached out to find the boundaries of his prison and felt metal and carpet. This, and the back and forth surge of gear changes, told him that he was in the boot of a car. He didn't panic; he'd been in this position before.

Eventually the boot was opened; Gladwin was blinded by the sun. "Get out," said a voice, not Gugs'. Gladwin obeyed, grateful to stretch his cramped frame. As his eyes became accustomed to the light, he looked around and saw that he was in a squatter camp. The nearby sand dunes suggested it was Khayelitsha, a sprawling township that developed between the Cape Flats and Muizenberg in the 1980s. He'd read about it, but never seen it.

He was hurried through a small, neat garden lined with bright yellow marigolds and honeysuckle, a declaration of optimism, or perhaps a dream of permanence for the resident of this corrugated iron shack. He wondered if Gugs lived there. A middle-aged woman, speaking *isiXhosa*, appeared in the doorway and invited him in, as if he'd driven the car instead of being shipped there in the boot. A young man pushed past him and scowled at the woman. "Don't look at me like that, boy, Gugs said we should treat him well. Come in Mr Nkulu, I've prepared some food for you."

As a diabetic, Gladwin had to eat regularly, and Gugs obviously knew that. It was a good sign. He hurriedly ate the *pap* and meat and thanked the woman. She nodded, took the plate, and left the shack, locking the door behind her. Gladwin was alone.

Time passed slowly. When Gladwin checked his watch it was 3pm, over an hour since he had been brought to the Khayelitsha shack. It was a two-roomed affair, with the living room/kitchen separated from the bedroom by a curtain. He reckoned that five people lived here from the number of mattresses he'd seen stacked in the bedroom. At least two of them, probably the young man and a teenage sibling slept in the lounge (he deduced this from the Grade 8 text books in a school bag), and the mother and a toddler (from the toys and smell of soiled nappies) slept in the bedroom. The fifth person was likely to be a man, as he'd seen two razors near the washing bowl. One was probably the scowling son's and the other Gugs'. Or maybe another man's if Gugs didn't live there.

He looked out the window and took in as much as he could of the sandy streets. Small shacks and lean-to's were crammed up against each other. Bare-footed children played loudly in the dirt and scrawny dogs with swollen teats kept out of their way. The window looked as if it had probably been liberated from a train at one stage and the door from a dump.

The inside of the shack was wall-papered with wrappers from Glenryck Pilchard tins, occasionally broken by Carling Black Label beer bottle stickers. The furniture was a mish-mash of things that were originally designed to be furniture and things that had evolved into furniture. The coffee table was two paint tins with a plank in between. There were two matching armchairs in a shade that Mrs Cohen would not be seen dead with, and a kitchen table covered in newspaper.

A two-plate hob was on top of the table next to a small television. Both were plugged into an extension cord that was fed through the roof. Looking out of the window, Gladwin could just make out where the extension cord was spliced into the municipal power supply – a fire hazard, to say the least, but a common occurrence in a place where the majority of people couldn't afford to pay for electricity. Not much had changed in twenty years, Gladwin thought wryly. The paraffin heater in the corner would be a godsend on a cold Cape night, but the reservoir was empty. It was getting colder. The winter sunshine had given way to more typical Cape Town weather: a biting wind and the first lashings of rain. He wondered if the shack was waterproof.

There was a knock on the door. It was the woman. "Mr Nkulu, Gugs is here, he wants you to go into the bedroom and wait for him. He says you must not try to look at him or escape. Do you understand?"

"Yes," said Gladwin, growing a little tired of Gugs' new persona as South Africa's man of mystery. But remembering the gun that he'd first felt between his shoulder blades in Soweto, probably the same one that had knocked him unconscious in Muizenberg, he complied.

The padlock was removed from the door and Gugs came in. Even from the bedroom Gladwin could smell him. Usually Gugs' sweat was faint, intermingled with the roasted *mealies* that he loved to eat, but this time it was as strong as a soccer player's after forty-five minutes on the field: Gugs had been exerting himself.

"You can come out now Gladwin," said Gugs.

Gladwin stepped out of the bedroom and came face to face with his old friend. Well, hardly face to face, rather face to balaclava.

"Is that really necessary?" asked Gladwin, his impatience growing.

"Yes, for your sake as well as mine. I told you, I've had some work done on my face, and I don't want you to be able to identify me. Come, let's sit."

Gladwin sighed and sat down in one of the armchairs. Gugs took the other.

"Have you injected your insulin?" asked Gugs, confirming that he knew about Gladwin's diabetes.

"Yes, just after I ate. Thank you for arranging that." Why was he thanking him, Gladwin wondered, he'd just been kidnapped.

"Was all this necessary, Gugs? Couldn't we just have sat down and had a beer like old friends? Why all the subterfuge?"

"Because I'm wanted by the police. They've been following you since you arrived in South Africa, hoping that I would contact you. This way, if they find out we've met, you can tell them that I kidnapped you and distance yourself from me. It's imperative that you're beyond reproach."

"Why?" asked Gladwin.

"Because I need you to help me without the authorities knowing that we're working together."

"Of course I'll help you. You didn't have to resort to this."

"When you find out why the police are after me, you might not be so keen."

"Why *are* they after you?"

"They think that I may be involved in some of these farm murders. You know, when the white farmers and their families have been robbed and killed. They can't prove it, but they think that someone may be orchestrating the whole thing. Some people think it's just criminal, but the *boere*, and their white farmers' union, think it's racial."

"Well, is it?"

"Yes."

"And are you the one orchestrating it?"

"I might be; if it furthered the cause."

"How can killing innocent people be furthering the cause?"

"Because there is no such thing as an innocent white!" Gugs bellowed, his voice reverberating around the tin shack.

Gladwin didn't want to antagonise him, so he kept quiet. Instead he asked: "What is your cause now, Gugs?"

"The same as it's always been: to return the land to those that it belongs to. The white farmers and all other so-called white landowners are occupying the land illegally. Their forefathers stole it from our forefathers and it's time they gave it back. We won't rest until they do."

"Who's *we*?" asked Gladwin.

"My comrades in the OCSR: the Organisation for Complete Socialist Reform. Me and a few others – men and women who haven't sold out to the white man – started working together when it became clear that our leaders in the liberation movement were not going to go all the way to free our country. Mandela's ANC and even the PAC – *viva* comrade Biko – have sold out to the parliamentary system. It's a white man's system, set up to maintain white privilege, and our leaders have fallen for it hook, line and sinker."

"But what about forgiveness and reconciliation? Comrade Mandela and Bishop Tutu have done it. It's the only way."

"Have you looked through this window, Gladwin? Look what forgiveness and reconciliation have done for our people. Two years after the first free elections and they're still living in shacks and the *boers* are still living like kings."

"The suburbs are more racially mixed than they've ever been. It's going to get better, not worse, given time."

"It might, but how long will it take? We can't wait fifty or a hundred years. We need the land back now. You're a gardener, right? Well have you heard of the *Ukuvuka* campaign?" Gladwin shook his head. "It's a campaign to get rid of alien plants. It's providing jobs for some of our people, but not enough. European trees are being cut down because they're a fire hazard and they suck up all the water. Some places look like wastelands without them, but it won't be long 'til the indigenous plants grow back. And then nothing will stop them."

"What's that got to do with me?"

Gugs was quiet for a while, scratching his sweating scalp under the balaclava. Then he spoke: "I need you to go back to England and wait to be contacted by Hans Larson. I believe you've already met him. Larson is a communist and believes that the world-wide revolution can still be achieved."

"He struck me as a millionaire businessman," said Gladwin.

"He's only posing as a capitalist so that he can help to fund the revolution. A bit of a contradiction, I know, and maybe he's not really a comrade at heart, but useful nonetheless. He wants to give us money and both of us think that you are the best channel for it."

"So what are you going to do with the money?"

"Buy land back; where we can."

"And where you can't?"

"We'll do what's necessary."

"But what if I say no? I was hoping to come back to South Africa, now that my amnesty's been granted. I've already applied for a job at UCT."

"I thought you might say that, so I've taken out a little insurance

The Peace Garden

policy."

"What's that?"

Gugs didn't say anything, but looked at his watch and grunted. Then he switched on the television. A news bulletin, in English, was just starting. The attractive black woman smiled at the camera then in perfect Queen's English, spoke to the nation:

"There has been another family murder in Cape Town. A police spokesman told SABC news it is believed that twenty-six-year-old Riaan Labuschagne killed his pregnant wife and two children at their rented holiday home in Fish Hoek this afternoon then turned the gun on himself. His wife, Isobel, was twenty-six, and eight-months pregnant. Their other children were four and two. Mr Labuschagne's uncle, Kobus Labuschagne, was also found dead on the scene – there were signs of a struggle and police believe that the elder man was trying to stop his nephew from shooting his wife and children.

"Initial reports suggest that Mr Labuschagne was depressed after the granting of amnesty to Gladwin Nkulu, the man who killed his father in 1976. Labuschagne senior was a member of the security police and was killed during the Soweto Riots. We hope to bring you more on this tragedy in our next bulletin. In other news, President Nelson Mandela told parliament today …"

Gugs switched the TV off then turned to look at his old friend. "D-d-did you do that?" Gladwin asked, feeling suddenly faint.

"Who really did it isn't important. What is important is that I can make it look like you did. I have a friend in the police force at the crime scene right now. One call from me and he can plant sufficient evidence to put you away for life."

"What evidence?"

"Have you seen your passport lately?" As far as Gladwin knew, it was back at the hotel; but perhaps not… "Then of course there's one of your insulin vials, some hair, a handkerchief … anything's possible. And where were you between 11.30 and 3pm today? Can anyone account for your whereabouts? Could that old lady at Rhodes Cottage prove that you didn't go to Fish Hoek after you left her? Then of course there's your train ticket – you could have got off at any point if you wanted to …"

"But I didn't get off at Fish Hoek."

"No, but can you prove it? Look," said Gugs, in a cajoling voice, as if trying to calm the nerves of a scared puppy or highly strung horse. "Don't worry; I'm not going to frame you for murder. You're my friend. You saved my life. But I also saved yours by producing those photographs for the TRC. You owe me a favour."

"You want me to go back to England and be a conduit for finances for your revolution."

"It's your revolution too. Don't tell me you don't believe that South Africa belongs to Africans and not Europeans."

Gladwin was silent; he couldn't dispute that. But he needed some assurances: "Okay Gugs, but you must promise me that no one will get killed because I've helped you."

"No one will die unless it's absolutely necessary. And if you do what I say, your family, here in South Africa, and in England, will be safe too."

"Don't tell me you're threatening to hurt my family!"

"Whatever's necessary, Gladwin, whatever's necessary."

Gladwin contacted me only once more – a postcard from London.

7 September 1996

Dear Natalie,

I'm safe in London. I don't want you to worry. Apparently there's been some sort of misunderstanding. It seems that Gugs was only joking with me. I sorted everything out and after saying goodbye to my mother and the Cohens took a flight home. If some things in my letters have scared you, forgive me – I wasn't myself. Please don't show them to anyone. In fact, you should destroy them. I should never have burdened you with all this. But thank you for lending a listening ear.

Kind regards,
  Gladwin Nkulu

Everything was sorted out? How? Some joke! But if Gladwin said everything was fine, it probably was. He was back in England. I wondered about that. Was he there because he wanted to be or because Gugs had forced him to go? I didn't know. I thought of telling someone about the letters – Gugs was, after all, a wanted criminal – but I never did. What if no one believed me? What if Gladwin denied everything? It would ruin our friendship. So I kept the letters, just in case, hidden in a shoebox in the top of my wardrobe. Looking back, Gladwin was right: I should have destroyed them.

Part Three:

"Lovers"

"The essence is control – control over nature by man. Without constant watchful care a garden – any garden – rapidly returns to the state of the country round it. The more fertile and productive your garden is, the more precarious its position."

(Hugh Johnson, The Principles of Gardening)

Chapter Thirty

September 2000

IT HAD BEEN three years since I'd last been to Jasmine Close – a fly-by-night visit, just before I started university. Now I was a graduate and feeling guilty that I hadn't seen my Grandma for so long, and more so because she was sick. Auntie Rose had written to tell me of her sister's cancer, begging me not to let the proud Iris know that I knew. So when I saw a position for a social work graduate to work in Newcastle and a chance to continue my studies through the university there, I jumped at the chance.

The job involved working at the local refugee centre, helping the stateless people to adapt to their temporary home. The centre had a constantly changing clientele depending on which war was raging in which part of the world at any time. In 2000 there were a number of Congolese, Rwandans and Burundians, although some of the Rwandans, particularly the Hutus, were beginning to return to their homeland.

But by far the biggest group at the centre was the Albanian Muslims who were fleeing the latest bout of ethnic cleansing in Kosovo. My supervisor told me that at least another fifty were expected in the next few months, and that the more long-standing African asylum seekers would be encouraged to leave and find their own accommodation to help make room for the newcomers.

Stateless people: what an awful expression. But I could identify with it as I had been 'without state' for most of my life. My parents' divorce when I was thirteen just made things worse: they were global nomads treating me like a timeshare investment. But I loved them both and they loved me. In fact my therapist (it was compulsory to have a therapist during Psychology III) said I was pretty well adjusted. And I suppose I was.

Well, at least that's what I thought on my good days, and this golden early autumn day in Jasmine Close was certainly one of those.

"When ya finish raking up those leaves, Natalie, come in and have a cuppa. Then we can have tea early and watch *Inspector Morse*."

"Okay Grandma. I'll be there in a minute."

I finished raking the leaves into the garden bags and hauled them to the bottom of the driveway, ready for the next morning's collection. Bert Storey was driving into the cul-de-sac and waved warmly to me. Grandma had filled me in on the gossip within minutes of me unpacking my suitcase, so I knew that Pam and Bert were separated. The final straw, according to Grandma, was when Pam insisted on renting a salon at the new shopping centre built on the remains of our Peace Garden. Bert didn't like it and that was that.

"Surely there was more to it than that, Grandma," I said as I unpacked my make-up bag and put it in the dresser drawer.

"No pet, there wasn't. Bert's a man and men don't like it when women do their own thing. And that's a fact!"

Well, fact or not, Bert and Pam were no longer a couple. Roger stayed with whichever parent he chose to when he couldn't manage in the real world (another of Grandma's diagnoses) and was currently living with his dad.

"At least he's learning a trade though; but what he'll do with the family business once Bert's gone only the Man Upstairs knows," said Grandma who had never warmed to the skinhead.

"And the Nkulus?" I asked.

"Aye, they're still here. The lad's not bad, he's always willing to help me around the garden, but his father's still an odd'n."

"Odd? In what way?"

"Oh, I don't know, he keeps to himself, that's all."

"But Gladwin's always done that."

"No pet, not like this. He was getting better, you know, not quite like the rest of us, but what d'ya expect from a foreigner?"

"Grandma!"

"Well he is, and nothing will change that."

"But he *was* changing, you said yourself."

"Aye I did. But when he came back from that trip abroad a few years back …"

"You mean the trip to South Africa?"

"Aye, that's it. Something must have happened over there, 'cos he came back all quiet and he's been like that ever since."

I didn't say anything to Grandma about the letters. I looked along the street to the Nkulu house but there was no car in the driveway. Thabo and his father must still be at work.

With the bags of leaves all packaged and ready to be collected, I turned to walk back into the house. But before I reached the doorstep an old friend greeted me. Gazza the Labrador, now a veteran of eleven, was clearly thrilled to see me and had obviously not held the past years of non-correspondence against me.

"Hello boy!" I said and scratched under his greying chin. He had put on quite a bit of weight and it took some effort to roll over and present his ample tummy for a tickle.

"He hasn't forgotten you."

It was Aktar. My, he'd changed. The last time I'd seen him, briefly, he had been fifteen. Now at twenty-three he was easily six-feet-four and very, very good looking. I looked over his shoulder, expecting to see Dullah – he wasn't there.

"So where's your partner in crime?" I asked.

Aktar laughed. "He's at the police station – on duty!"

Oh yes, I'd forgotten, the twins were both policemen now.

"And Fatima?"

"You haven't heard? Don't tell me your grandma hasn't said anything!"

"Why, what's wrong?" I asked, suddenly concerned.

"See for yourself."

With almost theatrical timing a red Golf pulled in the Rashid's driveway. The driver, a Muslim woman in full-length black robes and a veil, stepped out carrying a briefcase.

"Fatima?" I asked, not hiding my shock. Aktar raised his eyebrows and nodded in assent. My mouth dropped, but I had to pull myself together quickly; Fatima had spotted me.

"Nattie! What a surprise! Come over for tea tomorrow. Sorry it can't be now, I've got some studying to do," she said, patting her briefcase.

I composed myself and answered as cheerily as I could: "That's okay Fats, I'll see you tomorrow then!"

As I walked into Grandma's house and sat down at the tea table, she took one look at my face and smirked: "So you've seen Fatima then." I nodded. "Foreigners!" she said, and poured us both some strong Ceylon tea.

Chapter Thirty-one

"BUT WHY DID you do it Fatima? Aktar tells me that your mum and dad are heartbroken. He's asked me to talk to you; I think he hopes I'll make you change your mind."

"Oh you won't do that, Natalie, so don't even try."

"Don't worry, I won't, but I would like to know what made you do it."

It was a Saturday afternoon and Mr Rashid and the twins were watching a football match at St James' park. Mrs Rashid was in her herb garden. Fatima and I were alone in the lounge, sipping tea, with Gazza snoring at our feet.

Fatima sighed and pushed a strand of raven hair back behind her ear. At twenty-one she was fulfilling the promise of delicate beauty that everyone had expected and as she was studying medicine, the intellectual expectations too.

"I just didn't believe in their God anymore. He just didn't seem to *do* anything – not like Allah. And besides, it's not just the religion, it's the culture: I've finally found a place where I belong; a place that isn't *European*. I suppose I don't feel like an outsider anymore."

"Is that what you're trying to say with the *burkah*? I mean, is it necessary Fats?"

"For me, yes."

"But why? Loads of Muslim women don't wear it. And in this country, it's the majority. Why do you have to be so – so – *extreme*?"

Fatima laughed. "That's rich coming from you Natalie. Every thing you do is extreme."

"Not that kind of extreme. You know what I mean. Wearing that just sets you apart from everyone."

"Exactly. I want to be set apart. I don't want to be like everyone else; not everyone else in the West anyway."

I didn't know what to say about that so I sipped my tea. So did Fatima. I remembered all the times I'd sat in this house over the years then suddenly, one memory in particular came to mind.

"You know what Fats? Do you remember the time I cut my leg on the barbed wire and had to stay here?"

"An extreme example." She smiled.

I let it pass. "You know, I remember when your dad said Christianity was a world-wide religion, for everyone. Not just for the West. Don't you believe that?"

"He believes it but I don't. No offence Nattie, but Christianity will always be a white man's religion. Maybe it wasn't intended that way, but as soon as the whites got hold of it, they made it their own."

I thought of the multi-racial Christian group I visited back at the University of Manhattan, and wanted to tell her she was wrong. But I didn't. I believed that Christianity was the only true faith, but I knew too that to say it would only make me look like a bigot. I didn't want to give her any more fuel for the fire that smouldered in her eyes.

But she wasn't going to let me off the hook that easily.

"Do you believe in him, Natalie?"

"Who?"

"Jesus of course."

Now that was a direct question: I had to say something. "Yes, yes I do," I said with more trepidation than conviction.

"But do you believe that he's the only way to get to heaven?"

I was cornered now and said a little prayer asking the God I had just professed to believe in to come to my aid. I suddenly felt bolder. "Well, I suppose it's a matter of truth. If you're not convinced that what you believe is true, then you're wasting your time believing it. I wouldn't waste my time believing in a God who makes such sweeping statements about himself if there's a chance they're not true."

She smiled then and said, "Yes, I know what you mean. I wouldn't waste my time either."

Then she poured me another cup of tea.

Gazza stirred and gave a low growl. Then, more fully awake, pricked up his ears and jumped onto the couch near the living room window, not caring who or what he stepped on on the way. He started barking: a friendly 'oh I know who that is' bark. I looked out of the window and saw my Auntie Rose crossing the road from her sister's house to her own. She was carrying something under a tea towel: a pot or casserole dish, or something. I had needed a polite way out and this was it.

"That's my Auntie Rose, Fats, I'd better go and see her."

She nodded then walked me to the door. "So what're you going to tell Aktar?"

"I don't know. I suppose I'll just say you're searching for the truth."

"But I've found it Natalie."

"Oh, okay then," I said then ran to catch up with my great aunt.

"Hello petal," she said happily, her perfect pink mouth forming the words. Now eighty, she looked at least ten years younger, although some of it was due to a hairdresser's colour. "Mutton dressed up as lamb," my grandma would say. Perhaps, but a classy lamb nonetheless.

She sounded a little sad. Auntie Rose carried the ghost of her lost love in little sighs and wistful glances, but this was something more. She'd been crying.

"What is it, Auntie Rose?"

"Oh, it's just that stubborn grandmother of yours. Has she told you yet?"

"About the cancer? No. But she's running out of ways to explain her tiredness and weight loss. She also says she's going to the shops and comes back with nothing. That's probably when she goes to the doctor. Why won't she say anything Auntie Rose?"

The old lady sighed then led me to a newly installed bench in her front garden. The September afternoon was cooling down, and I had rather hoped we could go inside. But Rose wanted to enjoy the light before it slipped away, so we settled down on the wooden slats brushed with petals from a nearby rambler.

The Peace Garden   *171*

"Your grandma's a proud woman, Natalie. She's been running her life and everyone else's since the day our dad died when she was fifteen. She's eighty-three now and independence is a hard habit to break."

"But why?"

"Because to accept help from the likes of me means that she may have been wrong about me all these years. She couldn't admit that or her life would have been built on a lie."

"But she *was* wrong, wasn't she? You never thought you were better than her, did you?"

"I'm not sure. I always said that I never knew why she hated me so much when we were growing up, but maybe I just refused to see it. Our mother treated me like a princess, and if I had wanted to, I could have forced her to be kinder to Iris. Or I could have just turned my back on all that she offered me. But it's difficult to say no when the devil offers you the kingdoms of the world."

"Yes, but …"

"Yes, but nothing. Enough of this old lady's problems, it's too late to change anything now. So tell me, have you seen any of your old friends?"

"Yes, I just saw Fatima. She's become a Muslim now, you know."

"Yes, I heard. It has something to do with a boy."

"Why do you say that?"

"Well, I heard she met someone, a Muslim, and he wanted her to convert."

"She never told me that! How do you know?"

"Her mother told me."

"I don't think so, Auntie Rose. Even if there was a boy, Fatima wouldn't do something as serious as this unless she really wanted to."

"Don't be so sure; love makes us do crazy things, petal, you should know that."

"What do you mean?"

"Don't tell me you've forgotten the way you panted over the Nkulu boy that summer?"

"I didn't pant! And besides, even if I had, I was just a child. I'm not interested in him now."

"Oh? Have you seen him?"

"No."

"Then don't disqualify him until you do."

"What do you mean?"

"Oh, you'll see."

Chapter Thirty-two

"EEEEEE, IF IT ISN'T young Natalie. My, pet, ya've grown." Pam Storey teetered towards me from behind the black marble counter of her new salon. Her hair a breakable blonde, her eyes a charcoal smudge. She looked me up and down, her eyes lingering for a while on my now even breast-line, then to my straightened teeth and makeup-faded freckles. It was only a matter of time before she got her talons into my still unruly red hair.

"But yer quite the young lady aren't ya? How old are ya now?"

"I turned twenty-two in March."

"Aye, that's right, yer a year younger than the Rashid boys and our Roger. D'ya hear the twins joined the police? Both constables and training for the gun squad. They look very handsome in their uniforms too. Salima and Abe are so proud of them. Eeee, but it's a shame how the lass turned out, mind."

I bristled, suddenly defensive of the girl I'd always been uncomfortable with. "I think she's just fine. She's doing well at her studies and will make a great doctor. You can't do much better than that."

"Aye, but the Muslim thing. What's the lass thinking? They're all terrorists – and the way they treat their women!"

"They're not all terrorists," I said simply then changed the subject. "Can you give me a cut, Pam?"

"I thought ya'd never ask!"

For the next half hour, Pam and I went through the most up-to-date style books and discussed the pros and cons of the various fashions. "Ya know, I wouldn't mind cutting it quite short then feathering it into yer face and neck. I'll cut yer fringe short to frame yer eyes. They're very pretty ya know, that bluey green colour, and big. But ya can hardly see them under that curtain.

Aye, I think we'll go short. Yer quite a tall lass and slim – I think ya'll carry it off well. Ya've also got a nice neck but no one can see it under all this hair. It'll bring focus to yer form – and those boobs of yours will get the attention they deserve!"

I blushed then, considering this a supreme compliment from one so well endowed as Pam Storey. Although it had taken a few years, my mum had been right: my uneven breast development had been just a temporary blip. "All right then, let's go short." And I settled down to let the artist get to work.

Some time later Roger popped in. He was wearing blue overalls with '*Storey and Son Plumbers*' emblazoned on the breast and back. Pam told me that the skinhead had gone into business with his dad and was doing very well. I could just see the hulking young man flexing his muscles with a monkey wrench. But what was I thinking about his muscles for? Roger wasn't my type; although he obviously didn't see things the same way.

"Why if it isn't Natalie Porter! It's been a long time."

"Yes, three years."

"Eeee, but ya've changed in three years."

"No not really," I said, remembering the last time I was here Roger had still been fawning over Fatima, even though their childhood romance had fizzled out some years before. He must be over her now, I thought.

The young plumber, now twenty-three, flopped down in the chair beside me and turned his gap-toothed grin in my direction. The phone rang and his mother went to answer it. "So what ya up to?"

"Well, I'll be living here now. My grandma's not too well and she needs someone to look after her. And I've got a job at the refugee centre."

Roger scowled. "Whadya want to do that for? All ya'll do is encourage more of them to come here. The country can't look after everyone ya know, we're just a little island and there isn't enough jobs for our own folk."

"You don't seem to mind the Rashids."

"Aye, I know, but that's different. They're here on their own steam and have never leached off the state. Abe started his own business; he wasn't taking anyone's job. And besides, they came in the fifties when things wasn't so bad. It's different now."

"And the Nkulus?"

"Aye, they're not too bad either. Thabo's alreet. We go watch Newcastle play sometimes. But Gladwin's an oddball though; he's never learnt to speak proper English."

I smiled, knowing that Roger meant that Gladwin didn't speak English with an English accent; and worse still, that there was no Geordie inflection in his African tones. I wasn't exactly the best example of Geordie either, but that didn't seem to worry him.

"Well I'm glad yer back; maybe we can go out for a drink sometime?" He took out his mobile phone. "What's yer number?"

"Oh, I don't have one," I said truthfully.

"Ooooo you should get one," cooed Pam, joining us again. "They're all the rage. And you can get different coloured covers to go with your outfits."

"Never found a need for one yet," I said.

"Well you will soon. They're very useful to set up dates, I've been told." She winked at Roger.

"Oh Mam!"

I blushed as hard as he did then quickly changed the subject. "Am I finished yet?"

"Aye pet, I think you are. Whadya think?"

I looked at the reflection in front of me and was pleasantly surprised. The new cut made me look more sophisticated; a little like Nicole Kidman: just right to start a new job, I thought. "Ta Pam, I like it. You've got a nice set up here."

"Aye, I have, I just wish my Bert would see it the same way."

"Ahhh, don't start with that Mam. Ya know Dad was happier with ya running the business from home. He earns enough for both of ya; ya don't have to work."

"I don't have to, but I want to. Just like yer dad. He doesn't have to work either; we could just live on benefits. Is that what ya want?"

The two turned on each other then, slipping into the familiar argument, like a practice rally before a tennis match.

"Dad could never do that; he wants to make his own way in the world."

"And so do I son, so do I. Whadya think Natalie?"

I was already gathering my handbag and jacket, not wanting to get involved in the family politics. But they both looked at me as if I was the umpire, each hoping I'd make a decision in their favour.

"I think people should feel fulfilled in whatever they do. If a woman is fulfilled at home there's no reason why she shouldn't stay there, like Salima. But not all women are built that way, Roger. I'm not, and neither's your mum, you need to accept that."

"Yes, but ..."

"Sorry Rog, Pam, I've got to go. I've got to pick something up at Tesco for Grandma's tea." I gave Pam the money for the cut, smiled nervously, then retreated as quickly as I could. As the door closed behind me, I could see mother and son reloading their weapons with the ammunition I'd just left them.

I stepped out of Pam's salon and headed towards Tesco. The concrete shopping centre and regimented streets of the nearby housing estate were a far cry from the fertile earth of our garden from so long ago; our Peace Garden. The old oak was still there; bracketed by benches for foot-weary shoppers, but the tree house where the children of Jasmine Close had fought their battles and made their peace was long gone. Somewhere under the asphalt and concrete the fecund earth slept, and maybe, in generations to come, flowers would break through crumbling pavements, reasserting eternity over progress.

I walked through the Tesco car-park to the main entrance. I quickly had to step back to give way to a metallic blue BMW. It parked a few bays down from the entrance and a familiar figure got out of the passenger side. It was Gladwin. He bent back down to say something to the driver who was obscured from my view by a large Landrover pulling into the space beside them. I wondered if I should wait or approach him. Before I could decide, the blue car pulled off and Gladwin walked towards me. His face lit up with recognition.

"Is that *Khandlela*, my little candle?"

"Gladwin! How nice to see you." We hugged.

The Peace Garden 177

"I heard you were back. Will you be staying long?"

"Yes, actually, I'm here to stay. My grandma isn't well."

"So I heard. We've been taking turns doing shopping for her, when she lets us, but it's been hard for her to accept our help. A stubborn one, that *mkhulu* of yours."

"You don't have to tell me."

We both collected trolleys then headed through the automated doors, turning left into the fruit and veg section. We stopped in front of the avocados.

"I'm doing a post-grad course in social work at Newcastle University." I said, squeezing the fruit gently.

"A masters' degree?"

"Yes, and I'll be working at the refugee centre. Have you been down there?"

"No, I'm afraid I haven't."

"That's a pity, I'm sure you have a lot to share about your experiences as a refugee."

"Oh, I wouldn't have much to say."

"But your letters …"

Gladwin, seeing his son walking towards us, interrupted me: "Thabo, look who's here."

"Hello," said the younger man.

"Hi," I said, suddenly very nervous.

"What were you two talking about?" asked Thabo.

"Oh nothing," I said casually.

Gladwin smiled gratefully then headed off towards the dairy section, leaving me with his son. Thabo had turned his attention to a pile of South African fruit; his back was turned, so I could look at him without being noticed. He was taller than his father, perhaps six-feet-two; but not as broad. He was still well built though, just as he had been when I first saw him as a shirtless fourteen-year-old. I wondered what he would look like now.

"So whadya think?"

"About what?" I asked, defensively.

"The oranges. Not the best quality I've ever seen. Someone should speak to the manager."

"Yes someone should."

"But you haven't even looked at them," he said, tossing his neat dreadlocks away from his face. His eyes were wide, deep, and brown, and a smile played on his full lips.

"You haven't changed, Natalie."

"Whadya mean?"

"Your eyes are as clear as a mountain pool; showing every rock and fish."

"What's that supposed to mean?" I asked, scowling.

"Just what I said. I'll see you again, sometime." Then he turned back to his oranges.

"And maybe you won't," I said to his back then propelled my trolley down the nearest aisle, not caring that I was acting like a twelve-year-old again.

I passed Gladwin on the way out. "Look Natalie, about those letters, you haven't told anyone about them, have you?"

"No of course not, and I won't."

"Thanks. It was a difficult time for me; I just needed to get it off my chest, that's all."

"But why me?"

"I don't know. Perhaps it's because you've always told the truth. And that's rare."

That didn't make sense: he wrote to me because I tell the truth, but now he was asking me to lie. Oh well, he must have his reasons. I asked about Gugs.

"Oh don't worry about him Natalie; he's no longer in the picture."

"But how …"

"Just leave it *Khandlela*, it's all in the past now. Let it stay that way."

Chapter Thirty-three

GRANDMA'S GARDEN HAD aged well. There was the usual backdrop of gold and bronze foliage with nuts, berries and hips begging to be harvested. The crab apple was particularly brazen, with medlar fruit and hawthorn berries competing for centre stage. But the autumn stalwarts didn't have it all their own way and were forced to share the spotlight with some late blooming fuchsias and wine-red clematis. There was also a troupe of long-legged sunflowers, basking in the last of the season's rays. A new addition to Grandma's garden was a dusky pink hybrid tea rose, which was reported to keep on flowering right up to the first frost.

I was intrigued. Grandma had always sworn she would never cheapen her display with the roses so favoured by her sister.

"I see you've introduced a tea rose, Grandma."

"Aye, I did. Against my better judgement, mind."

"Oh? Why's that?"

"Well, yer Auntie Rose gave it to me on my birthday. She knows I don't like 'em, but she said that it was time to get rid of some of my prejudices. So I planted it, just to prove to her that I'm not that narrow-minded. She was trying to prove a point, and I beat her at her own game."

"What makes you think that?"

"Oh, she's been telling me for years that I've judged her unfairly, so by planting the rose I've proven her wrong."

"But haven't you?"

"What's that, pet?"

"Haven't you judged her unfairly?"

She inhaled quickly; then, just when I thought she would give me a tongue-lashing, she let out a long, painful sigh. "Yer aunt did me a lot of harm when we were young, but in the last years, she's tried to make up for it; sometimes a bit too hard. I've never been accused of not giving anyone a second chance, but I'm still waiting for her to prove herself."

"But how long are you going to wait, Grandma? She's been trying for over twenty-five years, ever since she moved into Jasmine Close. Don't you think it's time you just forgave her of whatever you have against her? I mean you don't have much time left."

The old lady pulled herself up on the rake she was using to spread mulch over her vegetable patch and glared up at me. "And who do ya think ya are, Natalie Porter, talking to me like that? I'm not one of yer social work cases!"

"Yes, Grandma, I'm sorry."

"Well, ya'd better be. And ya'll be surprised how much life's left in these old bones. Ya won't be getting yer hands on me money just yet."

"Yes Grandma," I said, seeing colour rise in her sallow cheeks for the first time in weeks.

The old lady sighed again, this time rattling as the air forced its way out of her diseased lungs. Iris Porter had never smoked a day in her life, yet somehow cancer had taken root in that proud chest. But she still hadn't officially told me of her illness; as if giving it a name would give it life and hasten its spread.

"Well, don't just stand there, we've got a lot to do before winter comes, and we'd better be ready. I'll carry on mulching if ya'll plant those spring bulbs."

"Are you sure *you* don't want to plant the bulbs, Grandma? I'll do the mulching and pruning; it's harder work."

"No, I don't think so. It's better if you do the planting seeing ya'll be the one who'll look after them in the spring. I want to make sure everything's ship-shape for the winter. If ya don't do it properly the garden won't have a good rest. Remember this, Natalie: it's not just how ya start, but how ya finish. It's no use leaving this world with people having to clear up after ya."

"What do you mean Grandma?"

"Don't play dumb, lass, I know that ya know. I'm just not ready for winter yet, that's all, but I know that I won't see another

The Peace Garden

spring."

"Oh Grandma!" I said, reaching out and taking her hand. It was dry and cold, despite the early autumn sun.

"Now don't go soft on me, we've got things to do. Get on with that planting or there'll be nowt to look forward to next year. And besides, ya don't want to be crying in front of that Nkulu boy. Now wipe yer eyes."

I looked up, holding back the tears, and saw Thabo coming around the side of the house, carrying some long-armed pruning shears.

"Hello Mrs Porter. Natalie."

"Hello son, thanks for comin'. I think the hawthorn and the crab apple need the most work. I asked Thabo to prune the top of the trees, now that I can't climb the ladder anymore."

"Oh, I could have done that for you, Grandma."

"Maybe ya could; but it's man's work and ya don't have enough fat to keep ya warm, never mind climb a ladder."

I was about to protest but a wink between Thabo and Grandma changed my mind.

"I think I'll go and lie down if ya young'uns will excuse me."

"Certainly, Mrs Porter," said Thabo, escorting the old lady into the house.

With his back turned I busied myself sorting the tulip, iris, crocus and daffodil bulbs, which I was going to plant for next spring.

"She's right, you know."

"About what?"

"You don't have enough fat on you to keep you warm. I'm surprised you're wearing shorts."

"I'm quite warm, thank you very much."

"I usually like my women a little fuller," he said, plopping himself down on the grass.

"Well it's just as well I'm not one of your women then," I spat, attacking the flowerbed with my trowel. He smiled, lying back on the sun-drenched lawn, his hands pillowed under his dreadlocks.

"Well, aren't you going to get to work?" I asked.

"Oh there's plenty of time. Besides, I thought I'd watch you;

make sure you plant those bulbs properly. I am a professional horticulturist after all."

Tired of sparring I changed the subject. "So, where're you working?"

"At the garden centre in Ponteland. I do a little bit of cultivation, but I'm just a glorified salesman, really."

"Bored?"

"A little. I've always seen gardening as a way of transforming society, but the only transformation I'm doing is adding a bit of greenery to housewives' lounges."

I laughed, then lay down my trowel and joined him on the grass.

"Well, I may have something you might be interested in."

"What's that?" he asked, propping himself on one elbow and turning towards me.

"Remember the Peace Garden?"

"Of course."

"Well I've had this idea ..." I stopped, holding my breath. Thabo was running his finger down my leg; tracing the old scar I'd acquired spying on him through the hedge.

"Go on," he said softly, his finger pad trailing from my knee to my thigh.

"Ummm ... well, it's about the asylum seekers ..." I whispered, closing my eyes.

"Mmmm. What about them?" His hand stopped then rested gently over my leg. So gently, I almost couldn't feel it. But it was there. And it wasn't just my leg that felt it.

"I ... I want to start a Peace Garden project at the centre. It will be a kind of therapy, getting the people to work together. It will also give them something to do."

"Yes, it's a good idea. It will help them to reconnect with themselves again by reconnecting with the earth."

"You understand," I said.

"Do you?"

"That depends on whether we're talking about gardening or not."

He laughed then pulled his hand away. He stood up, picked up his shears and headed towards the ladder lying next to the potting shed.

"Maybe we're talking about both. Now get on with those bulbs, or your grandma will have your hide."

Chapter Thirty-four

THE NEXT DAY was cold and overcast. As agreed, I met Thabo at the bus-stop and we caught the first bus to Newcastle. We sat in a two-seater, near the back, and though the vehicle was nearly full, we might as well have been alone.

He wore a bottle-green polo neck sweater over faded blue jeans. His boots had seen better days and had caked mud stuck in the cracks. Over everything he wore a black, hooded windbreaker, which was needed on such a blustery day. His shoulder-length dreads were pulled back into a ponytail by a band at the nape of his neck.

I was suddenly conscious of my cropped locks that barely brushed the top of my collar. Pam's blow-drying had been washed out, and the feathering into my face was now a corkscrew of curls.

I must have been toying with one of them because he said: "I like your new hair cut; it makes you look like a pot-scourer."

"Thanks," I scowled, and looked out of the window.

"Sulking?"

I didn't respond.

He took my hand. "Hey, I'm only kidding. Don't be so sensitive. It's cute, and it shows off your eyes."

"You like my eyes?" I blushed.

"Yeah, I've told you that before."

"When?"

"In Tesco's."

"No, you went on about rocks and slimy fish. Don't tell me that was a compliment."

"For me it was!" He laughed.

Yes, I suppose it was. The fact that I received any compliments from this enigmatic man still amazed me. I had to remember I was twenty-two now and not a twelve-year-old schoolgirl. If I had met Thabo for the first time as an adult, I certainly wouldn't be acting this way.

"So how's your dad?"

"Not so well. His diabetes is playing up again. The doctor said it's stress."

"What's he so stressed about?"

"I don't know, but it's been getting worse, ever since he came back from his trip to South Africa a few years back."

I didn't know what to say about that, but I certainly wasn't going to betray Gladwin's confidence. So I said: "Yeah, I was surprised that he came back. Wasn't he hoping to go back now that everything's cleared up there?"

"I thought so. I just don't understand him. Exiles from all over the world are going back now, but not him. It's as if he's scared to."

"Why?"

"I don't know. Maybe he's scared of facing all the real freedom fighters."

"That's not fair. Your dad's done a great job raising awareness for the cause."

"Maybe, but others, people like my mother, have paid a much higher price. They didn't run away."

"And neither did Gladwin. He didn't have a choice! He …"

"What do you know about it?" he said accusingly.

"Nothing. Nothing at all. But you shouldn't judge your dad for living in England. You came here as well, remember?"

He glared at me then crossed his arms over his chest. The conversation ground to a halt. The bus was heading over the Tyne Bridge. The river was not looking its best: choppy and murky and sporting some plastic bottles and a few beer cans in the shallows. Further along the river, outside the city limits, the water would clear and create a haven for animal and bird life throughout the valley.

I was uncomfortable with the silence. "You said your dad was stressed. Problems at work?"

"I don't think so," Thabo said coolly, having let go of my hand some time ago.

"What then?" I probed.

He sighed then turned to me. "Look, the Nkulu family are not subjects for a social work case, okay?"

"Okay! I was just trying to make conversation." It was my turn to cross my arms.

Thabo sighed. "Look, I'm sorry. I don't know what it is … it's lots of things … He makes and receives these long-distance phone calls."

"To South Africa?"

"No, to Norway. I've checked the printout."

"Who does he know in Norway?"

"Some guy called Larson."

Larson! Gugs' money man. I thought Gladwin said that Gugs was no longer in the picture. Maybe he wasn't. There were lots of Scandinavians called Larson. "An academic?" I asked.

"He says so, but I've never heard them talking about anything high brow."

"What do they talk about?"

"Money, mainly. Meeting times, building projects, their mutual friend in South Africa."

"Who's that?" I asked, suddenly suspicious.

"I don't know."

"Have you asked him?"

"I tried to, but he just closes down and says it's nothing that would interest me."

"And you just leave it?"

"Not everyone is the human incarnation of a bull terrier, Natalie."

"You saying I'm pushy?"

"Well aren't you?"

"Persistent, perhaps, not pushy."

"Mmm, and look where it gets you."

"Whadya mean?"

"Remember when you got that scar?"

At the mention of my scar, I edged slightly closer to him, trying to recreate the intimacy of yesterday's moments on my grandma's lawn. He felt it and took my hand.

"And it's not just the phone calls," he said.

He was clearly worried about the older man.

"Oh? What else?" I asked.

"He spends hours at a time reading the South African newspapers online."

"Well, that's not so bad. He obviously wants to keep track of stuff that's going on back home. Maybe some of it is research for his studies at the university."

"Maybe, but I don't think so."

"Why not?"

"Because of the type of stuff he's downloading. He's printed reams and reams of articles about white people being murdered on farms. Then there's some stuff about a man, an ex-policeman, who was tortured for twelve hours with a clothes iron before he was able to escape."

"My God!"

"Exactly! Then he's collected a box-load of stuff on an investigation into one family's murder. The parents and two little kids. The wife was pregnant too. Some people say it was suicide, but the case has never been closed. It happened in Cape Town when he was visiting my mother there. And the weird thing is: they're the family of the policeman my dad supposedly killed in 1976."

So Gladwin couldn't let it go. I wasn't surprised, but it didn't mean that Gugs was still around.

Thabo looked at me strangely. "What's wrong, Natalie?"

"Nothing. Why?" I asked defensively.

"Because the Natalie Porter I know would be asking me a million questions if I told her my dad had killed a policeman."

"I'm shocked that's all. I don't know what to say. Is that why he left South Africa in the first place?" I asked, not having to feign concern.

"Yeah, that's what he says. But he could have stayed and gone into hiding. Hundreds of others did."

"Why did he do it?" I asked.

"Apparently it was self-defence. He was trying to protect his friend, a guy called Gugile Sithole, who the cop was going to shoot."

"Then it *was* self-defence, in a way. Who do you think killed the guy's family? Gugile?"

"No, it couldn't have been. Gugs is dead."

I was stunned. "How do you know that?"

"My dad told me."

"When?"

"Last year. I was trying to get in touch with him but my dad told me that he'd heard that Gugs was killed in a car crash. My mother had heard the same; apparently his body was burnt beyond recognition."

"Why were you trying to get in touch with him?" I asked, relieved that the mysterious Gugs was finally out of Gladwin's life.

"Because he was more of a father to me than Gladwin ever was."

"Thabo, what a terrible thing to say about your father!"

"Well it's true. Gugs was there for me when my dad wasn't. And for my mum too. Look, we can talk about this later; we've gotta get off."

The bus stopped outside the refugee centre and we alighted. As we walked through the gates a group of mainly young African men were coming out of one of the residential hostels, carrying their luggage.

"Who are they?" Thabo asked.

"Mainly Congolese, but there're some Rwandans and Angolans as well."

"Where're they going?"

"They've got to move out to make room for the Albanian families that are coming soon."

"Oh great, the whiteys need somewhere to sleep so the black guys have got to move."

"Has anyone ever told you you're a bigot?"

"It's a fact. Research has shown that white people find TV footage of other whites suffering much more disturbing than the suffering of black people. They see black people killing each other as the norm so it's far less shocking."

"Well, for your information, the people of the Balkans have been killing each other, or being killed by other Europeans on their way

The Peace Garden

to the Holy Land, for well over a thousand years."

"I don't need a lecture!"

"Well you obviously don't know the facts! In this century alone, nearly a million people have been killed by so-called 'ethnic cleansing' policies in the Balkans."

"And over four million were killed in Rwanda in only one year!"

"It's not a competition, Thabo. These guys are leaving because they've been here for over a year. It's only supposed to be a temporary shelter until other accommodation can be found. We have an old block of council flats for the families, but single guys stay in the hostel. Now we need every bed we can get. If there was a sudden influx of Sudanese or Liberians, it would be the same, so don't play the race card with me."

"What do you know about being the victim of racism?"

"You think the victims of apartheid were the only victims in history?"

"You're saying we didn't suffer?"

"No, of course not. I'm only saying … "

"Go to hell, Natalie!" And with that he stormed off down the road, joining the other Africans.

I looked after him, furious. I was not going to follow him, I was absolutely not. Then something else caught my attention: a metallic blue BMW cruised slowly passed. Gladwin's friend? I wasn't sure; I couldn't quite see the driver. The car pulled up beside the stomping Thabo. He slowed down and bent towards the passenger window. He spoke for a while then straightened up as the car pulled away. He glared at me watching him. I tossed my hair in disdain and went into the centre.

Chapter Thirty-five

IT HAD BEEN a hard day at the centre. I had to tell my supervisor that the wondrous Peace Garden project I had promised needed to be postponed. He rewarded me with a backlog of paperwork that took me most of the day to wade through and produced a 'to do' list the length of my arm. I was grateful it was home time. But just as I was packing up I received a phone call from my university department secretary saying that two men had been around to visit. They didn't leave their names but apparently they'd left a message for me on my desk in the post-grad study.

I decided to stop off at the university on the way home rather than leaving it for the next day as I had an early start at work. Newcastle University was just a ten minute bus ride back across the river from the asylum centre in Gateshead. I grabbed my bag and coat and jumped on the first bus heading in that direction.

The red-brick campus was in the heart of the city, hedged between the Royal Victoria Infirmary hospital and Eldon Square Shopping Centre. The uni was going through a renovation with some old buildings being upgraded and others demolished and rebuilt. The social work department was in the latter category and we were soon to be re-housed while the demolition took place. Not a moment too soon, I thought, as the cranky plumbing and erratic lighting were not likely to last another winter.

We were going to be in the new premises by the time the undergraduates came back in a couple of weeks. But for now, the other post-grads and I were still in the old building, despite preparation work having started for the demolition. Scaffolding had been erected and entire sections sealed off while asbestos panelling was stripped.

It was nearly six by the time I reached the department on the fourth floor. As per usual, the old Victorian lift was on the blink so I decided to use the stairs. The whole third floor – which used to be the Geography department – was closed off for asbestos stripping and sheets of plastic hung from the ceiling. On the fourth floor, which was still in use, the halls were deserted. I turned left out of the stairwell and walked down the corridor towards the post-grad study.

I opened the door with my key and was stunned at what I saw: the whole room had been ransacked. Papers and files were strewn everywhere. Books had been pulled off shelves and scattered all over the floor; not just on my desk beside the window but the other five desks belonging to my post-grad colleagues too. The window was open and a strong breeze was helping to further swirl the papers. There had been a storm earlier, a little after five: had the window been open then? Was this simply the result of that? The secretary had called me a bit before five so maybe she'd dropped off the note then and been caught in the storm on the way home. But why didn't she close the window? It had certainly looked like rain for a while.

None of my colleagues were likely to have been working there. Two of them were on holiday. Another was concerned about the asbestos work on the third floor and didn't come in as a matter of principle; Mark was away at a conference and Annabel …

Suddenly, I heard the crank of old cables. The lift was working again. Someone was coming. Should I call campus security? Maybe it was campus security. I didn't want to look. I quickly closed the door, locked it, and then slumped to the floor below the glass pane. The lift bell pinged. The doors opened. Footsteps approached. Someone tried the handle. But of course the door was locked. Whoever it was then gave the handle a shake then a bit of a shove. Oh God, what if they tried to kick it in? Could I hold it? Should I try to pull a desk in front of it? I forced my weight back against the door and the shaking stopped.

I spotted the cable of a phone line under some papers. I tried to hook it with my foot and pull it towards me. The handset clattered loudly off the cradle. The person on the other side of the door tried the handle again and then knocked. Knocked? All of my colleagues had keys. They wouldn't knock. I dared not move again in case I alerted the intruder that there was someone in the room. I held my breath, bracing myself for an assault on the door. But then suddenly I heard an exasperated sigh and footsteps going away from the door and back down the corridor.

I kept low and crawled to the phone. I really needed to call campus security. I lifted the handset but there was no dial tone: the phone was dead. If only I had one of those new-fangled mobile phones. The enormity of the situation suddenly hit me: I was in a room that might have been targeted by thieves and one of them was still in the building. There was no way of phoning out and I was trapped here. What if they came back? What if they'd just gone to look for a crowbar or axe or something?

I was getting hysterical and needed to pull myself together. I looked around the room and noticed that the computers were all still there. If this was a burglary, why didn't they take the computers? I was letting my imagination run away with me. That was probably some colleague or campus security officer who had seen that the window was open and just wanted to close it. I started to feel embarrassed. Then suddenly I heard a window smash on the floor below. I ran to the study window and looked down. There was a leg clambering out of the window onto some scaffolding! There was no scaffolding directly outside my window, but a reasonably fit adult would be able to clamber up on what there was and reach it.

I needed to get out of there. I ran across to the door and sneaked a glance through the glass panel. The corridor was clear. Should I rush to the lift? No, not the lift, the stairs. I wavered for a moment then ran back to the window and shut it. There *was* someone on the scaffolding: I didn't wait around long enough to see who it was.

I ran out of the door towards the stairs and quickly down a flight. As I reached the third floor landing I heard the lift ping. I whipped a glance to the lift and saw that it had stopped on the second floor. Whoever was in the lift was below me. I decided to wait to see if it went down or up. If it came up I would run down before they had time to change direction, if it went down again, I would stay here

The Peace Garden

for a while to give them time to leave.

The lift went down. I exhaled slowly. I would just have to wait. Or maybe I should hide. I looked around but couldn't see any rooms or cupboards as most of the interior walls and panelling had already been removed. Plastic sheets hung as if suspended from washing lines, flapping in the stiff breeze from the broken window. The broken window! Was the man still on the scaffolding or was he going down in the lift? Were there two of them? The secretary had said two men had come to see me. Who were they? Where were they?

I heard a crunch of glass and a man cursing. Oh my God, he'd come back through the window! Then the lift pinged and the door opened on the third floor: another man stepped out. I gasped and ran into the stairwell. I ran down one flight then heard voices above me.

"Down there! She's heading down!"

I picked up speed and flung myself two, three steps at a time, propelling myself off the banister and into the chest of a large man who blocked my path from below. He wrapped his arms around me and held me in a crushing hold. "I've got her!" he shouted up to his friend.

Feet clattered down the steps then someone shouted: "Natalie!" I looked up and saw Gladwin.

"Let her go, please!" he said. "I know her."

"She was breaking into university property."

"I was not! I walked in on a break-in then I was chased."

The man loosened his grip on me and I turned round to see a campus security guard. I then noticed that the other man with Gladwin was also wearing a uniform.

"Who was chasing you Natalie?" Gladwin asked, concern written on his face.

"I don't know. There was a man trying to climb in the study window and ..."

"That was me," said the second security guard. "I heard someone in the study and when I knocked there was no answer.

"I had called in to say there was an open window ..." Gladwin chipped in.

"I climbed through the window on the third floor, but smashed a pane by accident with my truncheon. I was trying to climb up on the scaffolding to have a look in the fourth floor window. But someone closed it before I could get there," finished the guard.

I felt like a real idiot. There had been no break-in after all.

"What were you doing there, miss?" asked the guard who caught me, not convinced yet of my innocence.

"It's my study. I'm a post-grad here."

"Yes she is," Gladwin confirmed.

"Then why didn't you answer the door when I knocked?" asked the other guard.

"I – I – the room looked ransacked."

"Ransacked?" asked Gladwin, still concerned.

"That's what I thought. But it could also have been the wind. I'm not sure, you see I came in to pick up a message and …"

"Why don't you show us, eh?" interrupted the guard with Gladwin. So I did. We walked back up the stairs, down the corridor and into the study. I hadn't re-locked the door after my terror-ridden flight a few minutes ago. The room was as I left it: papers and files strewn everywhere.

"The window was open of course, so it could have been the storm …"

"What made you think it was a robbery?" asked one of the guards.

"I don't know, it just looked a bit – *deliberate*."

"Anything taken?"

"I'm not sure. All the computers are still here. I haven't had a chance to check the notes and files."

"Would there be anything worth stealing in your notes?" asked the other guard.

"I don't think so."

"Well, if there is, let us know. But without anything obviously missing I think we'd better just put this down to the wind then," he said, with a look at his partner that implied "and an overactive imagination." First Thabo this morning, now this. I'd had enough humiliation for one day.

Gladwin stayed to help me clean up then offered me a lift home.

The Peace Garden

There had been nothing obviously missing, but Gladwin was still concerned. As we drove towards Gosforth he asked: "Are you sure you didn't keep anything worth stealing in the study, Natalie?"

"Like what?"

"Oh I don't know. The letters, perhaps?"

"Your letters?"

"Well, yes."

"Who would steal those? What's happened Gladwin? Are you in trouble again?"

"No, no," he assured me. "Everything's fine. But maybe you should get rid of them anyway. In case Thabo ever finds them. I don't want that to happen."

"I doubt it will. We're not exactly close at the moment." Gladwin looked at me questioningly, but didn't comment. "But if you want me to get rid of them, I can. They weren't in the study."

"Where were they?"

"Safe." I said.

Before Gladwin could probe any more we pulled into Jasmine Close and he stopped outside my grandma's house. "By the way," I asked. "What were you doing at the social work department?"

"I was visiting a colleague downstairs in Geography," he said.

"But the Geography department's moved."

"So I discovered! All this shifting around of departments and offices; it's hard to keep up! Well good night Natalie. I'm sorry for all the drama with the security guards. Just a misunderstanding."

"No problem," I smiled then got out of the car. "Thanks for the lift." As he pulled off I realised I had forgotten to mention the two men who had come to visit me. And then when I thought of it, I had not found any message during the clean up either.

Chapter Thirty-six

BY THE NEXT morning the wind had dropped. It was still nippy though and I pulled my anorak a little closer as I waited for the bus. I didn't have time to drop into the uni before work, but when I had a chance I planned to call the department secretary and ask her about the message and the men. She would probably have had a report from campus security too, so I needed to make sure they hadn't put me in a bad light. I looked at my watch: 7.55am; the bus was late.

"Hey, wanna lift?" It was Thabo, pulling up in a garden centre truck.

"No thanks, the bus'll be here in a minute."

"Oh come on Natalie. It's my way of saying sorry." His eyes were hopeful. I couldn't resist for long.

"Okay then," I climbed into the passenger seat.

"Look, Nat, about the things I said yesterday …"

"Don't worry; I said some things I shouldn't have too. You're right; I think everyone's a social work case. I stick my nose in where it doesn't belong and I wonder why things go wrong."

"At least you care enough to try. I mean, if it hadn't been for you, my dad would still have been sulking behind his garden wall."

"And we wouldn't have found out who the plant thief was."

He laughed then and gestured to the assortment of plants and tools on the back of the truck. "Yeah, I've been at it again."

"You haven't!"

"No, of course not. I spoke to my boss and told him about the Peace Garden project, and he thinks the garden centre should sponsor it. It's good PR. So I'm here as an official representative of Ponteland Garden Centre."

"That's great, but when did you see him?"

"I went back to work after I left you at the refugee centre."

"Did you catch a lift with the guy in the blue BMW?"

"Who?"

"The guy you were talking to in the blue car."

"Sorry Nat, don't know who you're talking about."

"The metallic blue BMW. The same car dropped your dad off at Tesco the other day. Friend of the family?"

"There are lots of blue cars Nat."

"But you spoke to him. Yesterday, outside the refugee centre."

"What is this, an interrogation? Yeah I spoke to some guy – he was asking directions – but I can't remember what colour his car was. I didn't think I'd have to!"

I was sorry I had brought it up. We sat in silence. But it didn't take long for Thabo to give me a sideways smile. I smiled back, still unsure but keen to be friends again. He saw my discomfort and changed the subject.

"My dad said you had a bit of a run-in with campus security."

"Yeah, I thought there had been a robbery but apparently it was just the wind."

"Nothing missing?"

"Nothing that I could see. But how the wind would have blown the telephone off the table, I don't know."

"The telephone?"

"It was dead. I tried to call out."

"Must have been the storm. Why didn't you use your mobile?"

"I don't have one. Never seen the need before now."

"You can have mine". He nodded to the cubby hole.

"I can't take your phone, Thabo!"

"It's an old one. I've just got a new one for work. I was going to recycle it anyway. Should still have enough life to keep you going until you get another one. But it'll need charging soon. Remind me to give you a charger."

"Maybe I can ask Santa."

"Maybe you can." We drove on while I familiarised myself with the phone. Every so often I'd ask Thabo a question about how this or that operated. He also told me his new number and supervised as I plugged it in. "You may get a few calls for me; if you do, just give them my new number."

"Okay." With the tutorial over we crossed the Tyne Bridge.

"Those Rwandan guys I met yesterday were very excited when I told them what we were doing."

"They were?"

"Yeah, they said that even though they weren't living there anymore, they are still allowed to use the facilities, and they'd love to help out."

"Yes, of course they are. Did you think we were just throwing them to the wolves?"

"Well it had crossed my mind."

"Maybe they'll be the only ones, though. Some of the people I spoke to at the centre weren't so keen."

"No? Why?"

"Oh, I don't know. One Sudanese guy, he's a lawyer I think, said he hadn't come to England to become a gardener. Then there was this woman from Bosnia who said that gardening was man's work. She said that God had cursed men to work the soil and women to give birth."

"Don't worry, when they see what the place can look like with a bit of colour they'll come on board."

"You think so?"

"Of course. But even if they don't, we can just do the work and let them enjoy it."

"Maybe, but that's not really my vision."

"I know, Nat, but it's better than nothing. Things don't always turn out the way we want them to."

We arrived at the refugee centre at 8.15am, fifteen minutes before I would have got there on the bus. Parents were seeing their children off to school, mothers were hanging baby clothes on the line, and a small group of Eastern European men were sitting on a bench, smoking strong, filterless cigarettes.

The bench was set against a sunny wall in the sparse area that I envisaged for the garden. "You can park over here," I said.

"Is this where you want the garden?"

The Peace Garden

I nodded.

"Mmmm, it gets good morning sun but that block of flats over there will block it out in the afternoon." He bent down and poked around in the dust with his ignition key. "Yup, just as I thought: a lot of concrete dust and crumbled rubble from when they built the place. When was that?"

"Early Seventies, I think. Will it be a problem?"

"Well, it's not exactly brimming with life. But, like the poem says: *for all this, nature is never spent*."

"God's Grandeur."

"You know it?"

"Gerard Manley Hopkins. So there's hope is there?"

"Oh yes, it will just take a few seasons, that's all."

"But we don't have a few seasons."

"Look, it's taken nearly three decades to get the soil into this condition; it'll need a couple of years to bring it back to life."

"It didn't with our Peace Garden."

"No, but that was pre-development. And besides, I learnt a few lessons after that."

"You mean after you spent the night in a police cell."

"Abe Rashid came with my dad to pick me up. On the way home he said to me, 'don't worry son, one person will plant it, another will water it, and still another see it grow'. I spent some time with him in his garden after that. I learnt that gardens are about process not product. We garden because something inside of us wants to be connected with the earth: to be plugged into God's lifecycle, I suppose. The seasons pace us, balance us, stop us from rushing ahead. And the earth can never be owned. We may build on top of it, but the earth itself remains independent."

"You've become philosophical with age."

"Yeah, sorry," he said, and started to off-load the truck. By this time two of the Rwandans from the day before had arrived and lent a hand. The Eastern European men stayed on the bench.

There were a lot of potted plants and shrubs that Thabo placed along the dirt path near the wall. Particularly cheery were two barrels of sunflowers, which, Thabo told the Rwandans, were one of the easiest things to grow.

Samuel, a twenty-five-year-old Hutu, had been studying to be an English teacher at home when the war broke out. As we were marking out the flowerbeds for next season and digging out the chunks of concrete, the told us he had decided to flee with the rest of his village when he woke one morning to see his Tutsi neighbour dead in his potato patch. He'd been shot in the head. The wife was nowhere to be found. His family took two of the neighbour's children who had survived the attack and walked nearly two hundred kilometres to a refugee camp in the Congo.

By this time, one of the Eastern European men had sauntered over. His name was Gregor. His wife and five-year-old daughter hadn't made it out of Kosovo alive.

"What you do, Natalie?"

"We're making a garden. Do you want to help?"

"Why you do it?" He asked Thabo.

"Because it will make people happy. Soon, there will be grass here for children to play on, and flowers for your wife to pick."

"My wife dead."

"I'm sorry," said Thabo, stopping to stretch his back after failing to dislodge a stubborn boulder.

"I help you," said Gregor, rolling up his sleeves and calling his cronies from the bench. With spades and crowbars from the truck, the men managed to move the boulder. They seemed to like the physical labour and soon Thabo was directing them to other boulders that needed moving. By lunch, with the help of Gregor, Samuel and their friends, five flowerbeds had been created. Thabo added compost to the soil and declared that in a week, after the organic material had been well worked in, some planting could begin.

"Who plant?" Gregor asked.

"Whoever wants to," said Thabo.

"I want," said Gregor.

After that, we packed up the truck and headed to Ponteland. I spent the rest of the afternoon chatting to Thabo's boss about the project, and helping to plan the next phase. By 5pm we were getting on the bus and heading for home. I had forgotten to call the uni secretary, but it could wait until tomorrow now.

By the time we got to Jasmine Close the autumn sun was waning. "Want to have some dinner with me?" asked Thabo.

"Oh, I'm a bit too tired to go out," I said, regretting it the moment I opened my mouth. But fortunately Thabo didn't take it the wrong way.

"That's okay, we can stay in. My dad's going out, so we'll have the house to ourselves."

"Okay, I'll tell my grandma and clean up a bit. I'll see you in an hour."

Chapter Thirty-seven

JUST UNDER AN hour later I was knocking on the Nkulus' door. Gladwin answered; he was wearing his coat. "Hello Natalie. I don't know what you did to him, but Thabo's gone mad in the kitchen. I'm lucky if I can get him to fry an egg."

"It must be all the hard work; it's given him an appetite."

"Well something has. You must excuse me, I won't join you; I was just going out."

"Oh, where're you going?"

"I have a meeting."

"At the university?"

"No, Nancy Drew, not at the university, at a restaurant in North Shields. I'm meeting someone off the ferry."

"A friend?"

"Not exactly. Goodnight," he said, and closed the door behind him.

"I'll be out in a minute!" Thabo shouted from the kitchen. Then he popped his head around the corner. "If you need to use the bathroom, excuse the mess. Bert and Roger are putting in a new basin but at the moment there's just a big hole in the wall with a cupboard shoved in front of it" Then he disappeared back into the kitchen.

"Need a hand?" I called.

"No thanks," came the reply. So I mulled around the living room looking at photos of Thabo and Gladwin's family back in South Africa. The older woman must be Sophie and the elderly Jewish couple, the Cohens. A young white family – a husband, two young children and a wife – were likely to belong to Bryan Cohen. I looked for a black woman, around Poppy's age, but couldn't find any. Not surprising really, seeing they were separated, and this was

Gladwin's house, not Thabo's. Perhaps he had a picture of her in his room. Not that I was planning on seeing his room, of course, but …

The phone rang. I looked around but couldn't find it. It wasn't the phone on the hall table, so it must be … it was coming from my handbag. I scrabbled and finally found it, but it had stopped ringing before I managed to extricate it. The screen said: '1 new voicemail'. After a few false starts I managed to figure out what to press to access it. I listened. It was the voice of an African man: "We need to meet. Soon. The old man is not doing his job properly. Call me." There was no name or number that I could see. Maybe Thabo already knew the number. I let him listen to the message as soon as he came in.

"Sorry," he said. "I thought I'd given this guy my new number. I'll remind him my phone's changed." He took out his new phone and plugged in a quick text.

"Who's the old man?" I asked.

"Just an old employee at the garden centre who's retiring. That was my boss. He'll want me to take over the 'old man's' clients."

"But your boss isn't African."

"Not the one you met today, another partner. What is this? Twenty questions?" He switched off both phones and put them side by side on the coffee table. "Let's not have any more interruptions, shall we?" I smiled and settled into the proffered chair at the dining table.

Thabo had cooked seafood pasta: smoked mussels, some fresh garlic, an onion and a sprinkle of origanum from Mrs Rashid's garden. Then he'd added a tub of cream and a splash of white wine. A pre-packed salad from Tesco's completed the main course. It was simple, but delicious. I scoffed the lot.

"More wine?"

"Yes, why not."

"Seconds?"

"You mean thirds?"

"Oh really? You must like my cooking."

"It's delicious, but I don't have space for any more."

"Not even dessert?"

"Well, you could twist my arm. But let's have it later. I'll let this digest first."

I sat back and sipped my wine, listening to a blend of township jazz and classical strings. Thabo's hair was still slightly damp from the quick shower he'd managed to squeeze in while the pasta was cooking. A few loose strands from his braids glowed raven, silhouetted against the orange flames of the open fire. A warm red shone through the chocolate hue, partially from the fire, partially from the wine, and partially from me, I hoped.

An hour wasn't long to work a miracle but if I do say so myself I hadn't done a bad job. I wore a sage green figure-hugging knit dress: tight at the bodice and flowing from the hips. The neckline was low enough to accentuate my breasts, but not to flaunt them. I had chosen a cardigan instead of a stole to cover my shoulders, so it looked more casual, but after the second glass of wine, I discarded it.

"Hot?" he asked.

"A little."

"Perhaps I should let the fire die."

"No, don't do that. It's a nice fire. And besides it's …" I stopped, mid-sentence, realising that it was the wine talking.

"It's what?" he asked, leaning across the table and taking my hand. My skin looked whiter than usual against his.

"Oh nothing," I said, not pulling away.

"Well, I would have said romantic."

"Yes, so would I, if it was that sort of evening."

"Isn't it?"

"I don't know; that depends."

"On what?"

"On you. I don't know how you feel about me."

He stood up and pulled me to my feet. It was sudden and I stumbled slightly. He caught me against his chest then pulled my hands to his mouth. He found the blisters already forming from my day of digging and ran his tongue over them.

"Now do you know?" he whispered.

I didn't answer, but tilted my head to look into his eyes. They were warm and brown with the green reflection from mine adding

The Peace Garden

another hue. His eyes closed as his lips moved from my fingers to my mouth. His tongue was gentle, probing, and I felt my body surge, wanting even more of him.

It was only a few steps to the couch, and we sank into it to the strains of the Soweto String Quartet. We kissed, hungrily, and before I knew it my dress was hitched up around my waist.

"I – I – I don't ..."

He pulled away. "I'm sorry. I shouldn't have pushed."

"You didn't. I wanted to. I still do. It's just that ..."

"It's your first time."

"Well yes."

"There's nothing to be ashamed of."

"I'm not ashamed. I'd be more ashamed if I'd just slept with some random guy."

"A random guy?" Thabo's face clouded over. I pulled my skirt down.

"Not you. I didn't mean you. You're not a random guy. I meant ... Oh I've blown it! I'm sorry. I should never have come."

I got up and quickly gathered my things. I was trying not to cry.

"Nat ... Natalie ..." He came up behind me and put his arms around me. "It's okay. We can take it slow."

"How slow?"

"As slow as you like." I turned around in his arms and sank my head into his chest.

"What if – what if – I don't believe in sex before marriage?"

"That's a very old fashioned idea."

"I know. But I think I believe it."

"You think you do or you do?"

"I don't know. I think. I know. I don't know if I think ..." He put his finger to my lips.

"It's okay. Let's just see what happens."

"You're still interested then?"

"Of course. Who do you think I am? Just some random guy?" His voice was light, teasing. His body began swaying to the music and he rocked mine gently with him. My head was dizzy with wine and I stumbled again.

"Would you like me to take you home?" He asked.

"Yes," I said, wanting to say no. But it was too late. A few minutes later he walked me the short distance to my grandma's house, helped me get my key in the lock then kissed me goodnight.

"Sleep tight, my love." He pressed something into my hand. It was the mobile phone.

"Don't call me, I'll call you?" I quipped.

"Don't be silly. We just live two doors away! I'll see you in the morning." Unexpectedly, Gladwin's silver Passat pulled into the cul-de-sac. "He's back early," said Thabo. "Just as well we didn't…"

"Just as well!" I giggled. "Time you got your own place?"

"Maybe."

"What's stopping you?"

"Money. I'm not exactly on an executive salary."

"Is that all?"

"Yes Nancy Drew, that's all. Now good night." He kissed me again and gently pushed me over the threshold. I so wished Gladwin had not come home.

Chapter Thirty-eight

THE NEXT MORNING dawned bright and sunny: outside and in. It was Saturday and there would be no work. The whole day loomed large before me, full of possibilities. But foremost in my mind was Thabo. He had said 'see you tomorrow'. And tomorrow was now today. The whole sex thing had been a bit of an embarrassment, but he'd handled it well. I still didn't know what I was going to do about that, but I knew one thing: I was falling in love with Thabo. In fact, I think I'd always loved him. If he didn't share my beliefs about no sex before marriage, we'd have to deal with it, together. I knew my Christian friends back at uni would say I shouldn't even be considering a relationship with someone who didn't share the same belief system, but why not? Was I to deny myself the love of my life, if that was what he was, because we had different views? Was I to …

"Natalie!" It was my grandma. I looked at the clock and it said 7.30am. Grandma was usually up by now, making tea in the kitchen. But I couldn't hear any of the usual clattering. I rolled out of bed and put on my slippers. "Coming Grandma!" I called. I saw that her door was slightly ajar and she was still in bed. I opened it and sat down on the edge of the floral quilt.

Her hair was limp and hung scraggily around her pale face. "Shouldn't you be getting ready for work?"

"Not today Grandma, it's Saturday."

"Is it?" she said, squinting weakly at a calendar on the wall.

"Are you feeling all right, Grandma?"

"Aye, I'll be up in a minute."

"I'll make you some tea, shall I?"

"That'll be grand."

I went into the kitchen, boiled the kettle and put on a slice of toast. As I was getting a jar of marmalade from the fridge I looked out the kitchen window and saw Thabo coming out of his house. My heart leapt. Was he coming to visit me? Oh no! I was still in my Tweetie Pie pyjamas! I rushed the breakfast tray into Grandma's room and nearly spilt the contents over the bed.

"Steady, pet."

"Sorry Grandma. I've got to get ready."

"I thought you weren't going into work today."

"I'm not. I'm seeing a friend." I ran into my room, listening attentively for a knock on the door. I grabbed some jeans and a T-shirt and dragged a brush through my hair. Not perfect, but better than Tweetie Pie. There was still no knock. Should I pop my head out, I wondered, or would that appear too desperate? The milk! I hadn't collected it yet: a perfect excuse.

I opened the front door and picked up the newspaper. As I was reaching for the milk I cast a glance down the cul-de-sac and saw Thabo still standing there, as if waiting for someone. He didn't look up at me as he was engrossed in reading or sending a text from his mobile phone. He didn't even notice when Fatima stepped out of her house and opened the garage door. Just then, a metallic blue BMW pulled into the street, driven by a blonde man in his early fifties. Thabo looked over his shoulder at his own house, as if checking to see if someone was watching him then quickly climbed into the car. As it turned around I withdrew quickly into my house so the two men wouldn't see me.

He'd lied to me! He had known the driver of the blue car. But what was he doing with him? How could I find out? Fatima!

I grabbed my handbag from the kitchen bench, shouted a goodbye to Grandma, threw open the door and ran over to the Rashids' house. Fatima was just pulling her car out of the garage. I flagged her down. "What is it Natalie?"

"I need a lift! It's an emergency."

"Is it your grandma?"

"No, it's Thabo. Can you follow that blue car that just left? It should still be in the estate."

"Yes, but why?"

"I'll explain on the way."

The Peace Garden

"Okay!" Fatima flashed a worried look at me as she screeched out of the driveway. We caught up with the blue car as it was waiting at the intersection into the main road. We were nicely placed three cars behind it, so wouldn't easily be spotted. The blue car, then two more, managed to take the gap into the busy road. Damn! We were forced to stop. Hopefully we'd catch up again at the roundabout onto the A1 slip-road. It was essential to know whether or not it would turn north or south at that point.

"So what's this about?" asked Fatima. A silver VW flashed its lights at us, letting us in.

"Take the gap, take the gap!" I shouted. She obliged and slipped into the stream of traffic. The blue car was still in sight.

"I'll tell you when we get onto the A1."

"Look Nat, I don't want to be rude, but I've got a meeting to go to."

"I know Fats, but it's an emergency. I'll tell you, I promise. There! There! They're turning north."

Fatima shook her head and turned onto the A1, heading north. We kept at a steady sixty, with the blue car in our sights. It was time to tell Fatima the truth. But what could I say?

"It's Thabo. I think he might be in trouble."

"What kind of trouble?"

"He's been lying to me. He told me he didn't know someone and it seems he does. And he's been spending time with them." Fatima looked at me incredulously.

"Look Nat, if your boyfriend's had straying eyes I'm sorry, but it's not worth me missing my meeting about." She started to indicate.

"Where are you going?"

"I'm getting off the motorway and going back to Newcastle."

"No Fats, please! There's more to it than that. It's just hard to explain. You see Gladwin got involved with some terrorist types back in South Africa and …"

"Gladwin's a terrorist?" That caught her attention and she switched off her indicator.

"No, no! But there was some trouble when he went back a few years ago."

"I thought that was all cleared up. With the TRC and all that."

"It was. But when he was there he was threatened by some bloke who tried to recruit him for his cause. Something to do with them not being happy the way things are going in South Africa now."

Fatima gave me a sideways look. At least I think she did as it was hard to see her full face under her *burkah*. "Some white right-wingers tried to recruit Gladwin? Doesn't seem likely."

"No, some black left-wingers. Well, one of them's black. The other one's white and I think that's the guy in the car with Thabo." The blue car in front indicated and took a slip road off towards the A19. "Just as I thought. They're heading for the Tyne Tunnel. Keep on them Fatima." Fatima shook her head in exasperation and exited the motorway.

"How do you know about all this?"

"Gladwin sent me a series of letters when he was in South Africa."

"Why?"

"I don't know. But he did. I shouldn't even be telling you about them. He asked me to keep it confidential."

"Then why aren't you?"

"Because I think he's in trouble. He told me that this Gugs guy – Gugile Sithole, the left-wing terrorist – was just joking with him. Then he told me he was dead."

"Is he?"

"I don't know. But Thabo also said he was dead."

"So Thabo's in on this too."

"I didn't think so. Thabo seemed as worried about his dad as I am. Seems like he's been following the trail of this terrorist organisation back in South Africa; the OCSR. There've been some horrific murders."

"So is Gladwin part of it or not?"

"I'm not sure. He was supposed to be some kind of conduit for finance between Scandinavia and South Africa. His contact is someone called Hans Larson."

"The white guy in the blue car?"

"That's what I'm beginning to think. He matches the description Gladwin gave in his letters."

"Does Thabo know about the finance thing?"

"Gladwin said he doesn't."

"Seems like Gladwin said a lot of things."

The car in front had reached the Tyne Tunnel. We joined the queue behind it. Fatima drummed the steering wheel with her perfectly manicured nails.

"Why haven't you gone to the police, Nat?"

"I didn't realise anything was still going on until today. Well, the last couple of days really. I've seen the blue car around. But it could have been quite innocent. It might still be. I don't want to go to the police and jeopardise my relationship with Gladwin – or Thabo – if it's nothing serious."

"So is the guy in the blue car the one you said Thabo didn't know but now it looks like he does?"

"Yes."

"And you think this guy is Larson. The Scandinavian who is providing funds for terrorist activity in South Africa?"

"Possibly."

"You've always had an over-active imagination Natalie."

"I was right about the plant thief."

"Yes you were. But this is international terrorism, not a few stolen azaleas."

"I know Fats, I know; which is why I haven't wanted to believe it. But this morning when I saw Thabo climbing into that car when he had told me to my face yesterday morning that he didn't know the driver; and when Gladwin's been acting so strangely, and when I got that phone call …"

"A phone call?"

"Yes, on Thabo's old phone. It was from an African man and he said it was his boss but I know his boss is white."

"What did he say?"

"Something about the old man not doing his job."

"Gladwin?"

"That's what I think."

"Strange. What else?"

"Well my study was broken into."

"Really?"

"Well sort of. I think so. Possibly."

Fatima let out another exasperated sigh and began to indicate. She was going to pull out of the queue. But just then a large truck with a wide-load pulled up behind us and made a retreat nigh on impossible. At the same time the queue surged forward. Fatima didn't have any choice but to follow.

We sat in silence as we drove through the lit tunnel. I toed at a newspaper that was on the floor. It was the one I had picked up from the doorstep in my panic to spot Thabo. I must have still had it in my hand when I jumped into Fatima's car. I picked it up. On the front page was a photo of a dignified looking black gentleman with a goatee beard. His face was familiar. I looked at the article and it read:

'South Africa's new president, Thabo Mbeki, is due to give the keynote address at the opening of the new wing of Newcastle University at noon today. Security is being stepped up at the city's premier educational institution after death threats have been made against the president in anticipation of his UK tour. Mr Mbeki will be receiving an honorary doctorate in politics from the university. "We are very honoured that Mr Mbeki has agreed to receive his doctorate in person," said Professor Gladwin Nkulu, head of the politics department at the university. When asked whether he thought the death threats from the so-called Organisation for Complete Socialist Reform were credible, Professor Nkulu said to his knowledge there was no such organisation and that it appeared as if the threats were a hoax. "I'm sure however that the ultimate care is being taken with President Mbeki's safety by the British and South African security services," Professor Nkulu added.'

The article then went on to describe Gladwin's background and how he had been cleared by the TRC of murder. It also spoke about his academic work at the university.

"Oh my word, Fats! Listen to this!" I read the article to her.

"So what? Mbeki's coming to Newcastle. Where's the conspiracy theory in that?"

"Because," I said, trying to keep my temper, "it's evidence that

Gladwin has been lying to me and is lying to the press too."

"How's that?"

"This Organisation for Complete Socialist Reform, the OCSR, is the organisation that Gugile Sithole tried to get Gladwin to join. He has heard of it. Why did he lie?"

Fatima's fingers were drumming again. I waited for an answer. As we pulled out of the tunnel Fatima had an opportunity to skirt around and take the tunnel back under the river. But she didn't. She carried on following the blue car. It was heading towards the North Sea Ferry Terminal and North Shields.

"So why is it Thabo in the car with him and not Gladwin?"

"I don't know. That's what I'm trying to find out. Will you help me?"

Fatima was quiet for a disturbingly long period. Then she finally spoke: "Against my better judgement, yes. But after we see what Thabo is doing we go to the police, okay? Or at least, talk to my brothers. Deal?"

I sighed. I would be betraying Gladwin's confidence but I didn't have a choice. "Deal."

Chapter Thirty-nine

"BLOODY HELL, FATIMA, where did you learn to drive?" The little red Golf was zipping in and out of traffic on the road to the ferry terminal.

"Mecca," she said and tried to suppress a giggle. Fatima was starting to enjoy this.

As we approached the terminal we saw the blue car pull into the car park. Fatima pulled into the overflow area. Hopefully Thabo and his friend would not look back. They didn't. The two got out of the car and headed straight into the terminal building. A ferry was already in dock. Were they leaving the country? Neither of them had suitcases, although the blonde man did have a briefcase and Thabo a small backpack. Travelling light? If Thabo was going on a trip today, why didn't he tell me last night? This was the North Sea Ferry and ships left from here to Scandinavia and mainland Europe.

Fatima and I followed them into the terminal and held back as far as we could. I checked the queue for embarkation but it wasn't open yet. Disembarkation though was well under way. Among the parents carrying children, students with backpacks the size of small wardrobes and pensioners with bag-loads of duty free, a middle-aged black man came through passport control and stood looking around. Could this be Gugile Sithole back from the grave? Gladwin had never physically described him but there was something familiar about him.

"Who's that?" whispered Fatima, hiding behind a carousel of magazines at a terminal kiosk. I sidled in beside her.

"I think it might be Gugile Sithole. The guy who's supposed to be dead."

"Looks very much alive to me," said Fatima. "But he could just be an innocent passenger."

"Possibly," I agreed.

"Give me your phone."

"What?"

"Do you have the phone the African guy rang you on last night?"

"Oh, okay, yes." I scrabbled around in my bag and brought it out. Fatima took it from me.

"Your battery's low. When did you receive the call?"

"Last night. About eight."

"And have you had any calls since then?"

"No."

"Good." Fatima pressed a few buttons and found what she was looking for. Then she held the phone to her ear. Suddenly the African man cocked his head and reached into his pocket, taking out his phone. Fatima hung up before he answered. He looked irritated but before he could ring back the man I believed to be Larson, waved to him.

"It's him," said Fatima. "We can give this to the police as evidence."

But evidence of what? We needed more information before we went to the police. What had Thabo got himself into?

The three men met in the middle of the terminal and shook hands. They remained deep in conversation for a few minutes. Suddenly, 'Gugs' unzipped his suitcase and brought out a parcel wrapped in a plastic bag. 'Larson' looked shocked and appeared to berate him. Gugs hurriedly put it back into his suitcase then the three men ducked into a nearby mens' room.

"Damn! We can't follow them in there."

"Give it a few minutes," said Fatima. We did. Both of us pretended to look at the magazines on the carousel, but as most of them were fashion and lifestyle magazines and one of us was wearing a *burkah*, I didn't think our cover would have held for long.

It wasn't long though before the three men emerged. Without further ado they headed out to the car park, but this time Thabo was carrying the plastic bag. Fatima and I followed from a distance, hiding behind trolley bays and parked cars where necessary. The men got in the blue car.

"Can we follow them?" I asked.

"Of course! Looks like you were right Natalie. Sorry I doubted you."

"Thanks for believing me," I said. Fatima opened the car and we jumped in, buckled up and started tailing the BMW. We followed it out of the ferry terminal, past the Royal Quays shopping centre, down the road and to the Tyne Tunnel, through the tunnel and back onto the A19. But instead of linking up with the A1 South we turned onto the Coast Road and went into Newcastle then across the bridge to Gateshead. This was not the most direct route to Gateshead. Why had Larson bothered going through the tunnel under the river if he was just going to go back over the bridge later on? Unless … unless … "Do you think they know they're being followed, Fatima?"

"How could they?"

"I don't know. But we've never done this before and they are – they might be – international terrorists. They must know all about this stuff. Perhaps they've spotted us."

The car in front of us started slowing down and stopped in a familiar spot: outside the gate of the refugee centre. We stopped too: further up the road.

The three men got out and shook hands. The African man went into the centre and Larson and Thabo got back into the car. They spoke for a few seconds then Thabo got out his phone and punched in a number. Suddenly my phone rang. Fatima and I both leapt out of our skins.

"You'd better answer it," she said. "But pretend you're not here. He might not have seen us. Play it cool."

I nodded but was unconvinced I could pull it off. "Hello."

"Hey Natalie!"

"Hey Thabo."

"Where are you?" He wouldn't have asked that if he could see me, would he?

"I – I'm with Fatima. Shopping."

"Where?"

"Royal Quays." I said the first thing that came to mind and

regretted it.

"Why there? It's a bit far to go so early on a Saturday morning, isn't it?"

"Yeah, but Fats said there was a sale on at Next." Fatima raised her eyebrows and shook her head.

"I didn't know Fatima shopped at Next. That's a bit high fashion for her these days isn't it? Besides, there's a Next at Kingston Park, just five minutes from home."

"Yeah, I know, but we wanted to make a day of it. Have breakfast at the Quays."

"Oh, all right." He sounded convinced. I began to relax.

"So where are you?"

"Just down the road."

"Just down the road at home?"

"No, just down the road at the refugee centre. In the blue car you've been following from the ferry terminal. What the hell are you doing Natalie?"

I dropped the phone and shouted at Fatima: "Drive! He's onto us!" Fatima got the car into gear and started to pull off but had to wait for a break in the stream of traffic. It gave Thabo enough time to get out of his car, run down the road and bang on the passenger window. He looked furious.

"Phone the police, Nattie!"

"You do it," I said and tossed her the phone. Then I opened the window. He wasn't going to hurt me. This was Thabo. Whatever he had got himself into, he wasn't a violent man; I knew it.

"The battery's flat," said Fatima. "Hello Thabo."

"Hello Fatima." Fatima sat there, staring straight ahead; embarrassed.

"What the hell's going on Natalie? Why are you following me?"

"Because you've been acting strangely. Why did you leave so early this morning? And in the blue car that you said you didn't know? And who was the guy you met at the ferry terminal from Scandinavia? It was him on the phone last night! The one you said was your boss, but he isn't your boss, is he? And how do you know Larson?"

"Larson?"

"The blonde guy in the car." A strange expression crossed Thabo's face. Was it fear?

"That's not Larson. That's Karl van Lelyveld. A Dutchman. He's a horticulturalist from Holland. He's been helping us develop a new hybrid tulip."

Tulip bulbs? What kind of a fool did he think I was? "Then why all the secrecy?"

"It's the first in the world of its kind. We're going to premier it at the Chelsea Flower Show next year but we don't want it to get out before then. We could make a lot of money out of this but not if we fall victim to industrial espionage."

"Industrial espionage in the flower world? So that's what this is about?"

He looked at me fiercely, challenging me to believe him. I wanted to; I didn't want to throw away what we had. But there were too many unanswered questions. And what about Thabo Mbeki and the OCSR? Was that just a coincidence?

Thabo called suddenly to his blonde companion. "Karl! Bring the package."

Karl did not look too happy about it, but he did as he was told. He glared at us as he approached and passed the package to Thabo. "Are you sure you know what you're doing?"

"Yes. I know them. I'll make sure they don't talk." Thabo opened the plastic bag and then unwrapped a box covered in brown paper to reveal about a dozen bulbs. He'd been telling the truth.

"But who was the guy at the ferry terminal? And why did you drop him off here? And why was he coming from Scandinavia?"

"He wasn't. It was the ferry from Amsterdam. Check your facts Natalie before you start tossing around accusations. His name is Benoit Kigali. He's originally from the Congo but is a naturalised Dutch citizen. His nephew and family however are from Rwanda and are in this refugee centre. He's trying to arrange for them to be transferred to Amsterdam. His nephew told me about it the other day and I thought it would be a great opportunity to get the bulbs over from Amsterdam without them running the risk of getting lost in the post. I told Karl about it and he said he'd give me a lift to the ferry terminal. It was all last minute and I didn't have time to talk to you about it last night. I thought I'd get these early then come to your house for breakfast. But I guess that won't happen now."

He started rewrapping his bulbs.

"Thabo, please, I'm sorry."

"No Natalie, I'm afraid you've gone too far this time."

"But your father ... I still think he's in trouble."

"Stay out of my family's business, Natalie, I'm warning you." And with that, he and Karl stalked back to their car.

"Natalie?" It was Fatima. Her voice was drenched with sympathy. "Do you still want me to call the police?"

"No Fats. Let's leave it."

"But Thabo Mbeki and the OCSR! I still think you've got something there. Maybe Thabo's not involved, but ..."

"He's not. Can we just go home, Fatima?"

"Okay," she said and pulled away.

Chapter Forty

WE DROVE IN silence all the way back to Jasmine Close. As we pulled into the cul-de-sac an ambulance passed us on the way out. There was a police car outside Grandma's house.

"What's going on here?"

"Don't know," said Fatima.

We pulled up in front of the bungalow and met Dullah on the drive.

"What's wrong Dullah? Is it Grandma? Is she all right?"

"She's all right. Just a bit of a shock. That was her in the ambulance. Your Auntie Rose is with her."

"What happened?"

"There's been a burglary. My mam heard Gazza barking at something over your wall. He wouldn't stop. So she went to have a look and saw the back door had been forced open. She was just about to call for help when a man ran out of the house and knocked her to the ground."

"Is she all right? I asked, shocked.

"Yes, she's fine," said Dullah. "But she called me and when I went to check on your grandma, I found her tied up."

"Oh my God! Did he hurt her?"

"Not really. She just fainted; no doubt from the shock."

"Can you take me to the hospital please Fatima?"

"Of course, but I need to see my mother first. Is that okay?"

"Yes, of course." Fatima rushed into her house.

"I need to ask you a few questions before you go," said Dullah as Aktar came out of the house with a man in an overall carrying a briefcase.

"Finger printing unit," Dullah explained. "Any luck?" he asked his twin.

"No, whoever he was he was a pro."

"What do you mean?" I asked.

"No prints, no electronics taken, just a hell of a mess. It looks like he was looking for something specific."

"What?" asked Dullah.

"Don't know. Maybe Natalie can tell us. You'll have to have a look around and see if anything's been taken."

As soon as I stepped through the door I was struck by a distinctive smell: something that hadn't been there before. It was a combination of sour sweat and something else. I couldn't put my finger on it: fermented barley, roast corn, something like that. The smell was the least of my problems though. Grandma's pristine bungalow was a mess: drawers and cupboards pulled out, furniture sliced with a knife, stuffing strewn all over the floor. The guts of Grandma's safe were scattered over her bed but a quick perusal told me that nothing was missing.

Aktar nodded to the safe. "The work of a pro; he cracked the combination."

I couldn't see what was missing: the TV and sound system were still in their place, expensive ornaments were smashed, not stolen, and even the housekeeping money was still in the teapot. Grandma's wedding ring was on her dressing table and my jewellery was lying on my bedroom floor.

"Well?" asked Aktar. "See anything missing?" I shook my head.

"Come on Nattie, there must be something."

"I don't know, maybe, maybe not. The place is just such a mess. I can't see where everything is. And that smell!" I was struggling to hold back the tears. This on top of my fight with Thabo was too much to cope with. I sat down heavily in the nearest chair. What if it was all connected? What if I'd been right about Thabo all along? What if the bulb story was just a cover? Or maybe it was true. Maybe it was just a coincidence. I needed help. I looked up into Aktar's worried eyes. He'd been a good friend for nearly fifteen years. I could trust him.

"This is the second break-in in a week."

"Here?" the young policeman tossed a worried look at his brother.

"No. My study at the uni."

"Did you report it to campus security?"

"Yes, but they said there was no evidence of an actual break-in and that the mess could have been caused by the wind through an open window."

"But you think it was a break-in."

"Yes. It looked like they were searching for something. Just like here."

"What?" asked Aktar.

"I don't know. I ..."

But suddenly it dawned on me. I leapt up and ran into my bedroom. I grabbed a chair and reached into the top of the wardrobe: it was empty. The robber had got there before me and already pulled everything out. I jumped off the chair and started scratching through the piles of clothes and books on the floor. Then I found what I was looking for: a yellow shoe box turned upside down. I didn't have to turn it over to know that it would be empty. The letters were gone. I sat back on my haunches and looked up at Dullah and Aktar.

"Did Grandma or your mother describe the man?"

"He was wearing a balaclava, but my mam thinks he was black."

"There were two men in the uni break-in. One black and one white."

"Anything more specific?" asked Dullah.

"No. But the uni secretary will be able to tell you more. If you contact her you'll probably get a better description of them."

Dullah nodded and dialled a number on his phone. "Campus security please."

"Have you something missing, Natalie?" Aktar asked.

"Yes. Some letters. From Gladwin."

"Gladwin?"

"It's hard to explain. But I will. I just need to speak to Gladwin first if that's okay."

"Yes of course," said Aktar. "He's at home. He came out to see what all the commotion was about, but then went back in. He said he wasn't feeling very well. His diabetes has been playing up and he said he's running low on insulin. My dad has just gone to his shop to pick some up for him. So go speak to him then I'll take you to see your grandma at the hospital afterwards and you can tell me everything on the way. When Gladwin's feeling better we'll ask him to come to the station and give his side of the story."

"Actually, can we meet you at the hospital rather?" asked Dullah. "Fatima can take you. We need to go and see campus security, Aktar. They say they've got something to show us."

I ran down the road to Gladwin's house. I needed to tell him about the letters, but I also wanted to talk to him about Thabo before I spoke to Dullah and Aktar. I still wasn't sure how, if at all, Thabo was involved and didn't want to make my fraught relationship with him any worse. I hoped that Gladwin could shed some light on it all.

I knocked and waited but there was no answer. I knocked again. Just as I was about to turn away, the door opened.

"Natalie, what are you doing here?" He looked ill. His eyes squinted behind his glasses and beads of sweat clung to his brow. He was unshaven and his shirt un-pressed.

"There's been a break-in at my grandma's house."

"So I heard. Is she all right?"

"I think so. Dullah said she's just a bit shaken. I'm going to the hospital now."

"Good. Give her my regards." Gladwin started closing the door. I pushed my foot to stop it.

"I need to talk to you first, Gladwin."

"I'm not feeling well, Natalie, can it wait?"

"No. It's about the letters." Gladwin's eyes opened wide and he flicked them to the side as if indicating something.

"You can tell me later Natalie. You need to go and see your grandma."

"I will. But I must talk to you first. They've gone. The letters have gone and ..." Gladwin tried to force the door closed but I pushed back. "What the hell are you doing?" I propelled myself into the hall. Gladwin grabbed me and started pushing me back. He was shaky and obviously ill but still determined.

"Get out of here now!"

"Oh let her come in, Gladwin." A voice called from the living room.

"She's got nothing to do with it. Let her go."

"Shut the door Gladwin or there will be consequences." Gladwin shut the door.

As he walked by me he muttered: "You should have listened to me."

"Come in my dear," said the voice from the living room. Ominously, I stepped through the doorway.

It wasn't cold, but there was a fire in the grate and someone had been burning papers. A few scattered envelopes told me they were Gladwin's letters to me.

"Come in, come in," said the voice again. It came from a man sitting with his back to the door. Then he turned around. He was wearing a balaclava and next to him was a five-litre can of petrol.

"So you are Natalie Porter. I've heard a lot about you, *Khandlela*." He let out a rasping laugh. "She's a pretty one, Gladwin. I can see why you're interested. Come closer, my little candle."

Gladwin grabbed my hand and pulled me back. "Stay away from him Natalie." I obeyed.

"Aren't you going to introduce us?" asked Gugs.

"I know who you are," I said, sounding braver than I felt. "You're Gugile Sithole, the head of the OCSR.

"Ah, she's a bright one, Gladwin. How do you know all this, my dear?"

"Gladwin's letters." I said.

"Yes, the letters. The stupid fool put it all down on paper, didn't he? But why he sent them to a white girl like you I'll never know."

"I wish I never had," said Gladwin.

"But you have," said Gugs. "We can destroy the letters easily enough, but the girl, well that could be more challenging."

"Don't you lay a hand on her!" Gladwin stepped between me and Gugs. The seated man laughed again. "Ever the chivalrous one, Gladwin. Pity you weren't there to protect Thabo and Poppy though."

"What have you done to Thabo?" I demanded.

"Don't worry your pretty little head about it, my dear, Thabo is quite safe. I was talking about the past, when your friend here left his family in South Africa to fend for themselves. But thankfully, I was there. I was the one who comforted his mother at night. I was the one who taught Thabo to ride his first bicycle and play soccer. I was the one he called *Tata* ..." Gugs paused for effect: "and I still am."

"That's a lie!" I said. "Thabo loves his father. His *real* father. He thinks you're dead!"

Gugs laughed again. "Oh really? Is that what he told you? Then why has he been corresponding with me for the last six months? You don't look shocked, Gladwin. Did you know?"

"I suspected," said Gladwin.

"Yes, Thabo found out what you were doing for us and got in touch. He offered to take your place. At first I thought he was just trying to protect you but after a while I realised he was a true comrade. Then when you started becoming – how should I say – *unreliable*, he continued our work. He's never forgiven you for leaving him, Gladwin. You know that."

Gladwin lowered his eyes.

"It's not true! Thabo is a good man. He would never be involved in any kind of plot to kill the president!"

Both Gladwin and Gugs looked at me. "You old fool!" shouted Gugs. "What have you told her?"

"Nothing!" said Gladwin.

"I worked it out for myself. How could you be involved in something like this, Gladwin?"

"I'm not. I've been trying to get out of it."

"Then why didn't you just go to the police."

"I was trying to sort it out myself. I didn't think Gugs was serious."

"Oh I'm serious," said Gugs and tossed another letter onto the fire. "But that's not the real reason you didn't go to the police now is it Gladwin?"

I looked at Gladwin, waiting for an answer. But then Gugs' phone rang. He answered it. "Hello Thabo, I was waiting for you to call. How are you my son?"

Chapter Forty-one

GLADWIN AND I waited while Gugs spoke to Thabo. "Yes, they're both here. Gladwin and the white girl ... no, the Muslim girl's gone into her house ... oh was she? Then we'll have to deal with her later ... no, the cops have left ... yes, I know they'll be back soon which is why we need to finish this now ... all right, I'll hold out for now, but hurry. Is Larson with you? ... good. And the merchandise? ... excellent. See you soon, son."

He ended the call and smiled. "That was Thabo. He's just finishing off some business with Larson at the university in anticipation of the visit of our dear president."

"You'll never get away with this," said Gladwin. "There'll be security all over the place; you'll never get a sniper in."

"Who's talking about a sniper? With that son of yours we have access to unlimited fertiliser and nitrates: everything we need for a bomb. Why else do you think we asked you to scout out the abandoned Geography department? It's directly opposite the entrance to the Great Hall where Mbeki will be giving his speech: a perfect spot from which to detonate a bomb. A couple of your refugee friends work at the university as cleaners. They were able to place something in the Great Hall for us."

"But there'll be hundreds of people there!" I said.

"Sad, but true," said Gugs, not sounding very sad at all.

"If you're going to be killing the president why are you here?" I asked.

"Tying up loose ends," said Gugs. "Gladwin let it slip once that he'd got evidence against me; that he'd written letters when he was back in South Africa. But he never told me who they were to. But then Thabo told me that you seemed to know more about Gladwin's business than you should and it didn't take a genius to put two and two together."

Oh God, could it get any worse? When I thought Thabo and I were bonding he was just milking me for information. The bastard, the absolute bastard!

"Look Gugs, let her go. She hasn't seen your face and there's no way she can identify you."

"True," said Gugs and pulled off his balaclava. A surprisingly good looking man was revealed. His hair was greying at the temples but the dark skin, while marred in places by scarring, showed very few wrinkles. "Now she has. No Gladwin, I'm afraid your little girlfriend will die in the same fire you do. It will be a tragedy, of course, but who could have known that the ever-trusting young social worker would become the final victim of the mad professor who had planted the bomb to kill the South African president then killed himself by deliberately setting fire to his house? His poor son, a promising young horticulturalist, will be devastated. And the young Muslim medical student who was friends with the social worker will sadly die trying to rescue her. Anyone else we should include in this sad tale, Gladwin? Ah yes, the old lady. She only saw a black man in a balaclava, but it could easily have been you. But, perhaps for thoroughness …"

"Leave my grandma alone!" I ran at him, grabbing a statuette, and swinging it at his head. He ducked and lunged at me, pinning me to the ground. Gladwin jumped at him, but the fitter man tripped him up. Gladwin fell heavily and lay winded on the floor. Gugs stood up and revealed the gun that he'd had on his lap. No wonder Gladwin had been reluctant to tackle him. He trained it on us both.

"Get up now." I did and then helped Gladwin to his feet. He swayed weakly. His hands were clammy and shaking.

"He's ill," I said to Gugs. "He needs insulin."

"He's going to die anyway."

"Yes but it won't be very convincing if a post mortem reveals the terrorist who killed the president was too ill to walk never mind detonate a bomb in the hours before he died. He needs insulin. Let me get him some."

As Gugs was considering this there was a knock on the door.

"Answer it, but don't try anything funny," said Gugs, ushering me towards the door with his gun.

I opened the door. "Fatima!" I said, shocked to see my black-robed neighbour.

"Hi Nattie. Are you ready to go?"

"Sorry, I can't"

"You can't? But your grandma!"

"I know. I've just called the hospital and they say she's heavily sedated and it will be better if I come around in the morning."

"Oh," said Fatima, looking confused. I knew that she knew that this was out of character for me. Sedated or not, I would want to be beside my grandma. Hopefully she would mention this to her brothers; or perhaps not. I needed to give her another clue.

"So can you give me a lift tomorrow then?"

"Sure."

"We'd better go another route to the hospital then because of the roadblocks we read about in the paper today."

"The road blocks?" Suddenly Fatima's eyes widened. I nodded and gave her what I thought was a knowing look.

"Yeah, you're right." Fatima was getting it. I looked at her in relief. She squeezed my hand.

"That's all set then," I said. "I'll be staying the night here with Gladwin because my place is trashed. By the way, is your dad back yet with the insulin?"

"Yes, here it is. He asked me to give it to Gladwin. Can I see him?" she pushed a chemist bag into my hands.

"He's lying down. Don't worry, Thabo showed me what to do that day when I helped him plant the tulip bulbs."

"Yes, I remember that day. Where's Thabo now?" Gugs cleared his throat behind me. I needed to be careful.

"I'm not sure. He'll probably be back later."

"Okay then, see you tomorrow."

"Bright and early," I said.

"As soon as humanly possible," she said. She walked away, not bothering to adjust her veil that had slipped onto her shoulders. I closed the door.

"Make sure she really goes," said Gugs, indicating that I should look out of the window. I did, just in time to see Fatima closing the door of her house.

"I've got the insulin. But Gladwin needs some food before he can take it. Can I make something?"

Gugs was pacing in front of the window, checking his watch. "Okay, make something simple. But don't try to get out of the back door: I've got the key," he said, showing the evidence.

I slipped into the kitchen and let the door swing shut. I was sweating, and not just from the heat of the fire. What was I going to do? That lunatic was going to kill us all after the bomb went off. I looked at my watch: 11am. If I recalled correctly from the article, Mbeki was going to speak at noon. We had an hour.

I opened a drawer and fingered the carving knives. Could I do it? Could I kill Gugs? Probably not; he was a lot stronger than I was, and he had a gun. I'd never be able to overpower him. But if I had the element of surprise ...

"The syringe is in the bathroom." It was Gladwin's voice.

"Okay," I said. "I'll get it in a minute." I made a sandwich and took it to him.

"In the cabinet beside the shower. You'll have to reach right to the back."

"Okay," I said again.

"Right to the back. You may have to push some stuff out of the way to get to it."

I looked at him quizzically. "Got it. Right at the back."

I went into the bathroom and opened the cupboard. I scratched around but could find no syringe. I reached right to the back as instructed. What was Gladwin getting at? Right to the back. Push stuff out of the way. But what? The back of the cupboard? I pushed and the plywood easily gave way. The cupboard was blocking the hole that the Storeys had made when they started laying the pipes for the Nkulu's new wash-basin. It would be a tight squeeze but I could just about make it.

I wriggled and stretched and with a bit of effort slipped through the hole into Gladwin's back garden. I heard Gugs shouting and started to run, but just as I rounded the corner of the house someone was blocking my path: it was Thabo. He grabbed me and pinned my arms to my side. I thrashed around and kicked out at his shins, but despite me landing a couple of blows, he didn't let go.

"You bastard!"

"Calm down."

"Calm down? You're going to kill the South African president and frame your own father for it and you tell me to calm down!"

"I told you to stay away from my family. But you wouldn't listen. Why don't you ever listen?" He pulled me around and looked intently into my eyes.

I was just about to answer when there was a knock on the window. Gugs was there and beckoned us both inside with the gun. Thabo grabbed me by the wrist and dragged me after him. As the door opened and closed I thought I saw a black shadow in the Rashid doorway. Was it Fatima? Had she understood my message and called her brothers?

Gugs met us in the entrance hall and waved us inside. "Good, you've caught the bitch. Bring her in." Thabo dragged me in with him then tossed me into the armchair opposite Gladwin who was barely conscious.

"What the hell are you doing here? There's only fifty minutes until Mbeki gives his speech. You should be there for the detonation."

"Larson can handle it."

"I wanted you to handle it, son." Gladwin groaned and Thabo nodded to him.

"I will. Buy I've been thinking. It would be far more plausible if Gladwin was killed in the blast. Suicide bombing and all that. Far easier than starting a second fire here."

"What are you saying?" asked Gugs, his eyes narrowing.

"I've come to take him to the university. There's still time." Thabo went over to his father and started lifting him up.

"Put him down," said Gugs. "It's too late to change the plan now. And if you don't get there in time we'll have problems."

"I can make it." Thabo carried on lifting his father.

"I said put him down." Gugs took a step closer to Thabo and pointed the gun directly at his head.

"Gugs, my man, I'm on your side."

"Are you?"

"Of course."

"Then call me *Tata*."

"You said yourself we don't have time to waste."

"Call me *Tata*." This time he turned the gun on Gladwin and pulled back the safety.

"*Tata; Tata*!"

"I thought so. You treacherous little shit." Gugs swung around and smashed the gun against Thabo's head.

Chapter Forty-two

GUGS AND I were the only two conscious people in the room. Thabo lay on the floor with a large gash on his forehead. He was still breathing though. His father was slumped in his chair. I opened my mouth, about to say something, but Gugs pointed the gun at me. "Don't try to talk me out of it girl, it won't work. He picked up his phone again and dialled. "Larson? Where are you? ... Good. There's been a problem. Thabo's turned on us. ... yes, yes, I know you never trusted him. We'll talk about it later. Are you still on track? ... What? Shit. Okay, never mind. Can you make another plan? Good, good. Call me when it's over." He put the phone down.

"Seems like Mbeki's arrival has been brought forward to 11.30. That's ten minutes time. Earlier than expected so I'd better get to work." He pointed the gun at me again. "Don't move or I'll blow your brains out. Do you understand?" I nodded. "Good." Gugs got up, took the lid off the petrol canister and started splashing it around the living room. He went in the hall and splashed some more around there too. Thabo began to stir. He reached out and grabbed my foot.

"Are you all right?" I whispered.

"Yes," he said. "Don't worry, everything will be all right." He squeezed my foot. Don't worry? Well I'd say there was a hell of a lot to worry about!

"Oh God, there's nothing more we can do," I prayed. "Please do something. And if you don't mind me saying so: do it now!"

There was another knock at the door. "Shit, shit, shit!" It was Gugs. He ran back into the living room and peered through the net curtain. "It's that Muslim girl again. What's her problem? Okay, get up and answer it. Invite her in. Got it?"

"Invite her in to her death? I don't think so!"

"Just answer the fucking door!" Gugs swung the back of his hand at me and connected with my cheek.

Thabo started to get up. "Do what he says, Nattie." I looked at him, perhaps for the last time. His eyes were full of love and tears.

I got up and answered the door. "Oh Fats, we don't have any time for this. We've run out of time. We've ..." Fatima put her finger to her lips and shushed. But it wasn't Fatima. It was Aktar wearing her *burkah*. "Look, Fats, er – er – Gladwin would like to see you after all. He's not feeling too well. He's in the living room and Thabo's there too. He's not too good either – a virus I think. And they've got a friend visiting. Maybe you can have a look at them. Okay?"

Aktar gave a non-committal high pitched 'uh huh' and came in. As he did I saw his robe open and he held a gun. He motioned for me to go out the door, but as I made a move towards it, Gugs came out of the living room. He summed the situation up in an instant and started firing. Aktar threw himself in front of me and I heard the thump, thump of bullets hitting him before a searing pain pierced my leg. I fell in the doorway as I heard the scream of police sirens filling the cul-de-sac. Aktar was up and dragging me out of the house while firing off a couple of rounds. I couldn't see Gugs.

"Are you okay, Nattie?" Aktar asked.

"Yes," I said. "It's just my leg," I said sounding braver than I felt. "And you?"

"Yeah, body armour. Put pressure on the wound, we'll get you seen to as soon as we can."

Police were now swarming all over the garden, taking up positions. I saw Dullah leading some around the back.

"Back off or I'll kill him," It was Gugs' voice.

Gugs had dragged Thabo towards the door and was pointing a gun at his head.

"Okay, relax," said Aktar, still standing in front of me as blood started soaking through my jeans.

"Put down the gun! Put down the bloody gun!" Gugs screamed. Aktar did what he was told.

"Look, you won't get away with it, you're surrounded. Thabo told us about your plan to kill the president. Your friend Larson is being arrested now and the bomb squad is defusing the device. It's over."

Suddenly I saw flames licking at the living room curtains: "Oh God, hurry, Gladwin's still in there!"

"Listen to the cops, Gugs, you won't get away with this," said Thabo.

"Since when did you become friends with the police, Thabo? I remember when the mere mention of them would have you peeing. Remember when I came to get you from that hideaway in the Transkei? You were playing in your little garden, pulling up weeds with your hands. When I told you the cops were coming you asked me if you could come back to your garden. I said 'no, you'll never see it again'. You started to cry and you pissed in your pants. I thought then you were just like your father. I hoped for a while that you'd grow up to be like me, but I was wrong."

"Yes, you were wrong," said Thabo. "I'm just like my father, and I'm proud of it. My father did more for the cause than you ever did."

"Shut up!" yelled Gugs and looked as if he was about to shoot him when Gladwin hurtled out of the living room and bulldozed into him. The two men fell on top of Thabo in a tangle of arms and legs. Aktar leapt into the fray too and somehow managed to wrestle the gun away.

Gugs broke free and ran back into the burning house as Thabo and his father stumbled into the garden. The curtains had burnt away and I could see Gugs standing in the middle of the room, waiting for the flames to reach him. He stared steadily at us through the window. Gladwin started getting to his feet.

"What are you doing *Tata*?" asked Thabo.

"I must get him out. He's going to die."

"He wants to die, *Tata*, but I want you to live."

Gladwin grasped Thabo's hand and the father and son cried together as the flames enveloped Gugs.

Chapter Forty-three

April 2001

"DO YOU KNOW this is the place my Auntie Rose's husband proposed to her?" I asked. Thabo and I were sitting at the top of the ruined tower near Corbridge on a glorious spring day. We had been together now for seven months and I couldn't believe that two people could be so happy.

"No. Seriously? What happened?" asked Thabo, allowing my fingers to run through his like water through the pebbles of a stream.

"It's a very sad story," I said.

"But it's romantic, right?"

"Yes, it's romantic, you softy."

"Well let's hear it then; you can't waste a day like this on anything that's not romantic."

So I told him the story of Rosemary Ludlow and Richard Worthington: the lovers from different worlds. As I finished the tragic tale, he sighed, took my hand and led me down the steps and into a sunlit pool of daffodils. He picked a flower and gave it to me, trying to tuck it into my now shoulder-length red hair. It fell to the ground and we bent down together to pick it up, our hands meeting over the fallen bloom.

"Thabo?" I said, feeling a sudden sense of foreboding. "Will we end up like Richard and Rose?"

"Why do you ask that, Natalie? Aren't you happy?"

"Of course I'm happy, I've never been happier, it's just that I have a strange feeling that something is going to go wrong."

"With us?" he asked, seriously.

"Maybe, I don't know. I just feel strange, that's all."

"Don't be silly. I love you and you love me, what could possibly go wrong? Gugs is dead, Larson is in prison, Thabo Mbeki is alive, all charges have been dropped against me, Dad's on the mend and so are you." He touched the second scar on my leg – the one from the bullet – then kissed me until the shadows crept away.

"Feeling better?" he asked later as I lay on his chest with the ruin towering above us.

"Yes, I'm sorry. I suppose I'm just scared of becoming like my Auntie Rose: like something out of a Brontë novel."

He laughed and tousled my hair. "How's the old girl doing, now that your grandma's gone?"

"I think she's free," I said, then sank deeper into his arms.

As she had promised, Iris Ludlow Porter hadn't made it through the winter. The shock of the attack and the sight of Gladwin's burnt house when she came home took their toll. But she managed to garner enough strength to help the neighbours salvage Gladwin's garden in the weeks while he was in hospital and later in temporary accommodation while his house was rebuilt. The greenhouse was beyond repair, the glass shattering into a million pieces with the heat of the flames, and most of the plants inside ruined, but the English garden fared better. When he returned, Gladwin was deeply touched by what his neighbours had done and settled quietly back into his house and his old routines.

Thabo, meanwhile, had got a flat in Kingston Park but was a regular visitor. As winter approached, he spent many hours with his dad, getting the garden ready for the cold, dormant months ahead. When he wasn't with Gladwin he was helping me with the Peace Garden at the refugee centre.

The whole place had been in turmoil for a while as the police tried to dig out Gugs' mole. They finally narrowed it down to two Rwandan men and the rest were cleared. But Thabo lost his job at the garden centre because, although the terrorism charges were dropped, he had still stolen fertiliser and other chemicals from them for Gugs. However, the judge accepted Thabo's defence that he had only done it to maintain his cover and feared for the safety of his father. He was chastised for not contacting the police earlier but, in the end, only received a three month suspended sentence for it.

My grandma watched all of this quietly from her garden. As cold as it was she would ask me to help her outside at least once a day and she would sit, bundled up, surrounded by her floral legacy. I would sit with her, holding her hand, until I couldn't bear the cold any longer and insisted we go inside.

On Christmas Day Auntie Rose came to visit and brought a flaming poinsettia to put on Grandma's windowsill. "Will you make us some tea, Natalie? I'd like to talk to your grandma alone."

I nodded and went to the kitchen. Soon the tea was made and I waited with the tray in the lounge. With the bedroom door slightly ajar I could see the two elderly sisters through the crack and could hear nearly everything they said.

"Will ya look after Natalie, Rose?"

"Yes, of course, Iris. I love her as if she was my own."

"Aye, you would have made a good mother, Rose. It's a pity your Richard couldn't give ya any bairns."

"He did once. But I lost it after the shock of hearing about his accident."

"I didn't know that, Rose."

"There's a lot about me that you don't know, Iris."

"I know, Rose, I know. I'm sorry if I've been hard on ya."

"No you haven't."

"Don't lie to me Rose, I'm going to meet the Maker and we need to have some truth between us."

"Oh Iris, I only wanted you to love me."

"I know, pet, but ya tried too hard. It's time ya lived yer life to please yerself now. It's too late to please our mam, and there's no need to please me no more, just please yerself pet, with the time ya have left."

"Are you scared, Iris?"

"About what, Rose?"

"Dying."

"I don't think so. I've done what I can here, but there's still some stuff I need to do on the other side, if God'll let me."

"Like what?"

"I've got some unfinished business with George."

"Do you think he'll be there?"

"Where?"

"In heaven. I mean, he did kill himself."

"I drove him to it, Rose, I know I did."

"Oh Iris, you didn't drive him to it."

"Yes I did. I didn't love like you did. Like Natalie does. I wouldn't let him be himself. I told you, Rose, I haven't been wasting my time in this bed; I've been summing up the truth."

Summing up the truth. What was the truth? Would the truth of today be the truth of tomorrow? Would I look at things differently in fifty years? Would I still think that Thabo was the love of my life?

Never one for airs and graces, Grandma slipped away quietly just before New Year after summoning her brood to her bedside. The shops and shares were left to my dad Jim. I inherited the Jasmine Close house.

I was very happy about getting the house, and of course the garden, because I'd come to realise that I needed to belong somewhere, and that Newcastle bungalow was the place I felt most connected to the earth.

"Penny for your thoughts?" asked Thabo.

"Oh nothing. I was just thinking about Grandma and Auntie Rose." Thabo held me close again and gently stroked my hair. He eventually spoke.

"So, what have you decided then? About the Peace Garden project. Will you come with me to South Africa to get it started?"

"What about your dad?"

"I thought he would for a while, but now he's decided to take a job at the University of the Witwatersrand in Johannesburg instead; to be near my grandmother."

"She'll love that!"

Thabo laughed. "Too right! He's buying a house in Parktown, just down the road from the Cohens and Sophie will go and live with him. But get this: she's going to carry on working for the

Cohens as a maid and hire someone else to clean her place!"

I laughed. "Why?"

"I don't know. I suppose it's all she's ever known."

"It'll be great for her to see her son and grandson again."

"And you," said Thabo.

"Just for a little while though, right? We spoke about three months."

Thabo took my left hand and traced the circumference of my ring finger. "Let's see how it goes."

I looked at the Northumberland countryside stretching out around us. I felt the Northumberland grass beneath my back then I dug my fingernails into the Northumberland earth and whispered: "I don't want to go forever, Thabo."

"I know," he said, and kissed me again.